PSYCHIC
CONNECTIONS

PSYCHIC
CONNECTIONS

A Journey into
the Mysterious World of Psi

Lois Duncan
and
William Roll, Ph.D.

DELACORTE PRESS

To two good friends—
Betty Muench and Nancy Myer
L.D.

To my grandchildren—
David, Martin, and Jensen
B.R.

Published by
Bantam Doubleday Dell Books for Young Readers
a division of
Bantam Doubleday Dell Publishing Group, Inc.
1540 Broadway
New York, New York 10036

Portions of the material in chapters ten and thirteen originally appeared in *Woman's Day* in April and June 1992, and are copyrighted by Hachette Filipacchi Magazines.

ISBN: 0-385-32072-8

The text of this book is set in 12-point New Aster.
Book design by Blake Logan

Printed in the United States of America

June 1995

10 9 8 7 6 5 4 3 2 1

CONTENTS

FOREWORD

by William Roll

Throughout history people have experienced strange occurrences—events that can best be called psychic phenomena. As a parapsychologist, I have investigated such mysteries for more than thirty years. This book is an overview of psychic phenomena and the attempts by researchers to discover what really is going on.

The collaboration between Lois Duncan and me has its roots in a personal tragedy. It began when I got a letter from Lois telling of the murder of her daughter Kait Arquette. Strangely, Lois had described the killing in a suspense novel she had published a month before—a striking example of apparent precognition. Hoping to find the murderer, Lois consulted psychics, who pointed to an underground world of drug dealing and to a higher reality from which Kait seemed to communicate. Lois asked my opinion as a parapsychologist, and this book grew from there.

Are psychic abilities real, and if so, what are they good for? Some believe the best way to study psychic phenomena is to test them in scientific laboratories. This work is important, but the experiments do not show how to use psychic abilities for practical purposes, such as solving the mystery of Kait's murder. To deal with these issues, this book goes beyond the scientific evidence to psychic experiences from everyday life and to interviews with psychics who have learned to put their abilities to work.

Psychic occurrences show us that we are connected to each other and the environment below surface separations. As we come to understand our psychic bonds to each other, we may move naturally toward a time in which human beings enjoy more compassion and less conflict. When Lois found she was part of a realm of psychic connections, the tragedy of her daughter's death became a transformation to a new and richer life, a life that does not end with death. I hope this book will encourage readers to explore and experience the reality of our psychic connnections.

The case histories in this book are mine, Lois's, and those of our students and friends; some come from the files of researchers in the field. Several first-person accounts of ESP experiences have been condensed because of limited space, and, at the request of the subjects, several names have been changed.

Grateful acknowledgment is made to the following for permission to reprint excerpts from previously published material: *The Blue Sense: Psychic Detectives and Crime*, copyright 1991 by Arthur Lyons and Marcello Truzzi; *Parapsychology: The Controversial Science*, copyright 1991 by Richard S. Broughton; *Silent Witness: The Story of a Psychic Detective*, copyright 1993 by Nancy Myer-Czetli and Steve Czetli; transcripts of recordings in the "Psychics in Action" series of audiocassettes, copyright 1992 and 1993 by Robin Arquette, RDA Enterprises, 6110 Pleasant Ridge Road, Suite 3431, Arlington, TX 76016.

Last, but definitely not least, we wish to thank Donald Arquette for the many hours of research he contributed to this project.

CHAPTER ONE

EXTRASENSORY PERCEPTION: THE INVISIBLE CONNECTION

I have written for publication since I was thirteen years old and am by now the author of forty books. The most popular of these by far have been young adult suspense novels that have had to do with psychic phenomena. I incorporated this subject into my fiction because it made for good story material, not because I believed in it. From childhood on, I was always a hard-nosed skeptic about anything that did not conform to the most conservative view of reality.

It took a soul-shattering tragedy to challenge that ingrained belief system and to force me to open my eyes to other possibilities.

The roots of this true-life horror story go back to June 1989, when my book *Don't Look Behind You* was published. The heroine, April, was based upon the personality of my eighteen-year-old daughter, Kait Arquette. In the book a murder contract was put out on April's family because they were going to blow the whistle on an interstate drug ring. April was chased by a hit man in a Camaro.

One month later, on July 16, my daughter Kait was chased down and shot to death in our hometown, Albuquerque, New Mexico, while driving home from a girlfriend's house. A man who witnessed the chase told the police that, like the hit man in my book, Kait's killers were driving a Camaro.

Suddenly events from my fiction became hideous reality.

In *Don't Look Behind You*, April and her family were forced into hiding because of death threats. Three men were arrested for Kait's murder, and because the arrests were the result of our family's reward flyers, the relatives of one of the suspects threatened to kill the rest of us. Like April's family, we fled from our home and hid for months in a rented apartment with a security guard.

In my book, when April was forced into hiding, her name was changed to Valerie.

When our case appeared to be falling through, a private investigator from out of state contacted our family to volunteer his services. He was of Russian descent, and his name was Valery.

The man who was indicted for shooting Kait was named Mike, and a statement in the police file gave his nickname as Vamp.

My fictional hit man in *Don't Look Behind You* was named Mike Vamp.

As coincidence piled upon coincidence, I thought I was going crazy. In an attempt to salvage my sanity, I contacted Dr. Bill Roll, project director for the Psychical Research Foundation.

"What you've experienced isn't uncommon," Bill said reassuringly. "The fact that people, under certain circumstances, can see into the future is quite well established, and creative people seem to have more of this precognitive ability than others. When such people are authors, glimpses of future events may turn up in the fiction they write. This is especially true in regard to violence."

He went on to describe other instances when this had happened. The most startling example was a fictional story titled "Futility" and published in 1898, about a giant passenger ship called the *Titan* ramming an iceberg. This was fourteen years before the sinking of the superliner *Titanic*. Similarities between the real and fictional disasters were uncanny. Both the *Titan* and the *Titanic* were designated as unsinkable and were the largest vessels afloat. The story contained many details that were duplicated in the actual event, including the size of the ship, the number of stacks and propellers, the passage capacity, and the tragic lack of lifeboats.

"Psychic phenomena aren't supernatural," Bill told me. "The word *psychic* comes from 'psyche,' the Greek word for 'self, mind, or soul.' There are many experiences of the mind that we all have and consider very normal. Many people have had dreams about distant events, some so vivid they have left them shaken. Some such dreams are realistic; others are symbolic. Most of us have intuitive feelings that range from hunches to premonitions to clear insights about future events that later turn out to be quite accurate."

Bill explained to me that, beyond dreams and intuitive feelings, there are other kinds of psychic experiences that parapsychologists have separated into several categories. There are out-of-body experiences and near-death experiences. There are hauntings and ghost sightings. There is the "poltergeist" phenomenon, which often includes loud noises and the chaotic and sometimes violent movement of objects. There are mediums and channels—psychically sensitive people who claim to be able to make contact with the dead. There are other types of sensitive people who claim to be able to read minds and to see distant places and events without actually being there. Such people may use their abilities for everything from telling fortunes to predicting national disasters, and from solving crimes to acting as psychic spies for the military. There is even a mind-over-matter category of phenomena that includes metal bending, dice control, and long-distance healing.

There are two human abilities that parapsychologists believe are fundamental in explaining all of these different kinds of psychic phenomena—*extrasensory perception* and *psychokinesis*.

Extrasensory perception—commonly known as *ESP*—is the ability to obtain information without the use of the five basic senses: sight, hearing, smell, touch, and taste. Subcategories of **ESP** are *telepathy*, the direct transfer of information from one mind to another; and *clairvoyance* (which means "clear viewing"), the direct transfer of information from a physical object to the mind of the receiver.

The second category of psychic ability, psychokinesis—commonly referred to as *PK*—is the ability to use the energy of the mind to move or otherwise affect matter without physical contact.

"Neither of these abilities is magical," Bill told me. "There's nothing spooky or weird about either one of them. The only thing that makes them seem supernormal is that they don't fit the old-fashioned concept of reality, and we don't yet have a full understanding of how they work. In 1633, the brilliant scientist Galileo was convicted of heresy for proposing that the sun didn't revolve around the earth. A few centuries ago, natural science museums threw out their collections of meteorites because astronomers were convinced there were no stones in the sky. And it wasn't too long ago that physicists asserted that the atom was the smallest bit of matter. Now there is a whole science called quantum physics based on the study of subatomic particles. It's incredible the number of 'miracles' we accept today without question that yesterday's teachers of science told us were impossible."

When I considered that statement, I realized he was right. There was a time when the idea of a telephone seemed impossible, yet today few people are without one. The same holds true of a radio. And as a child I would have found the concept of television too ridiculous to contemplate, yet now I take it for granted that, at a punch of a button, a blank screen will come alive with all sorts of activity.

If we can accept our ability to communicate with friends from a distance through the use of telephones and radios, and the fact that a picture can be broken into bits and transported invisibly through space to reassemble itself in our living room, why should we find it hard to accept the possibility that a thought might be transmitted from one mind to another as in telepathy?

And if the energy generated by electricity can produce heat and light, and the energy generated by gasoline can move a vehicle, why shouldn't the energy of the human mind be able to generate heat and light and cause objects to move as in psychokinesis?

When you think of the power of the mind as just an alternate source of energy, these things *do* seem perfectly normal and a natural extension of the world we live in. As Bill observed, almost all of us have experienced ESP in one form or another without even realizing it—we've had hunches that turned out to be accurate, gut feelings about whether we could trust people, and times when we sensed what would happen before the events occurred.

And just as a high antenna usually works better than a

low one to capture the energy that causes our television sets to function, why shouldn't particular people with "high" psychic talent have a heightened ability to capture mental and emotional energy?

Bill Roll assured me that there truly were such people and told me that some of them were actively involved in police work.

The Albuquerque police had classified Kait's murder as a "random shooting" and refused to consider any other possibility. Our family was not satisfied with this off-the-cuff assessment and felt that there ought to be further investigation. We now decided to do something that was totally foreign to us and contacted several of the nation's top psychic detectives. To our amazement, they provided us with information that led to the discovery that Kait's boyfriend was

Kait Arquette, 1989—the year she was murdered. (courtesy: Kim Jew)

involved in interstate crime and that our daughter, who was breaking up with him, seemed to have been planning to expose it. Suddenly there was a possible motive for Kait's murder, and the random-shooting theory became much less plausible.

Those experiences—and others, which I will describe later in this book—convinced our family that there is a legitimate sixth sense that at times may even surpass the other five. At first we were reluctant to discuss this unorthodox belief for fear our friends would think we had totally "lost it." However, we did finally find the courage to do so and were astounded at the number of conservative, down-to-earth people who responded with stories of their own—stories they had buried for years for fear *they* would be labeled crazy.

Estelle told us how, after she was widowed, the occupants of two houses the couple had once lived in reported seeing her deceased husband in their living rooms, smiling and wearing a raincoat. Although those people didn't know it, he had worn a similar raincoat in a community-theater production of *Guys and Dolls*.

Gail recalled a time when she was critically ill and suddenly saw her dead mother standing next to her hospital bed. "It isn't your time to die yet," her mother told her. To the amazement of Gail's doctors, she recovered from her illness.

Holly dreamed that a particular branch of Trust Company National Bank was going to be robbed by three men, and that the bank's security system would videotape the robbery and the tape would be shown on the TV news. The following evening she turned on her television set and was confronted with a video of the robbery exactly as she had dreamed it.

Mark, a college student, had grown so used to having his premonitions prove true that he took them for granted. "When I sit in class during a lecture, I write down what the teacher is going to say before he says it," he said. "When I want to hear a certain song on the radio, I automatically flip to the station where it's going to be played. And when I get a sudden urge to call people on the phone, I just sit tight and don't do it, because I know that in a few minutes *they* are going to call *me*."

Madge was playing piano accompaniment for a very poor cellist and thought wistfully of her friend Blake, a highly talented cellist who had recently died. "I can just imagine how upset he'd be to hear his favorite composition played this badly!" she thought. At that moment, a candle on a table on the other side of the room rose out of its holder and zoomed across to strike the opposite wall.

Dorothy came home from school and entered the house to hear her mother's voice calling for her. "The voice screamed my name three times as I ran to the garage to check and see if Mom's car was there," she said. "The garage was empty. Then I heard the phone ringing. The call was from the emergency room. My mother had been in an accident, and they told me to hurry to the hospital because she was yelling for me."

Audrey recalled suffering a severe concussion after falling on the ice at age seven. She was unconscious for twelve hours and given only a fifty-fifty chance of survival. "I suddenly found myself in a beautiful, sunlit garden," she said.

"The flowers were large and colorful, like sunflowers or giant dahlias, and they stood waist high; I have never seen flowers like that on this earth. I didn't know how I got there, but I knew I belonged there, and I knew there had been a time when I had been there before.

"Then suddenly I wasn't alone there; I was joined by a Being who seemed to be composed of perfect love. The Being said, 'So you are going back?' and I said 'Yes.' He asked me why, and I answered, 'Because my mother needs me.' At that moment, I started down what seemed like a dark tunnel. The light got smaller and smaller, and when I could no longer see it, I woke up. I looked around and wondered why the doctor was there. I saw my parents and said 'Hello.' "

As a result of that experience, Audrey lost all fear of dying.

"I have work to do here, but when that's over, I look forward to returning to that wonderful place," she said.

Bill Roll, who has made a life study of parapsychology at Oxford University in England, at Duke University, and at Utrecht University in the Netherlands, does not find these accounts surprising.

"We are learning more about psychical connections every year," he says. "There was a time when scientists didn't know that things could be connected if there were no visible links between them. Today it's been proven that they can be through radio and TV waves. Modern physicists have even discovered that things can be connected when no sort of known radiation passes between them. They have found that when a tiny, subatomic particle is split and the two bits are separated, they can get a reaction from one of them by agitating the other one. It's as if they are telepathic. And exactly that same sort of thing seems to happen between people."

Bill views science as an ever-expanding growth process —a search for truth that is constantly being updated.

"We once believed that the earth was flat," he says. "Then, new truths emerged, and we decided that it was a ball that was the center of the universe and that the sun revolved around it. Then, we made further discoveries that caused us to decide that the sun didn't circle the earth, it was the other way around.

"Science sets up theories based upon all the facts that are currently available, but when new facts surface, those theories have to be changed. The exploration and testing of theories about psychic phenomena is what the field of parapsychology is all about."

The formal study of psychic phenomena began in 1882 at Cambridge University in England, where a group of scientists and scholars got together to form the Society for Psychical Research, headed by Henry Sidgwick, a highly respected philosopher. Before that, psychical research had been conducted so haphazardly that none of the data collected could be solidly documented. The Society for Psychical Research set out to approach the field as a science by establishing standards of evidence to use for case studies and also for experimentation in laboratories. The United States came into the action in the early 1930s, when J. B. Rhine established the Parapsychology Laboratory at Duke University in Durham, North Carolina, which became the hub of this country's first program of concentrated ESP research. Bill worked there for seven years.

Bill's personal interest in the subject began at the age of sixteen, when he started having experiences with astral projection. Born in Germany in 1926 of Scandinavian parents, he moved with his mother to Denmark in early childhood and was living there at the time of the Nazi invasion.

It was then that he had his first out-of-body experience.

"At the time I didn't understand what was happening," he remembers. "I got up in the night and walked across the room, and when I turned around to go back, I saw my body on the bed. Somehow I had stepped *out* of my body without realizing it!"

He continued to have these experiences once or twice a month for the next forty years.

"I've thought a lot about what may have started them," he says. "Out-of-body experiences are usually triggered by physical or emotional trauma, and at that time I was experiencing a tremendous amount of anxiety. For one thing, my mother had recently died, which had been a great shock to me, as she'd been in seemingly perfect health, and since she and my father were divorced, she had been the one stable element in my life.

"Secondly, I was deeply involved in the Danish resistance movement, working as a liaison between the chief of the movement in our area and his group leaders. The chief was constantly on the move to avoid arrest by the Nazis, staying in the same place for only a few nights at a time. I was the only one who knew his whereabouts, and I also knew the identities of all the group leaders. If I were to be captured I almost certainly would have been tortured and forced to reveal the names and locations of those individuals, and, once I did that, I undoubtedly would have been executed. I knew that arrests were usually made at night, so I slept in a peculiar way, with both ears open, always alert for the sound of a car pulling up and stopping outside the house.

"When I think back on that tense time, it seems fairly clear to me that the combination of those two highly stressful situations may have produced a subconscious desire to escape from the physical world and given me the impetus I needed to leave my body."

Since becoming acquainted with Bill Roll, I have grown more and more fascinated by the results of the research he and his colleagues have been conducting, both through experimentation in the laboratory and through investigating the psychic experiences of everyday people. When Bill asked if I would be interested in writing a book with him that would attempt to explain this "magic that isn't really magic," it didn't take me long to say yes.

Not only did I think such a book would be of interest to adults and teenagers alike, I also hoped that the process of writing it might help me to understand the startling new realities that had invaded my own life—the glimpses of the terrible future that had appeared in the fiction I wrote just prior to Kait's death, the ability of psychic detectives to extract valid information from items that Kait was wearing on the night she was shot, and the mind-blowing concept of out-of-body experiences—sometimes called *astral projection* —a subject I once had written about as fiction, but now was beginning to think might actually be possible.

Astral projection had been of interest to me for years, because of letters I had received from readers of my suspense novels.

Here is one of those letters:

Dear Lois Duncan,

I am twelve years old and just finished reading Stranger with My Face. *I think I may have had some experiences with astral projection and would like to get your advice on them.*

When I was young, about five and under, I used to lie in bed at night and feel myself rise. If I looked down, I would see my body on the bed. I never did it on purpose, though, as Laurie did in your book. It was just something that happened. At the time I had no idea what it was, so I never tried to move around. Usually I would shut my eyes to wait for it to be over. I would feel myself falling, as when you're going down a big plunge on a roller coaster, and then would hit the bed with a thud.

I lived in Massachusetts then, and when I was five we moved to the Philippines. Since then I have never had one of these occurrences. Maybe it was from the move or maybe just because I had gotten too old, I don't know. If you have any information that would train me to use this power, I would be very grateful.

Alicia

Like Alicia, I wanted to learn more about the power of the human mind, so I eagerly accepted Bill's offer to act as my guide on a journey into the fascinating world of "psi"— the letter in the Greek alphabet that stands for "the unknown."

CHAPTER TWO

OUT-OF-BODY EXPERIENCES

The concept of astral projection is far from a new one. The idea that the soul may be able to detach itself from the physical body at the time of death is the backbone of most religions.

For people who accept that concept, it should not be too great a leap to speculate that the human spirit might also be able to leave the body temporarily to make short trips on its own while the body is alive.

Still, to people who have never had this experience, the idea of astral projection is a strange one. Despite Bill Roll's description of his own out-of-body experiences and the letters I received from young people who told me about theirs, I had a hard time accepting the concept of OBEs. It wasn't that I thought people who claimed to have had them were lying; I just thought that they might have been experiencing very realistic dreams or, in the case of my teenage readers, that they might have related so strongly to the heroine of

Stranger with My Face that they relived the events in that book in their imaginations.

Then, one night, I had an OBE of my own.

In keeping with Bill's theory that out-of-body experiences may be triggered by emotional trauma, my first OBE occurred at the point at which we realized that the police had given up on Kait's case and it probably would remain unsolved.

Overwhelmed by grief and frustration, I cried myself to sleep that night, and shortly before dawn I awoke to the strange sensation of heavy vibrations starting in my feet and moving slowly up through my body to center in my chest. Then I experienced the sensation of being manually lifted, as if I were in a hospital bed with a back that could be raised mechanically.

A moment later, without having moved a muscle, I found myself in an upright position. I looked down at the bed, and saw that my body was still lying there. The instant my eyes caught sight of it, it drew me like a magnet, and I was snapped back into that body as if I were attached to it by an overstretched rubber band.

Too stunned to know how to react, I lay there trembling. I knew that what I had experienced hadn't been a dream. It had been far too vivid to have been imaginary, and the odd sensations that preceded it had been totally physical.

"I've just had an OBE!" I realized incredulously.

One week later, the same thing happened a second time, complete with identical sensations of vibrating and lifting. As before, when I glanced down at my body, I was jerked back into it.

The third time the phenomenon occurred, I was no longer startled and made a conscious decision that I wouldn't view my body, since that seemed to have the effect of terminating the experience. Instead, I decided to see what my "astral body" was capable of. This time, when I felt the start of the now-familiar vibrations, I turned my back to the bed and flew out the window.

That flight was the most exhilarating experience of my life! I went zipping along, about twenty-five feet above the street, looking down on the tops of cars and feeling like Superwoman.

Then I saw a traffic light looming ahead of me.

"That won't stop me!" I told myself confidently. "I'm going to zoom right through it!"

I was wrong about that. When I hit the light, I was abruptly jerked back to my room and returned to my body with such force that I jolted the bed.

I was terribly disappointed. It didn't seem fair that a red light would stop my astral excursion.

That experience temporarily ended my nighttime adventures, and it was almost a year before I left my body again.

Curious to find out as much as I could about the amazing thing that had happened to me, I asked Bill to recommend some books on the subject. On their pages I found exact descriptions of my own experience, including the vibrations and the sense of being manually lifted. I also learned that over 90 percent of all reported OBEs occur in the late night hours when a person is relaxed and inactive and that the sight of the vacated body is often such a shock to the OBEer that it abruptly ends the out-of-body experience.

In the course of my reading, I soon came to realize that there was nothing new about OBEs and that people throughout the world had been having them for a very long time. Paintings found in Egyptian tombs show spiritual bodies hovering in the air above physical bodies, and Eastern cultures such as those in India and China take the existence of the second body for granted. A number of Western religions also incorporate this belief, and the Catholic Church, in particular, is rampant with accounts of saints and other religious figures who experienced OBEs.

Although, in general, the scientific community has tended to be more skeptical, the concept that a human entity can exist outside of the confines of the physical body has generated the serious interest of a number of scientists.

When Hornell Hart, a professor at Duke University, submitted a questionnaire to 155 students in his sociology classes, asking them, "Have you ever actually seen your physical body from a viewpoint completely outside that body, like standing beside the bed and looking at yourself lying in bed, or floating in the air near your body?" fully one-third of his students said that they had.

Intrigued by this unexpected response, psychologists at the University of Virginia presented the same question to 1,000 students. One out of every four responded "Yes."

Other researchers then got into the act and conducted surveys of their own in an attempt to add to this growing fund of information. When the results were averaged, 25 percent of everyone interviewed claimed to have had an out-of-body experience at least once.

Research organizations both in the United States and abroad began to keep files of reported instances of OBEs to try to determine what, if anything, they had in common. Although the details of these experiences varied to some degree, all the participants described the sensation of having their consciousness detach from their physical bodies and move to a spot outside of them. In some cases, there was a sensation of movement to this other location, while in other cases the person was just suddenly *there*.

Perhaps the most common jumping-off point for an OBE is the hospital emergency or operating room in which doctors are trying to restart stopped heart or lung functions. Patients often report leaving their bodies and rising toward the ceiling to observe this process. Sometimes they also go to the waiting room to observe loved ones anxiously awaiting the outcome.

A doctor named Michael Sabom did a study in this setting that compared the description of the resuscitation process given by thirty-two OBEers with the "educated guesses" of twenty-five medically savvy patients who had not had OBEs. All were asked to describe what happens when a medical team tries to get the heart restarted. Twenty-three of the twenty-five non-OBEers made major mistakes, while none of the thirty-two OBE patients made any. They apparently had *seen* what happened while they were out of their bodies.

Brad Steiger, psychic researcher and author of the book *Astral Projection–Para Research*, has collected thousands of testimonials from OBEers.

Typical of these are the following:

Jane, age twelve, was left at home alone one night while her parents attended her aunt's funeral. As Jane lay in bed on the verge of sleep, she suddenly felt herself rise toward the ceiling. Then, without knowing how she got there, she found herself in a room with her parents, her grandmother, and other relatives, and realized to her surprise that she was at the funeral.

Jane was unable to attract the attention of family members, and eventually returned to her body and fell asleep.

The following day, she astonished her parents by describing the funeral in detail, including the color of her aunt's dress and the arrangement of the casket.

* * *

Robert was forced to miss two months of school because of illness. Lonely and bored, he discovered that if he concentrated on visualizing himself going to school, he could "project himself" into the classroom.

"The first time this happened a cloud seemed to pass before my eyes," he said. "I heard a funny sort of popping noise, and I was there in school in the middle of spelling class. One of my buddies was having a tough time spelling the word *geography*, and a couple of the guys were passing notes. The teacher caught them and made them stand in separate corners of the room for the rest of the period."

Later, a classmate phoned to see how Robert was feeling and verified the note-passing incident in the classroom. He also admitted misspelling the word *geography*.

Helen, a teenage girl in Idaho, woke up one morning with unbearable stomach pain. To her mother the symptoms sounded like appendicitis, and she called the doctor.

As Helen thrashed about in her bed, moaning in agony, the "thinking part" of her detached from her body and drifted to the ceiling.

"The pain remained down with my body on the bed," she later reported. "The *real* me couldn't feel a thing."

As she wondered when the doctor was going to arrive, she suddenly found herself with him in his car, stopped at a stoplight.

"Why do they keep these darn things going all night?" the doctor grumbled. "Why don't they just keep them blinking on yellow?"

Helen rode with the doctor for a while and then returned to her room, where her mother was weeping at her bedside. When the doctor finally arrived, he gave Helen's body an injection, and she was yanked back into it.

Later when she described her out-of-body experience, no

one would take her seriously, until she repeated what the doctor had said at the stoplight. There was no way she could have known that, unless she was in the car with him.

The OBEs Bill Roll experienced were less spectacular.

"I didn't take off for distant places," he says. "I never tried to leave the house during those experiences, except for one time when I seemed to project myself into the front yard."

Like mine, his OBEs usually occurred at night and were preceded by the feeling of vibrations in his head and chest.

"If I woke up in that state, I could lean forward, apparently out of my body, and then completely detach myself," he says. "The activity was rather slow and required effort. It was like getting up in the morning when your body is a little sluggish after a deep sleep. When the OBEs first started I didn't know what they were. Fortunately, a neighbor who had an interest in parapsychology loaned me books on the topic, and I learned there were many other people who were having these experiences."

Bill's out-of-body experiences bore no resemblance to dreams.

"I had no doubt during these incidents that my self had really left the body," he tells me. "My mind was as clear as during waking life, and there was nothing dreamlike or unusual about my surroundings. Getting out of the body did not mean a change of consciousness, nor did returning to it. I would go up to the body, then *in*, and a moment later I was fully awake in the body. It was like closing my eyes and then opening them again. It was only when I was back in the body that I reasoned that I must have separate OBE eyes in addition to my physical eyes, or I would not have been able to experience vision during these excursions. I enjoyed my OBEs in the way I enjoyed rides at an amusement park.

They were interesting and mildly exciting, but nothing more."

After graduating from high school in Denmark, Bill went to the United States to attend the University of California at Berkeley, but even in this new location his OBEs continued on a regular basis. In fact, he became so used to them that there were times when he didn't even realize he was experiencing one.

One afternoon, when Bill woke up from a nap, he discovered that while he had been asleep the sun had gone down and the room had become dark. He got up from the bed and went over to turn on the light. When he placed his finger on the switch, the finger moved through it without meeting any resistance.

"What's happened to the switch?" Bill asked himself in bewilderment. Then it struck him that there was nothing wrong with the switch; it was his hand that had no physical substance.

He had projected out of his body without knowing he had done so.

Although personal reports of OBEs make for interesting reading, only evidence gleaned under controlled laboratory conditions is convincing to scientists, and because OBEs usually occur spontaneously during sleep or at times of extreme stress, they are not easily induced in laboratories.

It was Bill's great hope that someday he would be able to induce his OBEs at will. If he could do that, his colleagues could set up a secret "target object" behind a screen or in a separate room, and he could attempt to project himself to that location to take a look at it. If, during an OBE, he could visit and identify a picture or object he had not seen with his physical eyes, this would be evidence that his mind really did extend beyond his body.

Although he never was able to accomplish this, the next

best thing happened. In 1973, somebody entered Bill's life who could bring OBEs on at will.

By now, Bill was head of the Psychical Research Foundation, a research center located on the campus of Duke University. Into his laboratory, as a test subject, came Keith Harary, an undergraduate psychology major who had been having OBEs all his life and claimed to have amazing control of them. Not only was he able to induce OBEs at will, he was able to project himself to preset destinations, and he claimed that on one occasion he had taken a friend with him.

Harary's report of this unique adventure is a fascinating one.

"One evening I went to bed in my home in New York City, thinking about a woman friend in Maine I hadn't seen for a while," he told the scientists at Duke. "Then suddenly I found myself floating free of my body. I'd had this experience so many times in the past that I wasn't surprised, and I decided I'd use this opportunity to go visit my lady friend.

"Then I decided to see if I could bring my friend George along with me. I concentrated on George, who lived in another area of the city, and soon was floating above him where he lay asleep on his bed. I woke George up, and he agreed to go with me, so I grasped his hands and pulled him up out of his body.

"On the way to Maine, George and I seemed to walk through wooded areas and up and down green, rolling hillsides. At one point, when we stopped to rest on the slope of a hill, George began to wander too close to a pool of hot, bubbling, pink liquid. I warned him not to get too close to it, because, even in our present out-of-body state, it was dangerous.

"When we reached the area where I thought my woman friend might be, we were surprised to find her waiting for us. She's an older woman, but quite attractive—a strawberry blonde with extremely high cheekbones. We visited with her for a long time. Then we said our good-byes, and George and I returned to our sleeping bodies.

"The next morning I awoke with complete recollection of the experience, but I said nothing about it to George when I saw him that evening. I wanted to see if he would remember it on his own. At first he didn't appear to, and then we started talking about dreams, and a startled expression suddenly came onto his face.

"'Last night!' he exclaimed, pointing a finger at me. Then he began to describe our out-of-body trip together. 'We visited a fantastic lady! She had reddish hair and high cheekbones. And there was something about a pool—something that was dangerous!'"

Keith Harary seemed to have remarkable OBE abilities.

How can science go about proving OBEs? Bill and his colleagues decided upon two forms of testing. The first of these involved having Harary attempt to leave his body and project himself to the research lab, where target objects were set up for him to identify. These targets consisted of large colored letters of the alphabet, which Harary was asked to describe when he returned from his "trip." On five of the nine occasions on which this experiment was conducted, Harary's description of the targets was close to accurate, but it was not impressive enough to be statistically significant.

Since Harary seemed to relate better to humans than to objects, the scientists then tried an experiment in which they divided a room into quadrangles and stationed people in various areas of the room. When Harary projected to the lab, his task was to pinpoint where in the room the target subjects were standing. He was highly successful at first, but as he tired, his performance dropped to average.

One interesting sidelight of this particular set of experiments is that Harary's out-of-body presence was detected by others. One of the participants reported seeing a misty image of Harary appear in one of the quadrangles at precisely the moment at which he experienced himself there. John Hartwell, a psychophysiologist and electronics engineer, who was operating television equipment at the visit site, also reported having strong impressions of Harary's presence there on four different occasions and once actually saw his image on the television screen. It was later confirmed that the times at which Hartwell experienced these phenomena coincided exactly with the times when Harary was projecting.

The fact that Harary's disembodied presence seemed to be sensed by observers at the research lab gave rise to a

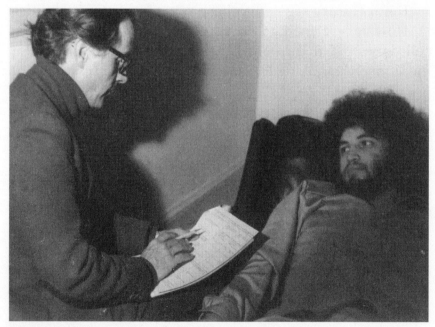

Keith Harary being debriefed by Bill Roll after one of his out-of-body experiences. (courtesy: William Roll)

Assistant experimenter Jerry Solfvin recording the brain waves of Keith Harary during one of his out-of-body experiences. (courtesy: William Roll)

third test that had never before been attempted. In this novel experiment, the detection device was a kitten.

Bill had long suspected that animals might be sensitive to psi. He based this belief on the many instances when people, intentionally or unintentionally, left their dogs or cats behind when they moved away and the pets tracked them down and found them. When a woman told the team of scientists that her cat would follow her "astral self" around the apartment when she was out-of-body at home, they decided to get two kittens and give them to Harary for pets. Harary liked cats and became very fond of the kittens, naming one of them Soul and the other Spirit. Then, once the kittens got used to Harary and became attached to him, the scientists conducted a series of experiments to see if his pets would respond when Harary attempted to "visit" them during his OBEs.

Helping to conduct this experiment was Robert Morris, a scientist who was completing his Ph.D. in animal psychology. Morris placed Harary's kittens in a large box, the floor of which had been marked off into a grid of twenty-four numbered squares. Morris's task was to measure the level of the kittens' activity by counting the number of squares they walked across and the number of meows they gave during periods of one hundred seconds.

That job proved more of a challenge than Morris anticipated. The active kittens took off in different directions, scooting from square to square like two fuzzy billiard balls.

"Sorry, little fellas," Morris told them, "I can't keep track of both of you."

He picked up Soul and removed him from the box.

Meanwhile, a quarter of a mile away, in a psychophysiology laboratory at the Duke School of Engineering, Harary attempted to induce an OBE so that he could visit his kittens and see if they would react to his out-of-body presence.

He later reported the experiment a failure.

"I thought I was in the laboratory," he said apologetically, "but I couldn't have been, because I saw only one kitten in the box."

Of course, there really *had* been one kitten in the box!

Bill considered this an encouraging "Spirit visit."

Harary's subsequent OBE visits seemed to produce meaningful results. Spirit appeared to respond to his owner's OBE presence with remarkable consistency. During the control periods, when Harary did not attempt OBEs, the kitten was restless, wandering from square to square and meowing thirty-seven times as if he missed his owner; but during the OBE periods when Harary went to visit him, he became much calmer, crossed few or none of the squares, and didn't meow at all. Odds against this occurring by chance were 200 to 1. Since then Harary has become a psi researcher in his own right and has written several books, including *Have an Out-of-Body Experience in Thirty Days: The Free Flight Program* (with Pamela Weintraub).

Bill and his colleagues weren't the only people conducting laboratory experiments on astral projection. Other parapsychologists in research labs in various areas of the country were also involved in research to try to find out whether OBEs could be proven.

Many of these tests involved assigning an OBEer a task that could not possibly be performed in a normal physical state, but might be performed in an out-of-body state.

One of the scientists involved in this research was Charles T. Tart, who was conducting experiments in a laboratory at a major university. His test subject was a woman, referred to in his reports as Miss Z, who claimed to be able to leave her body during sleep and agreed to spend four nights in a bed at the laboratory.

Tart wrote a five-digit number on a piece of paper and placed it on a high shelf, where it could be seen only by someone whose eyes were at least six and a half feet above the floor. Miss Z's task was to project herself out of her body and rise to a position near the ceiling from which she could look down and read the number.

During the experiments, electrodes were attached to Miss Z's head to measure her brain waves when she was out of her body to see if they were different from those that normally occurred during sleep. These devices served a second purpose also. Not only did they monitor her physiological responses, but the fact that she was attached to the lab equipment prevented her from being able to raise her shoulders more than two feet from the mattress without disconnecting the wires. Since any disturbance of the electrodes

27

would immediately show up on the recording equipment, there was no way she could sneak a secret peek at the paper on the shelf.

On Miss Z's first night in the laboratory, nothing occurred.

On the second night she reported having a nightmare at exactly the time that highly unusual changes in her brain waves were registered on the recording equipment. The dream, which Professor Tart recorded in a notebook, was about a teenage girl who was chased down and stabbed to death with a slender instrument. She had a strong feeling the killer was someone the girl knew and was driving a white car.

Two days later a report appeared in the local newspaper about a young girl who was stabbed to death with an ice pick on the same night Miss Z was having this OBE. The suspect, who was driving a white car, turned out to be the girl's boyfriend.

This was not at all what Tart had expected. It suggested that Miss Z might have somehow witnessed a tragic event at another location.

On the third night, Miss Z claimed to have left her body and gone to visit her sister in another city. Although there was no way to confirm this, another unusual brain wave pattern showed up on the monitors at the time she reported being "gone."

On the fourth night, the strange brain wave pattern was repeated. This time Miss Z said she "got up to the shelf" and read the number Tart had placed there, which she correctly reported as 25132.

Of the hundreds of OBE subjects tested under laboratory conditions, several proved so phenomenal that their names are instantly recognized by parapsychologists everywhere.

One of these was a New York artist and psychic named Ingo Swann, whose abilities were so extraordinary that he was enlisted by the CIA to head a project in the 1970s to help locate Russian submarines in the Pacific Ocean.

In experiments conducted at the American Society of Psychical Research, Swann was not only able to identify objects placed on a raised platform at a height that could be seen only if viewed from the ceiling (in one particular test he scored 40,000 to 1 against chance), but he also demonstrated an apparent ability to project himself to distant locations on the basis of their longitude and latitude coordinates. Upon his return he would attempt to prove that he had been there by sketching the terrain.

On another occasion, at SRI International (formerly the Stanford Research Institute), Swann was given the coordinates "latitude 49 degrees 20′ south, longitude 70 degrees 14′ east," and asked to give an instant response without looking at a map. He said immediately, "It's an island, maybe a mountain sticking up through cloud cover. The terrain seems rocky and very cold. I see some buildings rather mathematically laid out. One of them is orange." Swann continued with a detailed description of a complex on the supposedly uninhabited antarctic island of Kerguelen. He then stated that there were people there speaking French. This seemingly preposterous statement was ridiculed by skeptics, but investigation later revealed that the French government had built a meteorological station on that island. People *were* speaking French there.

To further test his powers of long-distance projection, which he termed "remote viewing," Swann decided to see if it was possible to project himself into space. When the *Mariner 10* spacecraft blasted off on its journey to Jupiter and Mercury, Swann blasted out of his physical body in an effort to beat it there, and reported that in eight minutes he

29

arrived at his destination. Eight minutes is about the time it takes light to travel from Earth to Mercury.

Upon his return from this astral space trip, Swann wrote down a description of the planets he felt he had visited and had these impressions examined by a lawyer and notarized. Later, when this report was compared with the electronic data sent back by *Mariner 10*, Swann's description of Jupiter was 92 percent correct. He described a ring around Jupiter that scientists denied existed but whose presence today has been confirmed. His description of Mercury was less accurate but still included such valid details as the presence of a very thin atmosphere and the shape of Mercury's magnetic field.

"When you first start doing remote viewing you have very limited senses," Swann says. "You see fragments and do well to get them together so you can make something

Ingo Swann, the extraordinary OBE subject who projected himself into space to visit Mercury and Jupiter. (courtesy: Ingo Swann)

concrete out of them. But as you get more experienced, you seem to have more senses than just the ones you have in your physical body. For instance, you can see ultraviolet rays and infrared light."

Swann also participated in an auditory out-of-body study that Bill conducted in North Carolina, although at that time Swann was living in New York. During this study, Bill and his colleagues had a cassette recorder playing tapes of different sounds—bells, sirens, yodeling, and musical instruments—in random order in an empty room. At given times Swann, in out-of-body form, would fly in and listen to the tapes. Then when he returned to his body he would call and report to the scientists what sound was being played.

All his reports were accurate.

Another internationally recognized out-of-body traveler is a businessman named Robert Monroe, author of the book *Journeys out of the Body*. Monroe didn't start having OBEs until age forty-two. At first, afraid that something had gone wrong with his brain, he sought medical help. Doctors assured him that his brain was fine and could find no reason for the mysterious nocturnal experiences that took him on trips, not only to locations on Earth but to what appeared to be other dimensions of space.

Eventually Monroe's family became so accustomed to his unusual ability to travel out-of-body that, on one occasion, his oldest daughter glanced nervously around her college dorm room and said, "Daddy, if you're here, I think you'd better go now. My roommate and I want to get undressed for bed."

Monroe wasn't there at that time.

In an effort to find out as much as he could about this phenomenon, Monroe presented himself at the Research Department of the Topeka Veterans Administration Hospital and volunteered to project while hooked up to a polygraph. There, doctors discovered that when he went out of body, his brain waves slowed and there was a shift in energy from the left to the right side of his brain. More startling still, when Monroe's brain wave tracings changed, his breathing got shallow and his skin became dry and hot.

What actually happens to people during OBEs?

Parapsychologists have come up with two possibilities.

One theory holds that during the out-of-body experience a literal second body detaches from the physical body, taking with it the physical senses of sight, hearing, and touch, which the OBEer can use when visiting distant locations. This theory is supported by the fact that, in certain cases, people at a place that is visited by an OBEer have reported seeing that person's image appear in a ghostlike form at exactly the time he or she projected into the area.

A second theory holds that there is no true second body, and that the sensation of leaving the physical body and occupying an OBE body is hallucinatory. This theory is supported by the fact that OBEers frequently return from such "trips" with a mixed bag of information, some of which is incorrect. In some cases they appear to move into a kind of fantasy world, and in others they visit a real location but get distorted perceptions of it, as if their minds add additional elements to the experience. For instance, when Keith Harary took his friend George on an out-of-body trip to Maine, although the men gave identical descriptions of the terrain there were aspects of their reports that were not realistic, such as the pool of hot, bubbling, pink liquid that appeared to be dangerous.

These conflicting theories offer us two possibilities:

(1) That the astral body, once detached from the physical, is able to move not only into the physical environment but into alternate dimensions of reality.

(2) That OBEs are only hallucinations, sometimes with the addition of ESP.

Michael Persinger, a brain scientist at Laurentian University in Canada who has collaborated in some of Bill's studies, has expanded on that second theory by suggesting that the OBE may result from an interaction between the left and right hemispheres of the brain.

"This makes sense," Bill says, "because our conviction that we are individuals separate from others is a product of our left-brain hemisphere, which is the educated, language-oriented side of the brain. If severe physical or mental stress threatens this left-brain self, where can it escape to? Right next door, so to say, to the right brain hemisphere, which is the place where we process spatial information. Like a pilot in the ejection seat of a fighter plane that is in danger of crashing, the emotionally threatened OBEer finds himself projected into space, perhaps the familiar space of his home or perhaps an imaginary place, because the right side of the brain is also the source of imagination. This would explain why OBEers may sometimes give incorrect information about the places where they seem to have projected."

If astral projection is projection into a mental, not a material world, how is it that OBEers often give *correct* information about the real world, such as Keith Harary's report that there was only one kitten in a box in which he expected to find two?

"The right-brain hemisphere is our main connection to ESP," Bill says. "If, when our OBE self is visiting in the right-brain hemisphere, our thoughts go to friends and loved ones and pets we are fond of, we may become aware of them, not only through memory and imagination, but psychically too. The term for this type of ESP is *telepathy*.

33

This OBE self may extend to *objects* beyond our immediate physical environment, as when Dr. Tart's subject, Miss Z, learned the five-digit number during her OBE. The term for this type of ESP is *clairvoyance*. ESP awareness may also include the future, as when Miss Z saw the sad fate of the girl who was soon to be murdered. The term for this type of ESP is *precognition*.

"The OBE self represents something that is very important to us—our image of ourselves as individual, living, human organisms. The capacity to project this body image in an out-of-body experience is an aid to our well-being, because it helps the conscious mind to escape from situations where the body and brain are overwhelmed by physical or emotional pain."

Because OBEs utilize memory, they are affected by habit. Bill thinks that the abrupt termination of my OBE excursion by a traffic light may have resulted from my ingrained habit of always stopping at red lights, and that if the light had been green I would have sailed right through it. He says he experienced the same problem during an OBE when he attempted to thrust his out-of-body hand through a wall. Since real life experience had taught him to believe that hands can't go through walls, it was an unpleasant feeling to do that, and he was only able to get the hand in partway.

Whatever else may be said about out-of-body experiences, they open a fascinating window on the creative reaches and limitations of the human mind.

CHAPTER THREE

LIFE AT THE TIME OF DEATH

For those who know about OBEs, the natural next question to ask is, What happens to the astral self when it is launched on the ultimate out-of-body trip? What does that self experience when the physical body dies?

There is no living person who can answer that question with certainty, and the dead are not available to be interviewed. There are, however, a surprising number of people who claim to have experienced the first lap of that final journey. These are the people who have had *near-death experiences* (or NDEs, as they are commonly referred to by scientists). Due to injury, illness, or complications during surgery, NDEers have come very close to physical death. In some cases they may even have been pronounced clinically dead with a flat brain-wave pattern and no heartbeat but eventually responded to efforts to resuscitate them.

NDEers report out-of-body experiences that start out like ordinary OBEs but progress far beyond that.

Typical of these is the experience of fifteen-year-old Natalie, as reported by William Serdahely, a professor of health science at Montana State University.

Natalie had an acute asthma attack and passed out in the office of her pediatrician. While unconscious, she suffered a seizure that nearly killed her.

Two years later, she described the amazing things that happened when she was on the verge of death. She felt herself ejected from her body; then she entered a tunnel. At the end of the tunnel she saw a bright light and people waiting to welcome her. Suddenly two friendly "light figures" appeared, one on either side of her. Each took one of her hands, and they carried her with them down the tunnel. Natalie felt a strong desire to get to the Light and was impatient because her companions were moving so slowly.

As they traveled through the tunnel, Natalie saw images from her childhood, one of which was her father pushing her in a swing. Then she saw an image of her mother and thought about how sad her family would be if she died. At that point the "light figures" set Natalie down and released her hands. Concerned about the grief her death would cause her loved ones, Natalie reluctantly turned her back on the Light, walked back out of the tunnel, and returned to her body.

For centuries people who have come close to death have reported experiences similar to Natalie's, but those accounts were taken seriously only by psychic researchers until a young medical student, Raymond Moody, became intrigued by them. For ten years, Moody collected and investigated the reports of NDEers, and in 1975 he published a book, *Life After Life*, based upon well over a hundred case reports from people who had had near-death experiences.

The consistency of these case histories was difficult to ignore and motivated other scientists to conduct their own surveys.

Although every NDE did not contain every one of the following elements, all contained at least some of them:

1. A release from pain and a feeling of peace and well-being.

Sam, a man who, at age seventeen, had a near-death experience on a battlefield, reported: "I was in a great amount of pain. . . . I must have passed out from blood loss. . . . I don't know how long I was in this blacked-out state, but I began to rise out of my body. I felt no pain as I just seemed to stand up right there on the battlefield. Ahead of me was a beautiful light that took away my pain. It was shining and beautiful, and I could just stand there on this horrible battlefield and be safe with it."

2. An out-of-body experience.

Vi, a thirty-six-year-old wife and mother, had major surgery during which she apparently died. She told Bill Roll that after she heard the doctor announce that her lungs were gone, "There was this little buzzing sound, and I felt myself leaving the body up through the top of my head. I was looking back at these people, and they were saying, 'She's dead,' and I really didn't recognize the body at first as being myself, and I thought, *'Who's* dead?' And then I thought, 'They're speaking of *me! But I'm truly alive for the first time!'*

"I had been in such agony before in that other body, but now I was standing and watching and felt no pain. I saw people gathered out in the hall, and I wondered what they were there for. My husband and daughter were there. She was dressed in a conglomeration of clothes, and I wanted her to leave and change, but I couldn't make her understand. I tried to tell my husband, and he didn't understand me either.

"A friend walked by and stopped and spoke to my brother-in-law. He asked him, 'What are you doing here?' My brother-in-law said, 'My brother's wife is sick.' The friend asked, 'What are you going to do this weekend?' And my brother-in-law answered, 'Well, I planned to go to Athens and see Uncle Henry, but it looks like Vi is going to kick the bucket, so I'll be sticking around and be a pallbearer.'"

Later, after Vi's recovery, her brother-in-law, with a red face, admitted the conversation had taken place exactly as Vi described hearing it.

3. The sensation of drifting through darkness, which in many cases took the form of a tunnel.

A teenage boy who, at age ten, nearly died from an unidentified illness, reported: "I don't remember the entrance, but in a little while I was in a dark tunnel. There was absolutely no sound, and all was black. I couldn't see to make my way through the tunnel, but I was being wafted along as a speck of dust, pitch black, but as I went along with neither sight nor sound, I felt at ease. It seemed as though I was discovering a new cave."

4. Encounters with guides, angels, or light beings.

Dean, a sixteen-year-old kidney patient, whose heart stopped beating when he was in the admitting room of the hospital, reported: "I reached a certain point in the tunnel where lights suddenly began flashing all around me. . . . At this point I also noticed that there was somebody with me. He was about seven feet tall and wore a long white gown with a simple belt tied at the waist. His hair was golden, and although he didn't say anything, I wasn't afraid, because I could feel him radiating peace and love. He wasn't

Christ, but I knew that he was sent from Christ. It was probably one of His angels or someone else sent to transport me to heaven."

5. Entering into a radiant landscape at the tunnel's end where the NDEer is united with departed loved ones.
As Vi's OBE continued, "guides" took her through a tunnel.

"We started through the tunnel, and I got the feeling of going up," she told Bill. "Suddenly we came out in this beautiful place. The colors—you can't describe them; they're much more brilliant than they are here. There is music, but not the church type. There was this open meadow, and there were my mother and grandparents. Both my grandfathers had died before I was born, but I knew immediately who they were when they came to greet me.

"All of a sudden I saw this baby, and he said, 'Look at me carefully so you can describe me when you go back.' I said, 'I'm not going anywhere,' but nevertheless I did as he said, and afterward when I was able to talk to my father, he admitted that there had been a brother between my sister and myself and that no one knew about it. The baby appeared to me as he was dressed as an infant, so I could tell my father. But immediately after I had absorbed what I was to know, he was in the prime of life."

This is an example of what are called "Peak in Darien" cases, where NDEers report encounters on "the other side" with people of whose death they had not even been aware.

"I had always been interested in FDR, *and I saw him!*" Vi continued. "He was sitting in a chair, reading a book. I had a girlfriend who'd died of polio, and I hadn't thought of her since I don't know when, and I saw *her!* I had worried about her when she died, because she died so young. Why was her

39

life cut so short? But now she assured me that everything was just great and it had been time for her to go."

According to Vi, people communicated by a kind of telepathy, but more intimately.

"You see, everything is one," she explained. "There can't ever be any misunderstanding about what's being said."

An even more fascinating account was given by a man named Monson who experienced an NDE after "dying" of a strangulated hernia. He described encountering his deceased daughter who told him, "Go back, Papa, I want Richard first. Then Grandma must come, and then Mama is coming before you." Monson survived and later reported that those family members predeceased him and passed away in that exact order.

6. A panoramic past-life review.

A man who, at age eighteen, had his chest crushed while working between carriages on a railroad reported: "There was something like a film went through my mind. It went that fast! You get every picture and think you have died. It appears to run for a long time although it is only a few seconds. It was the years of my life—what I had done, wrong or good. I think it was from the beginning of my life —what I have done, where I have been. When I think back I can still see the film running. I don't see any pictures anymore but I still have it in my mind."

The life review is usually not just an ordinary rerun of the NDEer's past activities. What he experiences is the pain or joy that his actions have given others.

A twenty-three-year-old woman reexperienced a childhood incident with her younger sister, not the way it was for her but the way it was for her sister.

"After the Easter egg hunt, I yanked my little sister's Easter basket away from her, because there was a toy in it that I wanted," she said. "In the review I felt her feelings of disappointment and loss and rejection."

7. Heading toward a cosmic being or place of light on the other side of a border or crossing.

After describing her meeting with loved ones, Vi told Bill, "I saw in the distance the City of Lights, and I wanted to go toward it. Then I heard my daughter's voice crying, 'Mom, don't leave me!' and my husband calling, 'Vi, come back!' I looked toward the City, and I knew that if I crossed and went into it, I could never return."

To enter the City, she said, would have been "reuniting with God."

8. A moment of decision about whether to continue on into the Light or to return to earthly circumstances. Sometimes this decision was left to the NDEer, and at other times it was made by the angel or guide.

Paul, who, at age ten, went into shock from internal bleeding caused by a ruptured spleen, reported: "At the end of the tunnel I was met by a Being who talked to me. I thought of him as a Greeter. . . . The Greeter was not in a physical form. He was more a feeling or an awareness. He told me that I could not stay in the tunnel, that I had to either go back or continue on. If I continued, there would be no return.

"I didn't make an actual decision to return, but I did get the idea from the Greeter that there was purpose to my life. While I was thinking about whether to stay or return, I felt myself enter my body. . . . For a while I longed for that Light. Then I realized that someday I would see it again. In the meantime, I had things to do."

* * *

41

The astonishing results of Moody's innovative study motivated another young scientist, Kenneth Ring, to conduct his own series of interviews with over one hundred people who had been close to death. Almost half of these reported having had NDEs that contained some or all of the elements that were cited in Moody's book. Ring's own book, *Life at Death*, was published in 1982.

With the surveys by Moody and Ring as a jumping-off point, other doctors, psychologists, and hospital personnel began to accumulate cases involving near-death experiences. They weren't difficult to find; a Gallup poll conducted the year Ring's book came out estimated 8 million of them. Over and over again, researchers received the same basic reports of out-of-body trips through tunnels, of meetings with deceased loved ones, of loving authority figures, and, above all, of the wondrous experience of being drawn toward a Light that was described as "beautiful . . . joyful . . . brilliant . . . golden . . . radiating love."

One of the leaders in NDE research was Melvin Morse, who became interested in the subject as a pediatric intern in a small town in Idaho when his ten-year-old patient, Katie, almost drowned in a swimming pool. Katie was not expected to survive, but after three days in a coma she miraculously regained consciousness and described an out-of-body journey that included a detailed report of activities in the emergency room; a trip through a tunnel accompanied by a guide named Elizabeth; a meeting with a deceased grandfather, and with two young boys named Andy and Mark who identified themselves as "souls waiting to be born"; a visit to her home where, invisible to her family, she watched her mother cook a chicken dinner, while her father sat alone on the couch in the living room and her brothers and sisters played with toys in their rooms; and, finally, a meeting with the Heavenly Father and Jesus, who asked her if she wanted to see her mother again.

Katie told Morse that when she responded "Yes" to that question, she was returned to her body and allowed to come out of the coma.

What set Katie's account apart from most other NDE reports was that part of it could be verified. She was able to identify by sight the doctors who had worked over her in the emergency room and to describe the techniques they had used in their attempts to resuscitate her, despite the fact that her body had been unconscious at the time. Her parents confirmed her report of what had been going on in their home during her out-of-body visit. Her description of the clothes family members were wearing, their physical location in the house, and the details of the activities they were involved in—including the fact that her brother had been playing with a G.I. Joe doll in a toy jeep and her sister had been combing the hair of a Barbie doll—were totally accurate.

Morse's experience with Katie spurred him to begin his own study of NDEs at a major hospital in Seattle. This research, which was centered specifically on the near-death experiences of children, eventually led to a best-selling book, *Closer to the Light*.

It also led to an exciting discovery. During the course of their study, Morse's team of researchers seemed able to identify the precise area of the brain in which near-death experiences originate. They found that when the Sylvian fissure, which is close to the right temporal lobe just above the right ear, is electrically stimulated, the same visions and sensations as an NDE are experienced. To Morse and his colleagues this suggested that the Sylvian fissure might be an area genetically coded to be a sort of launching pad from which the astral self can be ejected when death is imminent.

As might be expected, there were many scientists who considered this theory ridiculous. They felt that the discovery that the brain was involved in setting off an NDE meant that the near-death experience was only a hallucination, caused perhaps by a lack of oxygen. Morse investigated this possibility and discovered that, while it's true that a lack of oxygen can cause hallucinations, they are typically weird, frightening images that bear no resemblance to the lovely, comforting visions that are part of an NDE trip. In addition, the factual and objective reports of resuscitation techniques apparently observed during the initial stages of NDEs bore no resemblance to the distortions and fantasies that were the usual products of oxygen-starved brains.

Skeptical scientists came up with a second theory—that NDEs might be illusions caused by drug intoxication.

Morse investigated this possibility also and found that none of the medicines and painkillers with which his NDE subjects had been treated for their illnesses and injuries—including such drugs as morphine, phenobarbital, Valium, and codeine—cause hallucinations that are at all like NDEs. There were also a number of subjects, particularly accident victims, who experienced NDEs when they weren't being treated with any medication at all.

The well-known astronomer Carl Sagan came up with a third theory—that the near-death experience might be based upon a memory of the birth process. Sagan speculated that the dark tunnel with a light at the end might reflect the prebirth experience of traveling down the birth canal, and that the powerful figure waiting in the Light was constructed upon the memory of the doctor or midwife who ushered the NDEer into the world.

Arguments against this theory were that an infant in the

process of birth has its face pressed against the side of the birth canal and is in no position to see the light at its end; that the eyesight of a newborn is not developed enough to distinguish figures to any significant degree; and that experiments have proven that infants have little visual memory, which is why so few of us remember events from early childhood. Case studies also revealed that NDEers who had been born surgically by cesarean section and, therefore, had never traveled down the birth canal, gave the same report of the trip through the long, dark tunnel as those who had experienced a vaginal birth.

Morse's research uncovered what he considers evidence that NDEs are much more than mere hallucinations.

NDEers do appear to leave their physical bodies and, in many cases, the environment surrounding them. The typical NDE often begins as an out-of-body experience during which the NDEer observes things that he or she could not possibly see from the location of the inert and unconscious body.

At age eleven, a subject from Morse's study in Seattle experienced cardiac arrest and was without a heartbeat for twenty minutes.

"I heard a whooshing sound in my ears," he told the doctor. "I felt like you feel when you go over a bump in a car going real fast and you feel your stomach drop out. The next thing I knew, I was in a room, crouched in a corner of the ceiling. I could see my body below me. . . . I could see doctors and nurses working on me. My doctor was there and so was Sandy, one of the nurses. I heard Sandy say, 'I wish we didn't have to do this.' I wondered what they were doing. I saw a doctor put jelly on my chest. My hair was really messed up. It seemed greasy, and I wished that I had washed my hair before coming to the hospital. They had cut my clothes off, but my pants were still on. I heard a doctor say, 'Stand back,' and then he pushed a button on one of the paddles. Suddenly I was back inside my body. One minute I was looking down at my face. I could see the tops of the doctors' heads. After he pushed that button, I was suddenly looking into a doctor's face."

The boy's report was accurate in every detail.

In another well-documented case on file at the Harborview Medical Center in Seattle, a woman recovering from a heart attack reported leaving her body while being resuscitated and finding herself on a ledge of another story of the hospital, where she spotted a tennis shoe with a worn toe. With some difficulty, the hospital personnel checked the ledge, where they discovered the shoe exactly as the patient described it.

There is also the question of why the NDEs of thousands of individuals from a variety of backgrounds and belief systems were virtually identical. It would seem reasonable to expect that an atheist who did not believe in an afterlife, a fundamentalist who expected to be punished for his sins, and a child too young to have been exposed to religious concepts, would hallucinate differently. Yet almost all NDEers report the same experiences of leaving the body, speeding through a tunnel, meeting deceased loved ones, having a panoramic life review, and encountering the Light.

A third indication that NDEs may be more than neurological reactions to physical trauma is the dramatic and lasting effect they have on the people who experience them. In a large majority of cases an encounter with the Light appears to cause a radical change in personality and in the way people relate to the world around them. People who go through a near-death experience seem to become more psychic, more compassionate toward others, and more determined to live life to the fullest.

One teenager reported he was now more serious than most kids his age, but a lot happier.

"I don't feel like partying and drinking as much as my friends do or doing a lot of stupid stuff," he said. "I know that there is a better reason for living."

A teenage girl echoed those feelings.

"I see things differently than most people," she told Dr. Morse. "Little things that bother others don't really bother me. I feel calmer and more in control."

A study conducted by Bruce Greyson, a doctor of emergency psychiatry at the University of Connecticut, showed that almost all people who have NDEs during suicide attempts never again try to kill themselves. In contrast, a high percentage of those who attempt suicide, but do *not* experience NDEs, make further attempts to take their lives. The NDE has such a positive effect that desperate people who feel their lives have no meaning return from an NDE with a renewed sense of purpose.

NDEers also seem to lose all fear of dying.

In one study conducted in Australia, forty people, ranging in age from seven to fifty-eight, were asked if they feared death before their NDEs.

Seventy-eight percent responded that they did.

When asked if they now feared death, every one of them said "No." They felt they had been given a preview of what comes next and were certain it was going to be wonderful.

The same holds true for subjects in U.S. studies.

One teenage girl reported to Dr. Morse that the Light had been so incredible that at first she had not wanted to leave it.

Then she heard a voice say, "But look what you would be missing!"

"I saw a tall blond man walking with two children," the girl said. "The little girl jumped up and down, and her curls

47

shook. The other was a boy. I recognized this as being my future family. I felt a longing for my husband and children even before I had met them! I began to waver about the joys of being dead before I had even experienced the fullness of life. 'I want to go back,' I said. And I went back.

"But I realize now that death is not to be feared. The only real fear is in not accomplishing our work in this life."

This girl is now grown and married to a tall, blond basketball player. They have two children—a girl and a boy.

In Raymond Moody's second book on NDEs, *The Light Beyond*, he explored the long-lasting psychological effects experienced by NDEers. He found that NDEers usually have a new respect for people, for nature, and for all the world around them. Although this is a difficult concept for NDEers to put into words, they report a deep sense of interconnection with all things. This feeling of interconnection is reflected in increased psychic awareness of people and things. NDEers also report a new respect for knowledge. Many NDEers embark on new careers or new courses of study, not to advance their careers, but because they believe knowledge contributes to the wholeness of the person.

Moody has also observed what he believes are fundamentally different psychological reactions to crisis events from NDEers and non-NDEers. Crises like combat, auto wrecks, medical emergencies, and personal disasters often leave people emotionally stuck at that point in time. While the NDE is often caused by a crisis, the NDEer usually responds by taking positive action and moving forward with his or her life.

An additional fascinating discovery by Melvin Morse was that one-fourth of the adults who survive near-death experiences cannot wear watches; the watches stop running. Timepieces that work perfectly when worn by other people will not operate on the wrists of 25 percent of NDEers.

In his book *Transformed by the Light,* Morse speculates that the near-death experience may be so powerful that it permanently alters the electromagnetic forces surrounding the human body. "In short, people who have near-death experiences are 'rewired,' " he says. "In a large number of people there is such a profound change that their electromagnetic signature can actually stop a watch."

Bill Roll has a theory about what happens during the NDE.

"There appear to be three distinct levels of the NDE," he says. "First there is an out-of body experience; then a telepathic encounter with loved ones; and finally a merging with the Cosmic Being of Light, which many people call God."

Bill believes that these different states of NDEs result from our having three different levels of self.

He compares these three selves to a set of dolls that fit one inside another. The NDEer may experience one, two, or —for what is termed the *core NDE*—a third stage, that goes far beyond the others. When all three types are experienced, it is usually one after another, with each expanding into the next after some type of transition.

Typically the first transition takes the form of a tunnel, leading from the initial out-of-body experience to the encounter with loved ones; while the second takes the form of a crossing of some sort that takes the NDEer from the meeting with loved ones into the heavenly realm of the Cosmic Being of Light. The third stage of the death experience is beginning to merge with the Light. *All* NDEers return before the final merging.

"But unlike nesting dolls that, except for their ever-increasing size, are duplicates of each other, the three levels of the near-death experience are totally different," Bill says. "The self that experiences the initial OBE stage of a near-death experience is similar to the self that occupies the physical body. It usually seems to have a shape, including head and arms, and it sees, hears, and moves about like the physical body, though much more freely."

In fact, senses that were impaired in the physical body seem to function perfectly during an out-of-body experience. One seventy-eight-year-old woman, who had been blind since the age of eighteen, had an OBE while being resuscitated after a heart attack. In her out-of-body state she apparently regained her sight, for she was later able to describe instruments used to resuscitate her that had not been invented back when she could see. She also accurately reported the colors in the room and correctly stated that her doctor was wearing a blue suit.

"In the first stage of an NDE, the out-of-body self is concerned with all the same things that occupy the embodied self," Bill says. "For instance, Vi, the young mother who 'died' during surgery, wanted her daughter to look right by wearing clothes that matched. That was her everyday self talking, except that it had emerged from her physical body.

"The second phase of the NDE is reached by a transformation that's usually experienced as a dark space or tunnel that opens up into a realm of radiant light and love. Ordinary concerns, like dressing or looking right, which are important for everyday social relations and even for the first OBE self, evaporate like dew in the sun at this second level. The NDEer has now expanded into a larger Self of direct and joyful union with loved ones.

"The third level of an NDE is as different from the second level as the second is from the first. It, too, is reached by a transformation of the Self, this time often experienced as a river or border that must be crossed. Beyond this, there is a Being or Place of Universal Love and Light that exerts a powerful pull upon the NDEer. At the same time, there is the realization that once you merge with the Light, you cannot go back. At this stage, if not before, the NDEer must return to his body, or the *near*-death experience will become the real thing."

Bill believes that the three types of NDE are related to brain function, but in different ways.

"The out-of-body experience that usually occurs at times of physical or emotional trauma is the body's way of reducing stress," he says. "When consciousness is projected into a space that seems to be outside the physical body, the anxiety that results from the stress disappears, and the body is better able to heal itself."

There is another reason why Bill believes that the brain is involved in the creation of OBEs. Reports by OBEers suggest that astral projection may require bodily energy. When the Psychical Research Foundation team of scientists monitored Keith Harary's body during his OBEs, they found that his respiration and heart rate increased, indicating that effort was required.

"The second level of the near-death experience is different," Bill says. "The stage of psychic connections, which usually comes at the end of the OBE journey, is the result of a total letting go. Mind and brain are now completely relaxed and open to impressions, and there is not even the effort of astral projection.

"During this stage of an OBE, the Self, so to say, has one leg in the brain and another outside. Some of the experiences may be due to things going on in the brain—the result, for instance, of too little oxygen or too much carbon dioxide—but the psychic awareness of people and things beyond the reach of the brain and its sense organs cannot be explained by brain processes only."

This suggests to Bill that the individual brain and its mind are part of a larger psychic self that extends into space and time to include other people, living as well as dead.

"This psychic self exists before the birth of the individual and continues after death," he says. "It is not infinite, but mainly consists of people linked by family and friendship."

Then, there are some NDEers who actually approach the third level, a cosmic Self of light and love that permeates everything in time and space. Bill points out that the way this is described by NDEers is almost indistinguishable from the way modern physicists talk about the universe as consisting of intertwining fields of light energy.

"What physicists and astronomers study through microscopes and telescopes, the NDEer may experience directly," Bill says.

How can the finite human brain open up to the infinite?

"The brain is a filtering organism," Bill explains. "Many scientists believe that its primary function is not to produce experiences, but to filter them out. It's the fact that the brain stem, which is the primitive part of the brain directly linked to the spinal cord, regulates the flow of sensory information to which we are regularly exposed that prevents us from being overwhelmed by it. If we were sensitive to all the energies that surround us, it would be like a perpetual Fourth of July fireworks display. We would be unable to find our way in the world with all that chaos. The brain lets in only enough information to enable us to do what's necessary to find food and shelter and fend for ourselves as human beings.

"I propose that, as death approaches, the filters in the brain dissolve, and the Self becomes aware of realities it formerly blocked out, such as the fact that it is part of a living universe of Love and Light."

CHAPTER FOUR

APPARITIONS AND HAUNTINGS

A woman in Kentucky, who had just given birth to her second child in two years, felt guilty because she had been too busy to write her friend Betty, who had tuberculosis.

Then early one morning she awoke to the sound of the front door opening in the lower hall.

"I arose to see who it was," she says, "and, hanging over the banisters, I looked into the upturned face of Betty. She was steadily climbing the stairs, and, when she reached the upper hall where I stood, she put her arm around me and said, 'I just couldn't go by without seeing those two wonderful children you've been telling me about.'

"I took her into the room where they slept, and she went from one crib to the other, hanging over them and admiring them. Then she said, 'I must go now,' and I took her to the head of the stairs, where she told me, 'Don't bother coming down with me. I can let myself out.'

"As I stood watching her, she moved down the stairs and out the door."

The incident made the woman feel guiltier than ever, and she immediately wrote Betty the long-overdue letter, describing the details of what she referred to as "a very vivid dream."

Weeks later she received a letter from Betty's father, saying that Betty had died on the same date and at the very same time that her friend had experienced the visitation.

The young mother's explanation for this seemingly incredible coincidence is that "Betty stopped by to see us on her way to her 'new environment.'"

A woman named Florence reports a dream in which she entered her father-in-law's home in another state and found him lying in an adjustable hospital bed.

"He reached up and put his arms around me and sobbed," she says. "At that point, I awoke. Then a man's voice called, 'Florence!' I thought it was coming from outside the window. I turned to look out, and there, standing alongside my bed, was my father-in-law. I saw every feature just as though he were in the flesh. He looked right in my eyes and spoke my name again. He said, 'Florence, the Lord is my shepherd, and we go in peace.' This vision was enveloped in a very pale blue light. Then it just seemed to dissolve and fade away.

"The next day a telegram came saying that Dad had passed on. In due time a letter came from my mother-in-law giving us the details of his death. She said they had to get a hospital bed for him, just as I saw in the dream. She said when he was dying he said, 'The Lord is my shepherd, and we go in peace.'"

A woman in Maine describes an incident that occurred when she was ten.

"My father was in the hospital recovering from surgery,

and I was sent next door to stay overnight with my girl-friend," she says. "I woke up, and at the foot of the bed was the most beautiful light I had ever seen. There was my father, with his arms open to me, and as I watched, he was rising up. I called to my girlfriend, telling her my father was dead. We got up and lit the light. It was just ten after four in the morning.

"Soon my uncle came from the hospital to tell us my father had passed away, and that he called to me as he was dying. He passed away at exactly ten after four."

These are only three of the over fourteen thousand accounts of psychic experiences compiled by Louisa Rhine, a noted researcher and author of the book *Hidden Channels of the Mind*. Unlike the misty wraiths that float through Hollywood spectaculars or the traditional sheet-clad spirits that symbolize Halloween, the apparitions in real life reports appear to be solid, in some cases even casting shadows, and are dressed in clothing consistent with the situation.

Tales about ghosts have been recorded in virtually all cultures throughout history. According to a Gallup poll, one in every four Americans believes in them, and one in ten claims actually to have seen one.

The sheer number of such reports makes them difficult to ignore. People are reacting to something—the question is *what*? Are they really seeing disembodied spirits? Do the dead continue to exist on this earth in a nonphysical form that occasionally can be detected by the human eye?

There are those who believe that they do, but there are other possibilities.

Many skeptics contend that apparitions are nothing more than hallucinations experienced by people who have lost control of their faculties due to intoxication, illness, grief, or mental disturbances.

There is no doubt that there are times when this is the case. In fact, it's highly probable that in the largest number of instances of ghost sightings the apparitions are the product of overactive imaginations.

It is also true that a number of reputed sightings are instances of out-and-out fraud. There have been plenty of cases in which convincing accounts of supernatural activity have triggered best-selling books and box-office hits, and then turned out to be cleverly orchestrated hoaxes.

On the other hand, some reports of ghostly visitations cannot be explained away so easily.

One of the most famous of these is the Chaffin Will Case.

In 1905, a North Carolina farmer named James Chaffin made a will leaving everything he owned to his third son, Marshall, with nothing to go to his other three sons or to his wife. In 1919, he evidently thought better of this, for he made a second will, dividing his estate equally among all his sons, under the condition that they would take care of their mother.

Chaffin told no one about this second will, which he placed in the family Bible. He did, however, write a note saying what he had done with it and sewed that into the lining of his overcoat.

In 1921, Chaffin died from a fall. Since his family knew nothing about the second will, the first will went through probate, and Marshall inherited everything.

Four years later, in June 1925, Chaffin's second son, James, had a dream in which his father appeared wearing his overcoat and announced, "You will find my will in my overcoat pocket." James was so affected by the dream that he inquired around about the overcoat and learned that it had been given to his oldest brother, John.

In July, he went to visit John and looked in the overcoat pocket. In the lining he found, not the will itself, as the dream had indicated, but the note saying where it could be located. James then went to his mother's house and searched the bookshelves until he found the ancient Bible with the will between its pages.

This new will, which was in Chaffin's handwriting, was declared valid and admitted to probate. It took precedence over the old will, and Chaffin's estate was redistributed.

What makes this case so noteworthy is that the probate of the wills makes the dates and circumstances a matter of legal record, and James's claim to have learned about the second will from his deceased father is difficult to challenge. Who else could have given him that information? If James had known about the existence of the second will at the time of his father's death, he would not have waited four years before claiming his inheritance.

The term *apparition* is defined as "the visual appearance of a person who is not really there."

The three case histories at the beginning of this chapter are reports of what scientists refer to as *crisis apparitions*, seen when the subject is right at the point of death or suffering from a serious illness or injury.

Are these experiences due to out-of-body visits from the dying to comfort the living and to say a final good-bye, or is there another explanation?

Parapsychologists hold different opinions.

Some are convinced that the image sighted is the astral self, free of the body and on its way to another dimension.

Others believe that crisis apparitions are the result of ESP. They theorize that during a serious illness or accident, an emotional alarm is sounded that can be picked up telepathically by people the traumatized person is close to and that produces a hallucination in which a visual image of that person is seen.

In support of the ESP theory is the fact that apparitions

are not always of dead people. There are also apparitions of people who are still alive and in the best of health and who are not having an out-of-body experience when the apparition is seen.

I once appeared as an apparition to my father.

My father was having triple bypass surgery in a hospital in Minnesota, while I was hundreds of miles away in New Mexico. I had spent the day worrying about him as I sat by the telephone, waiting for news.

Finally, after eight long hours, the phone rang. It was my stepmother calling to tell me the operation was a success and my father was out of surgery and in the recovery room.

I was so relieved that I jumped up and down and clapped my hands.

The following day, my father phoned me.

"I saw you yesterday," he told me. "When I was coming out from under the anesthetic I opened my eyes and saw you standing in the doorway. You were grinning from ear to ear and clapping your hands. That's when I knew I was going to be okay."

Since I was not having an out-of-body experience when my father had that vision, it seems reasonable to believe that in that moment of intense emotion, I telepathically transmitted my relief and jubilation to him without being aware that I was doing so.

Among the thousands of apparition reports collected by Louisa Rhine there are many that might best be explained as instances of telepathy.

What other explanation can there be for a story like this one?

A woman in Wisconsin went to bed early after a tiring day.

Two hours later she awoke from a nightmare.

"I saw my husband standing in the bedroom door, his face all bloody and beaten up," she reports. "His clothing was covered with blood, and he was saying, 'Don't be alarmed, Mother. I just had a little accident.' I jumped out of bed, turned on the light, and there was no one there. I looked at the clock, and the time was nearly ten-thirty.

"I went back to bed, and around midnight I was awakened again. There, standing in the bedroom door, was my husband, face all beaten up, clothing all bloody, looking just like I had seen him two hours before. He said, 'Don't be alarmed, Mother. I've just had a little accident.' I said, 'What time did this happen?' He said, 'Around ten-thirty.'

"Two brothers had beaten him up about an old grudge."

Stories like this suggest that there may be a sort of mental telephone line connecting people who care about each other and that instances of shock or violence on one end of that line may make the "phone ring" at the other end.

Accumulated case histories indicate that children may be particularly sensitive to this kind of communication. The Louisa Rhine collection contains a number of stories like the following:

A family in Wisconsin was returning home from a trip when the four-year-old in the backseat suddenly asked, "Did Aunt Myrtle and Uncle Charles have a wreck with a train?"

"What are you talking about!" his father exclaimed.

"I see'd they did," the child said matter-of-factly.

The following day word came that the aunt and uncle had stalled their car on a railroad crossing. Luckily they were able to get out of the vehicle before it was hit and demolished by a train.

This occurred at the very same time their nephew reported "seeing" them.

* * *

Telepathy may be a feasible explanation for a crisis apparition, but what about apparitions that are seen, heard to speak, and even experienced physically, after the subject is dead?

Kim, one of Bill's parapsychology students, says that when she was eight years old she saw the apparition of her grandmother at the woman's funeral.

"My grandmother and I had always been very close, and I was taking her passing very, very hard," she says. "At the funeral home I stayed by her casket most of the time. Once, during the afternoon, I became aware of a change in the atmosphere around me. I began to feel very cold, and I decided to look around to see where the chill was coming from. When I turned around, I saw what appeared to be my grandmother. She was standing beside me, looking down at her physical body. As I stood there in shock, she turned around, looked at me, and then smiled at me. I quickly closed my eyes, I guess with terror, and when I opened them again, she was gone."

Another of Bill's students, Cynthea, reports having experienced a visit from her grandmother two years after the woman's death. In her case, rather than being frightening, she found the visitation comforting.

"My grandmother died right in front of me when I was six years old," she says. "It was a frightening experience and very disturbing to a young child. I felt very lonely and upset and had terrible dreams. Then one night when I was eight, I woke up in the middle of the night, and found my grandmother lying beside me in bed. I remember cuddling up to her and feeling such a burst of love and comfort. I swear to this day that she was in my bed and rocked me in her arms. My parents told me it was just a dream, but I don't believe that. I really think it was my grandmother helping me get over the tragedy of her death. My nightmares about her dying ended after her 'visit.' "

Stories like those of Kim and Cynthea suggest that the mental and emotional connection between people who love each other may continue to exist even after one of them dies.

It may even span generations.

"My daughter, Mary Lynn, never knew my mother," my friend Jim tells me, "but when Mary Lynn's little girl, Emily, was two years old a strange thing happened. My daughter heard Emily apparently talking to somebody in her room. Then she heard Emily say something like, 'Carkey! Carkey!' Mary Lynn assumed Emily meant 'car key,' even though she had never used that word before, and asked Emily who she was talking to. Emily replied, 'Mama's grandma.' Mary Lynn asked her what the grandma lady said to her, and Emily said, 'She said "I love you." ' Mary Lynn is open to psychic phenomena, and, suspecting that the 'grandma lady' might be her paternal grandmother, she called and asked me what my mother's maiden name was. I told her, 'Carkeek!' "

Michael Grosso, a renowned philosopher and psychic researcher, reports an even more incredible experience.

"I was living in Jersey City at the time," he says. "It was a very hot night, and I was unable to sleep, so I moved into the living room and lay on the couch. I drifted off, and at dawn I woke up and looked up, and there before me was an apparition of my deceased grandmother and another woman whom I had never seen before in my life. They were just sort of peering at me, and then they disappeared."

Later, when Grosso described the vision to his mother, she said, "That second woman sounds like your great-aunt Kate."

Grosso, who had not known his great-aunt, asked his

mother if she had any pictures of the woman, and his mother dug out an old photograph of a group of ten people, four or five of whom were women, all approximately the same age.

"Immediately, I was able to recognize this woman," Grosso says. "I picked her right out as the woman I had seen in my apparition. This was a very impressive experience for me, because I had never seen the woman, yet I saw an apparition of her many, many years after she died. Why I saw it, I can't imagine."

Bill Rolls's term for the concept of interlinked selves of both the living and dead is the *longbody*. The longbody concept originated with the Iroquois Indians, who used it to refer to the "tribal body," a web of living connections with other members of the tribe both living and dead. Other people throughout the centuries have had varying names for this cluster of psychic connections, Christians generally referring to it as "the Body of Christ."

"According to this concept, we are all bound mentally and even physically to the people we care about, as though, in some way, we are part of a single organism," Bill says. "The closest I can come to explaining it is to compare it to my body. My kidneys are quite different from my lungs, my heart from my liver, my right hand from my left hand, so each has a separate identity; at the same time, all are part of my body and are connected by a single bloodstream and nervous system. In that same way, the members of my longbody are connected by telepathy, and that telepathic connection does not seem to end with death."

Apparitions of the deceased that appear in familiar surroundings are seen most often at the time of death or soon afterward, with these instances decreasing rapidly during the following days and weeks, although images of people who died suddenly or violently may persist much longer.

Bill's student Andrea reports seeing the apparition of her grandfather when she was helping sort through his belongings weeks after his death.

"My grandfather passed away at home," she says. "It was in a house where he and my grandmother had lived for a long time. After his death, my grandmother and my sister and I were cleaning out his bedroom, when, for some reason, something made us all turn around to face the attic stairs. There on the stairs stood my grandfather, gazing straight at us! He looked the same as he did before he died, except his eyes were red as if he had been crying. We just stood there in shock, unable to make a sound. Then my grandmother called his name, and he disappeared. I'm absolutely certain this was the ghost of my grandfather, because all three of us saw him; we were amazed and frightened, but we could not all have imagined the same thing."

It's possible that some apparitions seen after death may represent the conscious spirit of the dead, while others may not. Bill's teacher at Oxford University, H. H. Price, felt that many cases of hauntings could be explained as *place memories*. Price discovered that memories, or something resembling memories, may not only reside in the brain, but also in the places where events take place. Like brain memories, place memories of hurtful events last longer and have a stronger impact than others. They can therefore be picked up by people who visit the location even long after the events.

"I've had two different people tell me that they were overcome with feelings of rage when camping in areas that, in one instance, they later discovered was a battleground from the U.S. Civil War and, in the other, an Indian battleground," Bill says. "Their experiences included sounds and visual images consistent with the histories of those places."

Price believed that place memory might provide an explanation for *psychometry*, the ESP method by which an object may be used to obtain information about the events associated with it. Psychometry is used extensively by psychic detectives to gain information during murder investigations by handling an object or an article of clothing that was on the body of the victim at the time of death.

Bevy Jaegers, head of the United States Psi Squad, a team of psychometrists who pool their talents to act as group consultants to law enforcement agencies, attributes the success of psychometry to the fact that human energy has the ability to impress its force into inanimate objects.

"Let's suppose you have a ring, watch, or bracelet that you wear very often," she says. "During the time you're wearing this item, your personal force field is penetrating it. After a time this item will carry a sort of signature of you, which anyone trained in psychometry will be able to read."

Jaegers says that if more than one person owns or wears an item, the item will absorb the personalities of all of them.

"But they don't meld into one," she says. "They always remain separate. When you psychometrize the object, you may get the first owner and then the second one, or it may be the other way around. You can also get impressions about people who are closely associated with the wearer and can pick up impressions about the places in which the wearer spends his or her time."

Jaegers, author of *Psychometry: The Science of Touch*, also believes that objects absorb energy from other objects with which they have had close contact, and that this energy continues to link the two objects even when they are separated.

"This became very clear when our psychometry team took on the task of predicting earthquakes," she says. "We were startled to discover that a given rock from a certain fault zone would actually start to feel hot to us when a quake was about to occur in the area from which it was taken. One night a rock sample given to me by Dr. Jeffrey Goodman from a fault zone near San Diego started heating up, and I spent the whole evening trying to reach Goodman to warn him. The quake occurred the next morning, and it was a big one. The only way I can find to explain this is that the rock may have retained an attachment to the place from which it was taken and had enough of a lingering relationship with that area to be an indicator of a major event like an earthquake."

In another interesting, though less dramatic, experiment, an archaeologist challenged Jaegers to psychometrize fragments of shell and shards of pottery from archaeologic digs to see if she could determine where they came from.

"One tiny piece of shell gave me a picture of a civilization to the west of me," she says. "I got the styles of houses, decorations and styles of pottery, and the name *Zuni*. From a fragment of a pot I got entirely different styles of dwellings, pottery, and decoration, and the word *Aztec*. I identified three more fragments, one of them *Hopi*. The archaeologist verified that all these impressions were accurate and said he did not believe that any professional archaeologist could have done better unless he had spent a lifetime working with Indian artifacts from those particular civilizations."

Bill Roll feels that place memories may be one explanation for the phenomenon of hauntings.

"The longbody does not only include people," he says. "It also includes things and places that are important to us, like our homes and belongings. When you make a study of hauntings, you find that ghosts are nearly always reported in areas that the deceased person spent time in when he or she was alive. This seems to indicate that the memories of the deceased are still attached to these physical portions of the longbody."

Place memory may provide an explanation for a haunting case Bill investigated on the *Queen Mary*, the old transatlantic liner that is now permanently docked in Long Beach, California.

Bill spent ten days on the ship at the request of the producers of the TV program *Unsolved Mysteries* in order to interview people who had reported what seemed to be haunting incidents and to try to discover the source of their experiences.

One of these people was a young woman named Nancy Waznik who was working her way through college as a tour guide. One night after the tourists had gone, Nancy saw the apparition of a crew member in the area where a man who looked like the apparition had been crushed to death when a watertight door closed during a fire drill.

Another report came from one of the ship's security guards. During his first four years on board, the guard had been assigned to the graveyard shift between the hours of eleven P.M. and seven A.M. He told Bill that sometimes at night, long after the tourists had gone and the area was empty of people, he would hear voices in the bow.

A second witness, who had been the chief engineer during the *Queen's* last voyage from England in 1967 and who stayed on after the ship was docked in Long Beach, also reported hearing voices there.

"It was my job to keep an eye out for leaks in the hull," he said. "One night when I was checking the bow compartments from the top deck, I heard water running down below. I thought that a pipe must have burst or that the hull had sprung a leak, so I hurried below to inspect the damage. As I approached the bow, the sounds of water faded and were replaced by tapping sounds and then a sensation of shuddering and vibration, which was followed by human voices shrieking and moaning and a gravelly voice that seemed to be talking in the distance."

The engineer told Bill that this recurred on eight occasions. He never saw anything unusual, he just heard the sounds.

These stories were of intense interest to Bill because of one particular incident in the *Queen Mary*'s history.

During World War II, "The Grey Ghost," as the ship was then called because of her wartime camouflage and her great speed, was a troop carrier. On an October day in 1942 she was approaching Scotland with 10,000 U.S. soldiers on board. Forging ahead of her were six antisubmarine destroyers, and chugging along by her side to protect her from air attacks was the Royal Navy cruiser *Curaçao*.

As the *Queen Mary* was steaming along on a zigzag course to avoid the torpedoes of German submarines, a tragic combination of miscalculations by the navigators of the two ships led to their collision. The huge *Queen Mary*, weighing 81,000 tons, plowed straight through the 4,200-ton cruiser, slicing her in two like a knife cutting cheese. Three hundred forty officers and seamen on the *Curaçao* lost their lives, and the bow of the *Queen Mary* was crushed inward eight feet.

The agony and terror these men felt when the *Queen*'s bow crushed them must have been excruciating.

The first time Bill removed the safety cover from the hatch in the bow of the *Queen Mary*, he heard what he thought were two men talking down below. When he investigated, however, he found that all the compartments were empty.

Deciding that the best way to explore the phenomenon would be to attempt to record the sounds, Bill bought a voice-activated tape recorder and installed it in the bow on the second deck from the bottom, which was the area that had been bashed in by the collision with the *Curaçao*.

During one of the next nights, the recorder picked up a strange sequence of noises. There were heavy blows of metal, sounds of rushing water, and voices, one of which was low and gravelly and almost intelligible.

When the engineer listened to the tape, his eyes filled with tears.

"Those are exactly the sounds I've been hearing," he said huskily.

By now Bill's wife, Lydia, had joined him on the *Queen*.

Bill Roll examines one of the haunting sites of the Queen Mary *with a magnetometer. (courtesy: William Roll)*

Lydia often worked with Bill on his investigations, and the two decided to spend a night in the bow, hoping to hear firsthand the sounds that had been recorded. The early hours of the evening passed uneventfully, but shortly after midnight Bill and Lydia heard faint voices that seemed to be coming from a distance, and just before dawn they heard what seemed to be a conversation in a foreign, perhaps East European, language.

Did the bow somehow capture actual conversations on the ship or were the voices due to place memories? Bill couldn't be sure.

"If there is a connection between the wartime tragedy and the sounds in the bow of the *Queen Mary*, what is the explanation?" he wonders. "Are we to suppose that the spirits of the dead sailors are still reliving their final moments of terror, locked in the huge body of iron that came crashing down on them? Or did the collective barrage of pain and terror experienced by hundreds of men imprint itself on the environment and become part of the place memories of the bow?"

Whatever their source, the voices have been captured on tape.

Place memory is only one of several possible explanations for alleged hauntings. Another, which Bill feels may also be valid in certain cases, is that the apparition is created by the witness.

A self-produced apparition is known as a *thought form* or a *psi projection*.

"There's reason to believe that a person with strong psychic abilities may be able to create an image and project it into space," Bill says. "And, incredible as this seems, it appears that, in some cases, it may also be possible for that visual image to become so solid that it can be seen by other people as well."

"I first ran into that phenomenon while investigating the haunting of a furniture factory in North Carolina. The apparition that was seen in the factory resembled a previous owner who had been dead for ten years. The new owner had known this man, and often when he had business problems and needed somebody to look over his shoulder and give him advice, up popped this supportive ghost figure, who knew how to run things in the factory. Not only did the new owner see it, other people did too. Employees had gotten so scared they were quitting their jobs."

Bill feels that this explanation may also apply to a haunting case that involved a young family in Atlanta.

The husband, a traveling salesman, was away a lot, leaving his wife and three-year-old daughter alone. When her husband was gone, the wife kept hearing footsteps, and on several occasions she glimpsed the form of a man out of the corner of her eye.

At first she tried to tell herself that she was simply imagining things. Then one day a visiting neighbor saw the man also. A few days later, when the woman was vacuuming the living room, she again caught sight of the shadowy figure walking by. At that exact moment, her little girl cried, "Man! Man!" and pointed to an empty corner.

The woman went into a panic and phoned the college to see if there was somebody there who knew about hauntings.

Bill took his parapsychology class with him to visit the house. After talking with the woman, he came to realize that she was desperately lonely for her husband. It seemed possible to Bill that longing for her absent husband might have caused her to subconsciously create the image of the missing male who would fill the void in the family and to project that image into the environment where her friend and her daughter could see it also.

This made sense to the woman, and the sightings stopped.

"Since then, whenever I've investigated haunting situations, I've looked at the 'psi projection' concept as one possible explanation," Bill says. "There are times when it doesn't seem appropriate, but others when it does."

According to Bill there have been a few startling cases in which the person responsible for the "haunting" unknowingly used *psychokinesis* (the mind-over-matter energy also known as *PK*) to move and activate physical objects.

It's his feeling that this may explain some of the mysteries surrounding the much publicized haunting of a Japanese steak house in the South.

Bill was summoned to this restaurant by the manager, who had requested help in dealing with bizarre disturbances. Lightbulbs were regularly unscrewed, footsteps were heard, toilets flushed in unoccupied rest rooms, alarms went off, and locked doors were found unlocked and open. Most disturbing of all, the stove and the deep fryer in the kitchen were repeatedly found on when the staff came to work in the morning.

"The fryer is operated by gas, and the on-off valve is operated manually," the manager told Bill. "There's no possible way that it can slip. Every night we turn it off, and in the morning it's back on again. This is dangerous, because the thing could explode. With as many gas lines as we have in this building, it could blow the whole block off!"

Apparitions of two men had been seen on the premises on a number of occasions, not only by the manager, but by the head waitress, the sushi cook, the cabaret entertainer, and a visitor. The manager and staff were convinced that these were ghosts and that they were responsible for the strange occurrences in the restaurant.

The ghosts were described as bearing little resemblance to each other. One was a slim, solemn man about six feet tall, who wore a white shirt and dark pants and seemed sober and responsible. The manager saw this apparition most often after a busy evening when the figure would appear behind the bar, in the lounge, or on the back staircase.

"The busier it is, the more often he turns up," the manager said.

The second ghost was short, sloppy, and overweight, and was most frequently seen when rowdy parties were in progress.

These apparitions appeared so frequently that they had begun to seem like real people, and the restaurant staff had dubbed them Harry and Charlie.

The manager also reported unexplained localized cold spots throughout the building.

"All the hair on your body will stand up when you pass through one of those," he said.

Drawing upon his prior experience with hauntings, Bill formulated a broad-based investigation involving multiple techniques. To begin with he had each member of the restaurant staff who reported having seen the apparitions fill out a lengthy questionnaire about the physical appearance of the ghosts and the details of the sightings. He also gave them floor plans of the building and asked them to mark the specific areas in which they had seen apparitions, heard unexplained noises, or encountered cold spots.

Then Bill assembled a group to conduct a *psi scan*. The group consisted of nine people who had psychic abilities, four of whom were professional psychics, and a number of parapsychology students with no history of psychic ability to act as controls (in this case, individuals with no special psychic abilities). One by one, at ten-minute intervals, the psychics and controls were sent through the restaurant with copies of the floor plan on which they were to indicate any areas in which they sensed ghostly presences. By using controls, Bill hoped to be able to distinguish between those areas of the building that any normal person would consider spooky, perhaps because of poor lighting conditions, and areas of psychic activity to which only a person with psychic abilities might be sensitive.

Bill's team of investigators also included three scientists. Since research suggested a relationship between local magnetic field intensity and haunting phenomena, the scientists physically evaluated the restaurant using a sensitive magnetometer, as well as infrared photography and sound and video recorders.

Finally, in view of Bill's interest in psi projection, psychological and neuropsychological tests were given to the manager. The neuropsychological tests were designed to look for signs of unusual activity in the temporal lobe, which is a part of the brain that appears to be involved in psychic experiences.

"We've found that people with what we call 'temporal lobe lability' are more inclined than others to see apparitions," Bill says. "Such highly sensitive brains are also easily aroused by magnetic fields, which may help trigger ghost sightings."

Bill thinks there are more hauntings reported now than in earlier times because of such things as high tension wires, microwave ovens, TV sets, and computers, all of which produce strong magnetic fields. He investigated a haunted music hall for the TV program *Sightings* and found that the bed of one of the main witnesses was only about five feet from an electric transformer that produced a strong magnetic field. Unknown to anyone, the young man's brain had for years been bathed in this field, probably resulting in his haunting experiences.

It's no great mystery how magnetic fields may affect the brain. A magnetic field that surrounds a person (and any other electrical conductor) produces electric current that can affect the body, including the brain. This may result in hallucinations that the person believes are ghosts. In some individuals, however, the electric current may not merely produce images that only the person can see but may also activate his or her psychokinetic abilities and trigger movements of objects and other real physical incidents. This seems to have happened in the restaurant, usually when the manager was around. Bill also believes that individuals with labile temporal lobes, such as the manager, may unconsciously project images that others can see, somewhat like the pictures that are projected in a movie theater.

The results of this elaborate study were interesting. The psychics were able to describe the tall ghost, while controls failed at this task. The psychics could not locate the haunted areas, but the scientists did! Using magnetometers, they found abnormally high magnetic fields in the locations where the witnesses had reported phenomena attributed to Harry and Charlie.

The neuropsychological study of the manager was also very interesting, as it indicated temporal lobe instability. Since this is the area of the brain connected with imagination and creativity and is the seat of some hallucinatory experiences, Bill thought it possible that the intense magnetic fields in certain areas of the restaurant might have triggered psi projections when the manager was under stress as well as the physical incidents he and others reported.

Although the manager was a bit surprised by these findings, he took them seriously enough to make efforts to change his lifestyle and to become less single-mindedly obsessed with the business.

He later moved up in his company and left the restaurant.

Harry and Charlie were not seen again.

Telepathy, hallucination, place memory, and thought forms may provide valid explanations for many instances of haunting phenomena; yet there are others that are hard to explain in these ways.

Bill's student Mark has this story to tell.

"I was in the Army and on night maneuvers in Yakima, Washington," he recalls. "I was driving a five-ton truck, towing an eight-ton Howitzer, and had lost my convoy in the hills of the desert. During night-move training you're not allowed to turn on your headlights, as they can be seen for miles by the enemy, so I was driving in the dark.

"I came around a bend, and there in front of me were three white crosses. I asked my sergeant what they were, and he said they'd been placed there to show where soldiers had gone off the road and crashed during training exercises.

"The sergeant dozed off, and up ahead I saw another row of white crosses. Beside them there stood a man with a lantern, motioning for me to slow down. I pulled the truck to a stop and woke up my sergeant, and we got out to see what was wrong. When we reached the front of the truck, the man had disappeared, but we discovered that he had been standing on the edge of a cliff. If it hadn't been for the lantern, I would have barreled right over it!

"After we got through shaking, my sergeant told me he had heard stories about a dead soldier who sometimes appeared to guide the living through the narrow passages at night."

Mark has no doubt that he owes his life to a ghost.

CHAPTER FIVE

CHANNELING AND MEDIUMSHIP

As I have come to know all too well since my daughter's death, the longing to be once again in the presence of a loved one who has died is one of the most intense of all human emotions. Those who lose people they love are desperate to renew contact.

This universal reluctance to let go of the deceased is what has popularized the practice of *mediumship.*

A *medium* is a person who professes to use psychic abilities to communicate with the dead. Because grief-stricken people are so vulnerable and so eager for reassurance that their beloveds are still available to them, fakery abounds in this area of psi activity.

One of the earliest highly publicized cases of mediumship in the United States involved the children of a blacksmith named John Fox. In December 1847, Fox and his wife and two daughters, Maggie, fourteen, and Kate, twelve, moved into a spooky old cottage in Hydesville, New York. Almost immediately the family started reporting strange noises—banging and rapping and the sound of furniture being dragged along the floor—and made a public announcement that the house was haunted.

Maggie and Kate began to communicate with the resident "ghost" through a code they invented. They would call out the letters of the alphabet, and the spirit would rap to indicate which letter he wanted them to write down. In this way he was able to spell out the message that he was the ghost of a traveling salesman named Charles Rosma who had been robbed and murdered by a former occupant of the house and was buried in the cellar.

People flocked to the Foxes' home to witness the rappings, and the teenagers' older sister got the idea of charging an entrance fee. Eventually the Fox girls became so famous that they started traveling around the country giving *séances* (demonstrations of mediumship). During these séances the *sitters* (participants in the séance) would ask questions, and the teenagers would repeat the answers they allegedly received from the spirit world. The longer they toured, the more wondrous the effects became, with objects moving about on the stage of their own volition and musical instruments played by invisible "spirit hands."

On one occasion Maggie and Kate told reporters that they had created the raps themselves by cracking their toe joints, but they later recanted this statement, saying they made a false confession to embarrass their older sister, who was cashing in on their success.

Years later the skeleton of a man was reportedly found in the cellar of the Foxes' old cottage after a wall collapsed, which suggests that their initial experiences may have been authentic, even if the road-show séances were not.

There is no way of knowing for certain whether the Fox girls were total fakes, but there seems to be no doubt that at least some of their theatrical effects were the result of fraud. Even so, the imagination of the American public was captured by the intriguing idea that it might be possible to communicate with the dead, and mediums suddenly began popping up all over the country to hold séances for people who wanted one last visit with the deceased.

This practice became very popular, died down for a while, and reemerged with new trappings in a more sophisticated era. In most cities today, all you have to do is open the yellow pages and you can take your pick of a dozen or so alleged mediums who will be happy to bring you greetings from your great-aunt Gertrude. There are even "pay-by-the-minute" telephone services you can dial to get a reading by a self-proclaimed psychic.

In view of all this it's little wonder that mediumship in general has a bad reputation.

There are two basic categories of mediumship—*mental* and *physical*.

A *mental medium* receives mental impressions, such as thoughts or images that seem to come from the departed. A *physical medium* not only does that, but is also the center of moving objects and other physical incidents supposedly caused by spirits. Some mental mediums go into a *trance*, a state induced by hypnosis or self-hypnosis, which superficially resembles sleep. During trance, the familiar world is blocked out, and the medium becomes aware of another reality. A trance medium usually sits in a chair in a room with ordinary lighting. Then she (most mediums are women) starts to speak, often in a voice very different from her natural one, as if someone else has control of her vocal cords. These visiting entities are called *controls* or *spirit guides* and appear to communicate through the medium as if she is a telephone line, passing along messages to the client from deceased friends and relatives. On some occasions these controls play the role of teachers and give lectures about spiritual matters. Mediums who give voice to these sermons are called *channels*. There are also many mediums who receive their information in a state very close to waking.

Physical mediumship has the same general format as mental mediumship, with a few added frills. In a case of physical mediumship the séance is usually held in a darkened room and the performance includes special effects. Furniture may rise from the floor, bells may ring, and knicknacks may float about or appear out of thin air. There is a special group of physical mediums called *materialization mediums* who seem to be able to give physical form to the departed from a substance called *ectoplasm*. Usually the room is too dim for these effects to be seen clearly, suggesting that many of them are parlor tricks that could be duplicated by any good stage magician. There are few genuine physical mediums.

Bill Roll once investigated a famous physical medium in Mexico named Luis Martinez. Several witnesses had told Bill this man was amazing, including a general in the Mexican army who said he had seen Martinez float over the heads of those present in a process known as *levitation*. But Martinez was best known for materializations of spiritual teachers, as well as of departed relatives of the sitters.

During the first séance Bill attended, about twelve people crowded into a small room in an apartment in Mexico City belonging to a couple named Lopez and seated themselves along the walls. At one point an altar with figures of the Virgin Mary and various saints interrupted the row of chairs. Martinez, a short, heavyset man, sat in an easy chair inside the circle. The sitters were asked to hold hands to create psychic energy for the materializations.

The lights were then turned off, and Martinez was hypnotized by an assistant. Shortly afterward, small "spirit lights" formed and floated around the room. Then a larger light in the form of a face appeared, and finally a full body in a glowing garment. This was supposedly the first of Martinez's many spirit teachers, among whom were St. Francis of Assisi, an Asian sage, and a psychic healer who ministered to ailing sitters by passing his hands over the afflicted parts of their bodies. Later there were apparitions whom the participants seemed to recognize as their departed loved ones, though Bill thought all their faces looked very much alike.

Bill had brought a camera with infrared film, hoping to photograph the spirit entities, but this was impossible since both his hands were held. But his feet were free, and when one of the apparitions came up to heal the person next to him, Bill stuck out his foot. He hit something hard, which he thought might be a shoe. And something else was suspicious. All the apparitions were the same height and build.

Bill first suspected that Martinez dressed up as the entities, but they were slim, while he was heavy. Perhaps, Bill thought, somebody quietly entered the room and put on the ghostly show, but this seemed unlikely because the row of sitters blocked the door. But there was a third possibility. Señora Lopez was sitting next to the altar and was holding the hand of only one person, who happened to be her sister-in-law. Bill wondered if Señora Lopez left her seat when the lights were off and dressed up as the apparitions. There was a compartment below the altar where he thought the sheets and other stage props might be hidden.

The next time a séance was held, Bill came prepared to test his theory. He filled the top of a jar with toothpaste and placed it in the arch of his left shoe. During the séance he slipped his shoes off and dipped his right toe in the toothpaste. When one of the apparitions approached, he stuck his foot out and again hit something hard. At the end of the séance, when the lights came back on, there was a telltale white smudge on one of Señora Lopez's shoes.

Martinez's apparitions had flunked the toothpaste test!

It is as important to debunk false claims as it is to validate genuine ones, and parapsychologists have been active in both efforts. There are people who have made careers out of debunking the paranormal and have dedicated their lives to exposing fraud. Thanks to them, a good deal of fakery has been exposed, yet there have been mediums who have managed to survive investigation.

One of these was the British mental medium Douglas Johnson. Johnson, who has since died, was a good friend of Bill's and often stayed in his home when he visited the United States. During these times he participated in Bill's program of ESP tests, but his results were never as good during laboratory testing as when he worked with clients who came to him with their personal problems.

Johnson claimed to have had his first psychic experience at age fifteen when the spirit of a long-dead Chinese man named Chiang began speaking through him. From that time on he kept seeing discarnate people who appeared to him to be as solid as their flesh-and-blood counterparts.

One evening Johnson was in a bar in London having a drink with a West Indian man when he saw the apparition of a dark-complexioned woman standing next to him.

"The man you're sitting with is my son," Johnson heard the apparition say. "He is planning to do something very foolish tonight. I want you to stop him."

When Johnson quoted this to his companion, the man turned pale and said, "That can't come from my mother, because she's dead."

"Tell him I was blind from birth, but I can see in the spirit world," the woman said.

When Johnson repeated that, the man believed him.

"Tell her that I'm not going to do it," he said.

He later confessed that he had been planning to act as lookout for a bank robbery that night. He dropped out of the conspiracy and escaped being captured with the others.

One of the most respected mediums of all time was Eileen Garrett, who displayed psychic ability very early in her childhood in Ireland. She had just turned four when she raced into the house to announce to her startled family that she had seen her aunt Leone coming up the pathway carrying a baby in her arms. Her aunt looked tired and ill and, as Garrett reached out to greet her, said, "I am going away now and must take the baby with me"—words that Garrett would remember for the rest of her life. Leone lived twenty miles away, and the little girl was punished for lying. The next day the family received word that Leone had died in childbirth and the newborn baby had died also.

Orphaned when she was an infant, Garrett was raised by an aunt and uncle who were cold and unloving. They lived on a farm in the country, and she had a lonely childhood.

Then one day when she was playing by herself in the garden she was joined by the apparitions of two girls and a boy. These youngsters, whom she called the Children, became her constant companions. They took her to places in the woods and fields where flowers bloomed especially abundantly and to the newborn animals on the farm. But her aunt punished Garrett for talking about the Children and for leaving her room in the evening to play with them outside.

The Children remained the girl's closest friends until she was sent off to boarding school at the age of thirteen.

"It's possible the Children were projections of her mind reflecting a need for human companions," Bill Roll says. "If so, the thought forms were amazingly long-lasting and played a very important part in Eileen Garrett's early life."

Garrett's psychic abilities accelerated every year. As an adult she volunteered to serve as a subject in many parapsychological tests and proved to have remarkable ESP abilities. She was also a gifted writer and a successful publisher and was founder of the Parapsychology Foundation, which supported scholarly and scientific research. She did not accept money for her séances, and her reputation for honesty remained unblemished throughout her fifty-year career as a medium.

The reporter and author Adela Rogers St. John went to Garrett for a reading when her son Billy was killed in combat during World War II. Billy's death had not yet been reported in the papers, and Adela did not tell Garrett why she had made the appointment with her.

As soon as St. John entered Garrett's hotel suite, the psychic stopped, stared into space, and then tilted back her head as if looking up at a very tall person.

"Well, here's Billy!" she exclaimed.

The grieving mother could not believe her ears. Not only had Garrett not known that St. John's son was dead, she had never met the young man and had no way of knowing that Billy had stood six feet four inches.

"He's wearing a uniform," Garrett continued. "It looks like a British uniform. What's he doing in a British uniform? He's American, isn't he?"

"It's Canadian," St. John said shakily. "He joined the Royal Canadian Air Force before we got into the war."

Garrett then passed on messages that St. John was convinced were from her dead son. Where else could a virtual

stranger gain access to details about a mother-son relationship that included pet names and personal details about
events in Billy's life?

Apparently only Billy had known these things.

Only Billy—and his mother, Adela St. John.

Garrett, who was a trance medium, received most of her
information about the departed from two spirit guides.
These, she thought, were split-off parts of her subconscious
mind. She was less definitive about the deceased communi-
cators. Sometimes they seemed to be personalities constructed by her own mind and based upon impressions she
got telepathically from the sitters; other times Garrett felt
they were independent personalities.

Some parapsychologists believe that, rather than actually communicating with the dead, mediums may use their
psychic abilities to pick up information from their living
relatives and other existing sources and then imagine the
communication. Since Eileen Garrett was renowned for her
gift of telepathy, it does seem feasible that she might inadvertently have drawn information about Billy's unusual
height and uniform from the highly charged mind of his
grief-stricken mother and that the reassuring messages that
Billy was happy in his new existence might have been projected into Garrett's receptive subconscious by St. John.

Indisputably Garrett obtained information by ESP. But
whose intelligence was she tapping? Was she reaching beyond the veil and dipping into the mind of the dead airman,
or was she dipping into the mind of his living mother?

Either possibility is fascinating to contemplate and
many honest mediums are as confused about the issue as
anyone else. They know that information that they have no
conscious access to keeps popping into their minds, but
they cannot say for certain how and why it gets there.

Sometimes mediumship is conducted through what

parapsychologists call *motor automatisms*. The term refers to physical movements of an intelligent and purposeful kind that seemingly occur on their own.

One popular vehicle for *automative mediumship* is the Ouija board.

The Ouija board, which is produced and sold as a toy, is a rectangular piece of plywood that is bordered by the letters of the alphabet. During a Ouija board séance two or more people sit around the board with their fingertips resting lightly on a pointer. The pointer then appears to take off on its own and dashes about from one letter to another spelling out messages.

Many mediums credit their discovery of their abilities to the Ouija board.

One such medium is Betty Muench, who professes to converse with the deceased through *automatic writing*. Muench asks questions of unseen entities she considers her spirit guides, and her fingers type out messages seemingly of their own accord.

"I was fooling around with a board in the home of some friends when it started addressing messages specifically to me," she says. "I became so intrigued that I purchased a board of my own and began using it by myself. One day it spelled out the question 'WLUCUM?' At first this appeared to be gibberish, but then I realized the spelling was phonetic; it was asking, 'Will You Come?' I was a little bit scared, but I felt I had to say yes.

"Then inside my right ear I heard a voice tell me, 'Write! Write! Write!' It was just as clear as if the speaker was sitting next to me. I went to the typewriter and sat down, and the voice started dictating. I typed out a message that said that I would do four things—'see the future, hear the future, travel without leaving your home, and perform healings.'"

The control or spirit guide who Muench believes dictated this message was soon joined by others, each with a distinctly different personality. Muench refers to this group of guides as her "Friends in Source," and for over twenty years she has been channeling their answers to personal and spiritual questions through automatic writing.

"I sit down at the typewriter, and the guides take over," she says. "What I see first is a flood of colors that relate to the reading. Various psychics interpret such colors differently, but, in my case, red stands for anger, gold stands for love, green stands for healing, blue stands for tranquillity, white stands for spirituality. After that I get symbols, and then I get words. I never know what the messages will say until I've typed them."

These messages are worded in a way that is very different from Muench's natural way of speaking, and some of them convey disturbing information.

Over one four-month period in 1978, Muench received a series of frightening messages about her husband, Paul, who was a stunt flyer. They read as follows:

1/11/78: You will experience soon the loss of one loved by you.
2/20/78: Your work with Paul will soon be brought to an end, and you will not be the one to create this.
3/19/78: Comes a severance with Paul which will be of his own doing . . . this will come within the year.
4/26/78: There will come the leaving off with Paul, and it will come through him, and you will not know much more time with him.

On October 4, 1978, Paul Muench died in a plane crash while flying in a stunt show.

On the day of the funeral, Betty Muench channeled a message that she believes came from Paul himself:

There is a sense of disorder in some of my thoughts. I made a mistake in my flying. . . . The visual reading at the time of my beginning was incorrect.

"That statement proved true," Muench says. "The mistake referred to in this reading was confirmed by the FAA. According to their report the plane crash was due to pilot error. Paul had just gotten new glasses and wasn't used to them. That may or may not have been the cause of the terrible mistake he made, but he evidently set the altimeter for that particular airfield two hundred feet short of what was needed in order to do three loops, touch the ground, and then take off again. In effect, he was attempting to fly two hundred feet into the ground."

How is it possible for people to receive intelligent messages through a frivolous board game?

"Obviously, the board has no power in itself," Bill Roll says. "It's a tool for recording involuntary movements which may reflect the subconscious mind of one or more of the players. The information that emerges during one of these sessions may be coming from that hidden level—in other words, the player may be providing the information without realizing it. But we mustn't forget that the subconscious mind is the part of our mind where ESP impressions are processed. Messages received by the player through telepathic contact with the minds of others also may influence the Ouija board marker."

I have personal knowledge of one incident when this seemed to be the case.

When our son Donnie was ten, his bicycle was stolen. We reported the theft to the police, who told us that bicycle theft was rampant and there was little chance that the bike would ever be recovered.

Donnie and two of his friends decided to consult a Ouija

board, which over and over again spelled out the word *AIR*. This made no sense to the children, or to my husband and me when they told us about it. In fact, I lectured them about being so silly and superstitious.

One week later, as we drove to the airport to pick up friends, Donnie almost jumped out of his seat.

"There's my bike!" he shouted.

Chained to a fence in front of a run-down apartment directly across from the airport was a bicycle that did resemble his. We stopped the car, and my husband got out to check the serial number. Incredibly, the bicycle was Donnie's. We phoned the police, who went to the apartment and retrieved it.

The word *AIR* had apparently been Ouija board shorthand for *AIRPORT*.

Donnie had no way of knowing his bike was by the airport, so where did that information come from? Did he pick it up telepathically from the mind of the thief, or was some friendly, disembodied spirit trying to help him?

There is no way to know.

During most Ouija board séances the spirits who allegedly spell out messages are people the sitters knew in life, but occasionally there are messages that seem to be from spirits the sitters don't know.

Such uninvited guests at a séance are called *drop-ins*.

If the sitters themselves are responsible for providing the messages at Ouija board séances, where do they get information about people unknown to them?

It is possible, of course, that in some instances one of the sitters may have gained access to information about what appears to be an unknown drop-in communicator by having read his or her obituary or, in the case of someone famous, an article or biography, and stored the details in the subconscious. There have been cases, however, in which the information presented by the drop-in was so difficult to obtain that this would seem to be impossible.

One such case concerns an apparent spirit communicator who dropped in on a Ouija board circle in Cambridge, England, at the end of World War I and spelled out a series of messages over a two-year period. He identified himself as Harry Stockbridge, a second lieutenant attached to the Northumberland Fusiliers, and said he had died on July 14, 1916. He also spelled out "Tyneside Scottish . . . Tall, dark, thin . . . large brown eyes . . . I hung out in Leicester . . . Leicester holds a record."

The sitters became excited about their spirit visitor and made an attempt to verify his statements. They interpreted "Leicester holds a record" as meaning that Stockbridge's name was on a war memorial in Leicester, but that proved to be incorrect. Their other efforts to check up on the information were equally unsuccessful.

It was not until fifteen years later that Alan Gauld, a senior lecturer in psychology at the University of Nottingham in England, became interested in the case. Gauld started an investigation of his own and discovered that a Second Lieutenant H. Stockbridge of the Northumberland Fusiliers was listed in a publication entitled *Officers Who Died in the Great War of 1914–19*. The date of Stockbridge's death was given as July 19, 1916, not July 14, 1916, as the spirit communicator had stated. However, when Gauld continued his investigation, he discovered that the Army Records Centre gave the date of Stockbridge's death as *July 14, 1916*, exactly as the drop-in had said.

A record card in the War Office Library said Stockbridge had been a member of a Tyneside Scottish battalion, and his death certificate showed that he had been born in Leicester.

When Gauld tracked down Stockbridge's brothers, they confirmed the fact that the man had been tall, dark, and thin, with large brown eyes.

Although Stockbridge's name was not on the war memorial in Leicester, Gauld did find it on the war memorial in Stockbridge's old school in Leicester.

Skeptics cringe when confronted with a case like this one.

Bill Roll does not encourage the use of the Ouija board by young people.

"It can be dangerous because it's an opening to the unconscious," he says. "It's true that the unconscious often contains ESP information, but that information may not always be good for you. And the unconscious also contains all kinds of buried psychological stuff that a young sitter may not be ready to deal with."

For scientists to accept the legitimacy of mediumship, more evidence like the Stockbridge readings is needed. And it must be proved that the information comes from the minds of the departed and is not due to ESP by the operators of the board.

Dr. Raymond Moody, the same creative thinker who pioneered the study of near-death experiences, has taken on the challenge of finding a way to induce visitations from the dead in an institutional setting in which such encounters can be observed and documented. In his book *Reunions*, Moody tells of his research on what he calls *facilitated visionary experience*, which is created by setting up conditions under which volunteer subjects may be able to experience reunions with lost loved ones, based upon methods used in the days of ancient Greece when there were special institutions to which people journeyed to visit with the dead.

What Moody has done is create a special environment that seems to enhance the same sort of altered state of consciousness that facilitates psi events such as OBEs. Throughout history people in all areas of the world have reported seeing three-dimensional visions when they stared into crystal balls, the still surface of bodies of water, or mirrors. One of these people was Eileen Garrett, who wrote in her autobiography that as a child she saw visions while staring into the polished darkness of an old dresser or into a mirror misted over by her breath on the glass.

When Bill and I met with Moody at his home in Alabama, to get firsthand information about his controversial project, he had just returned from a research trip to Greece, where he had visited the site of the ancient oracle of the dead at Ephyra.

In Moody's own apparition chamber, which he calls the Theater of the Mind, the subject is seated in a comfortable chair in a black-draped room in front of a large mirror in a

The old converted mill in which Dr. Raymond Moody has constructed his Theater of the Mind. (courtesy: Lois Duncan)

Raymond Moody describes to Lois Duncan his experiments in facilitated visionary experience. (courtesy: Lois Duncan)

position in which he is unable to see his own reflection. With nothing to distract his attention from the hypnotic sheen of the glass, he relaxes and waits for whatever is to come next.

Moody carefully screens the subjects for this experiment, eliminating anyone who has a history of mental or emotional instability, and confines his study to mature, intelligent people who have a strong desire to communicate with deceased loved ones.

Of the first twenty-seven subjects who participated in Moody's experiment, sixteen saw apparitions of deceased loved ones appear in the glass, and six subjects reported having had verbal communication with these visitors that ranged from a few loving words to lengthy two-way conversations.

An editor of a large newspaper came to the chamber hoping to see her son, who had committed suicide. He appeared and told her that he was fine and he loved her. During another session a man saw his deceased mother, who seemed surprised to encounter him and asked him how he had come to where she now was.

The results of these experiments went far beyond what Moody had anticipated. One man was startled when apparitions of three of his departed relatives actually emerged from the mirror and surrounded him. Thinking this must be a joke and the figures were actors, he reached out to touch one of them and was stunned when his hand went straight through it. One woman reported the physical sensation of being hugged by her grandfather.

And there were additional surprises. Three people who did not see visions during their sessions in the apparition chamber reported seeing them after they left. And the people they saw were not always the people they wanted to see. One woman who had gone through the session in the hope of seeing her dead husband experienced, instead, two encounters with her dead father.

All the people who reported seeing apparitions were convinced that they were not hallucinations.

When Moody asked one subject if he felt the experience could have been a projection of his own mind, he said firmly, "Oh, no! *I saw my mother!*"

Moody subjected himself to a session in the chamber in the hope of seeing his maternal grandmother. She didn't appear, but later, at another location, his *paternal* grandmother abruptly appeared before him.

"I wasn't even dozing," he told us. "I was just sitting in a chair, and suddenly, there she was! At first I didn't even recognize her; I thought she was some stranger who had somehow gotten into my room. We had a long talk, and she told me some things about our family that I hadn't known before. I hadn't cared much for that grandmother when she was alive, but I liked her as an apparition."

Moody is quick to point out that these experiments carry no weight scientifically because they were not conducted under controlled conditions. He believes, however, that they are a first step in exploring a fascinating new form of mediumship that has the potential for true laboratory testing. If apparitional sightings can be induced in a laboratory, it will be possible to monitor the brain activity of the people who experience the visions. It will also be possible to test the theory that magnetic fields and other forms of radiation enhance the perception of apparitions and to attempt to photograph and record the apparitional activity.

Another unusual method that is being used in an attempt to communicate with the dead is *electronic voice phenomena* (also known as *EVP*). With EVP, voices, supposedly of the dead, are imprinted directly on audiotape.

EVP had its origin in 1959 when a Swedish painter and nature lover named Friedrich Jürgenson was out in the forest recording bird calls. When he played back the tape, he was astonished to hear, between the bird songs, human voices speaking several different languages. One of the voices was that of his deceased mother calling his name and saying, "Friedrich, you are being watched!"

During the next four years Jürgenson experimented with his tape recorder and picked up thousands of what he believed were messages and greetings from his deceased friends and relatives. Sometimes he got these over his radio

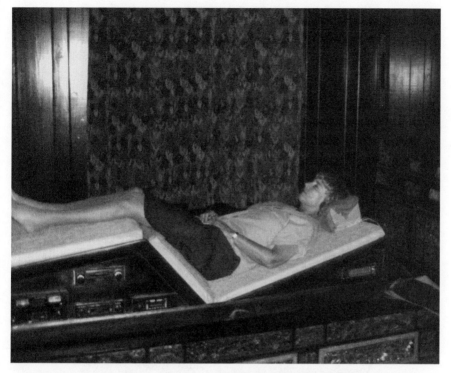

Lois Duncan goes through a relaxation exercise in preparation for taking part in a facilitated visionary experiment. (courtesy: Lois Duncan)

receiver and at other times by taping normal conversations in everyday life and then finding extra voices on the tapes when the conversations were played back.

In 1964 Bill Roll spent time with Jürgenson both in his home and in a physics laboratory in Germany. In his home Jürgenson used a standard radio receiver, moving the tuner until he thought he heard a voice, usually on an empty but noisy part of the band. Then he turned on a tape recorder so that the sounds could be preserved and studied. In the laboratory, the equipment was more sophisticated and allowed for better testing, but, although interesting, the results were

95

An apparition appears to be beginning to take form in the mirror during Duncan's experiment. (courtesy: Lois Duncan)

inconclusive. While at certain times previously unheard words did turn up unexpectedly on the tapes, there was no clear proof that these voices were those of the dead.

Jürgenson's explorations encouraged a German psychologist, Konstantin Raudive, to become involved in this research. Raudive recorded, analyzed, and cataloged close to 80,000 "spirit voices" before writing a book, *Breakthrough*, which inspired both professional and amateur researchers to purchase electronic equipment and pursue their own investigations of this phenomenon.

Though some skeptics believe that what Raudive heard and recorded might have been nothing more than fragments of radio transmissions, transformed into messages from the dead by his wishful imagination, Sarah Epstat, the founder of the American Association of Electronic Voice Phenomena, is convinced otherwise.

"As a psychic investigator, I was at first very skeptical about the phenomena, but I decided to try it and see if I could get voices," she says. "I did after only seven days."

Epstat points out that with today's technology the early problems faced by Jürgenson and Raudive have been eliminated. Today it is possible to cut out ambient sound and radio signals, and members of the society who are involved with EVP research are careful to use only new, commercially packaged audiotape to guard against the possibility of voices bleeding through from previous recordings.

She believes the voices they hear when they play back these tapes are voices of the dead.

I myself have never heard the taped voice of a dead person, but I have watched Betty Muench sit down at her typewriter and "take dictation" from her spirit guides, the Friends in Source. In many cases these messages have contained information that has later been verified—information that Muench could not possibly have obtained on her own.

Here is one of those cases:

After Kait's death I wrote a book called *Who Killed My Daughter?* in the hope of bringing informants out of the woodwork who could help us in our quest to learn the identities of her killers. When the book came out I received letters not only from tipsters, but also from grief-stricken parents who had lost children of their own and wanted me to know that their hearts went out to us.

"We understand," they wrote. "We know how you feel."

All of these letters were touching, but one broke my heart. It came from a woman named Dodie Peckham, whose twenty-two-year-old daughter, Julie, had hanged herself. Dodie had been outspoken about her disapproval of Julie's lifestyle, and since Julie had not left a suicide note, Dodie was tormented by the thought that something she had said or done might have driven her daughter to kill herself.

"I am struggling to believe she is not lost to me forever," she wrote.

This letter was filled with such anguish that I did something I had no right to do—I sent the letter to Betty Muench and requested that she ask her Friends in Source why Julie had committed suicide. I told myself that if the reading was comforting I would forward it to Dodie, and if it turned out to be upsetting, she would never know about it.

Muench did a reading and mailed it to me.

This was an interesting and very different reading, as they all are. I get an image of an eye opening which seems to indicate that Julie is just waking up. She seems to look just past Dodie, over her left shoulder, as if she is ashamed and does not yet want to meet her mother's gaze directly. Yet she is now reacting to the voice of her mother (the voice is expressed as strongly in handwriting as when spoken) and is quickly becoming aware.

This reading suggests strongly that this suicide was caused by something that perhaps a thicker skinned person would not have taken so seriously. I don't get that Julie was involved in anything sinister, but there was a situation that she did not know how to handle, some kind of challenge to her by an authority figure that made her feel inadequate, something done wrong that she felt she would never be able to set right. This is what drove her to suicide, not something out of the home. Her family was not responsible.

I sent the reading to Julie's mother, who responded as follows:

Thank you, thank you, thank you, a thousand million times for sending my letter on to Betty Muench. Now I can quit wallowing in my grief and guilt. I didn't know this before, but my husband tells me that when we were cleaning out Julie's apartment he found a letter from the District Attorney. Julie had needed money and apparently had forged two checks, and the D.A. was threatening to prosecute her. She was drinking and using drugs and apparently was in such a disoriented state that that letter shoved her over the edge.

And the part of the reading that says Julie is ashamed to look me in the face does not surprise me in the least. It was her lifetime pattern never to be able to face up to wrongdoing. We were never able to make her understand that she had to learn to face the consequences of her actions.

I called Betty on the phone, and she told me how to reach Julie. I did that this morning, and it was indescribably wonderful. I just kept telling her it was okay and I love her, and finally I had a strong sense she came and sat on my lap and cried and cried as if her heart would break. All I could do was hug her and tell her it was okay and I love her and ask her, please, to stay in touch with me, because I miss her and want to know she's okay.

Where did Muench get the information about the authority figure whose "challenge" had driven Julie to suicide? Certainly not from *my* subconscious. Nor, it seems, could she have gotten it from the subconscious of Julie's mother, who knew nothing about the letter from the district attorney.

There are sure to be people who pronounce the concept ridiculous, but to me it seems reasonable to believe that the information came from Julie.

CHAPTER SIX

TELEPATHY AND CLAIRVOYANCE

During World War II a woman named Gladys woke up in the night, weeping uncontrollably.

"Jack is dead! Jack is dead!" she sobbed. "I dreamed that I saw his plane go down in flames!"

Her husband tried to reassure her by reminding her that, although their son Jack was in the service and stationed in the Pacific, he was in the Army, not the Air Force.

Gladys refused to be comforted and became more and more hysterical, until her husband was forced to seek medical help for her. The doctor prescribed sedatives, and when they had no effect, the woman, who had a history of emotional problems, was hospitalized.

Days later word came that Jack had been on a plane that had crashed in flames, just as Gladys had stated. During his terrified final moments his mind had apparently sent a telepathic shock wave to his mother's, for the crash had occurred at exactly the time of her dream.

* * *

Telepathy, the transference of information from one mind to another, is perhaps the best-known form of ESP. It is particularly common between people who have a deep emotional bond such as husbands and wives, parents and children, and brothers and sisters, especially when they're twins. The word *telepathy* means "distance suffering," and is often about hurtful things that are happening to people who are close to us. Bill Roll calls it our "longbody pain sensor."

At times this pain sensor may even reach out to people we don't know personally, but who are part of our longbody-link to all humanity.

Robert Muller, former assistant secretary general of the United Nations, says he has had many nightmares in which he experienced all the sensations of falling in an airplane, only to wake in the morning to learn that there had been a plane crash.

"I have lived dozens and dozens of airplane accidents," he says. "I feel all the terror of the people falling out of the sky, knowing this is the end of their life. One day my wife opened *The New York Times* and said, 'Robert, you didn't tell me you had a dream last night. There was an incredible airplane accident! Didn't you dream about it?' No, I didn't, and when I read the newspaper article I understood why—the people were killed immediately, and there was no suffering."

Some people believe that this sixth sense is a heritage from our ancient ancestors who lived in a time when physical danger was everywhere and man was comparatively defenseless against more physically powerful predators. In that time the ability to sense danger and to telepathically warn other members of the tribal longbody would have been an invaluable asset in ensuring the survival of the group.

While telepathy involves mind-to-mind contact, there is

a second form of ESP that takes place without feed-in from a second person. *Clairvoyance*, which means "clear seeing," is the process of acquiring information about a distant place, event, or object, without contact with anyone else.

One woman described a clairvoyant experience in which she was awakened in the night by the odor of scorching paint, which she immediately recognized as the smell from her old-fashioned water heater when she forgot to turn off the fire. What made this bewildering was that she no longer lived in the house that contained that water heater.

Although what she was experiencing seemed impossible, the odor grew stronger, until she got up, got dressed, walked six blocks to her old residence, and awakened the new tenant. As soon as he opened the door, she knew that she was right—she now experienced with her nose the same odor she had experienced with her mind.

"Did you forget to turn off the water heater?" she asked the tenant.

He sniffed and smelled it also.

When they went together to turn off the heater, they discovered that it was red hot and that the wall next to it was scorched and blistered.

Young children seem to be naturally endowed with ESP, particularly in regard to their mothers. Before birth the child is, in a very real way, one with the mother, and that shared identity appears to continue to exist on some level throughout the child's early years, lessening as he or she becomes more independent.

The Institute of Parapsychology has numerous reports on file about incidents in which young children have voiced their mothers' thoughts before they were spoken, in some cases mentioning names that they had never heard, but which were in the mothers' minds.

One mother reported an occasion on which she was

thinking angry thoughts about a man she had hired to do a maintenance job. The man had walked out on the job before it was finished and had not bothered to come back and complete it. At dinner that night this woman was trying to decide whether to ask her husband, who was under stress of his own at work, to give the man a call.

Suddenly her three-year-old daughter looked across the table at her and said, "Aron Kraus," the name of the workman the woman was thinking about phoning.

To her knowledge the child had never heard this man's name and certainly had no way of knowing that her mother had him in her mind at that particular moment.

This psychic ability of children, while apparently strongest in regard to the mother, appears to encompass other family relationships as well.

One report in the Louisa Rhine collection involves three-year-old Vic, whose younger brother Chris had been left to nap at their grandmother's house a block and a half away.

"Suddenly, about forty-five minutes after Vic and I got home, he began to run to the window, looking down the street and calling frantically to me that Chris was crying," the mother reported. "I was busy, and it was only two-ten; I didn't expect them till three. I told Vic he was mistaken and went on with my work. He was very persistent and burst into tears, wailing, 'Chris wants you, Mommy!' "

In about five minutes the grandmother arrived with a tearful Chris, saying he had awakened crying at 2:10 and had then run all over the house sobbing, "Mommy! Mommy!"

In another case, recorded by H. H. Newman of the University of Chicago, a pair of twin girls seemed able to telepathically transmit answers back and forth to each other during school exams. On one occasion, when they were pressed for study time, each twin reviewed half the course material. Their answers on that test were so similar that they might have been accused of cheating if they had not been under very tight supervision and seated on opposite sides of the classroom.

Some people retain the psychic sensitivity of childhood into adult life. One of these was Eileen Garrett. Lawrence LeShan, who served for many years as chief of the Department of Psychology at New York's Trafalgar Hospital and Institute of Applied Biology, described an experiment he conducted with Garrett that convinced him of her psychic abilities.

LeShan presented Garrett with three identical plastic boxes. In one he had placed a lock of hair from the head of his twelve-year-old daughter, Wendy; in the second, a tuft of hair from the tail of his neighbors' dog, Charlie; and in the third, a rosebud from his small backyard garden. He allowed Garrett to hold the boxes for twenty seconds without seeing what was in them, and then took them from her and placed them out of sight behind a screen.

He then had Garrett thrust her arm through a sleeve in the screen. One by one, in a random order, he slid the boxes under her hand and asked her to identify what was in them.

The first box contained Wendy's hair.

"Oh, that's your daughter!" Garrett exclaimed immediately. "I think I'll call her Hilary; she'd like that."

Although Hilary wasn't her real name, at the age of four, Wendy had developed a crush on a nursery-school classmate named Hilary, and for over a year had pleaded with her parents to change her own name to Hilary. Her "Hilary period" was a long-standing family joke.

The second box contained the tuft of dog hair.

"Oh, he's a nice dog," Garrett said. "He gets a lot of burrs in his coat. I think he once had a very bad pain in his paw. It really hurt him badly."

The first two comments were not particularly significant, since many dogs are nice and get burrs in their coats, and as the dog was not his, LeShan didn't know the history of his injuries. When he consulted the owners, however, they told him that the previous year Charlie had cut a paw on a piece of glass and the wound had become infected. He had spent six weeks at the veterinary hospital and had not been expected to live.

LeShan shoved the remaining box under Garrett's hand.

"This is a rosebud," she said. "It comes from a very small garden. The garden needs a lot of work before it's ready for the summer. The soil is too acid for things to grow well."

All these statements were true.

This kind of experiment may involve both telepathy and psychometry, the process by which a person may pick up information about events through contact with an object connected with them. In LeShan's test of Garrett, she might have picked up the information about the contents of most of the boxes from the mind of the experimenter, but he was not aware of Charlie's injured paw, so she could not have gotten that from picking his mind by ESP. That information apparently came from the dog's owners or from Charlie himself.

Bill Roll believes that psychometry may be an important key to understanding the psi connection. He suggests that the longbody includes things the person has owned or has had prolonged contact with. The tuft of Charlie's hair was part of his longbody and of the longbodies of his owners, so when Garrett was in contact with it, she was connected also to both the dog and the family to which he belonged.

In most everyday instances of ESP, a psychometric object is not necessary, because the distant person is already a part of the receiver's longbody and the key factor is telepathy and its literal meaning, "distance suffering."

* * *

One example of this was reported by a California grand-mother who awoke at 3:45 one morning with her heart pounding from a dream in which she saw her infant grand-son smothering in his blankets. She hated the thought of waking the baby's parents, who lived on the other side of town, but she felt compelled to.

Her son-in-law answered the phone.

"What on earth are you calling for at this hour?" he demanded.

"Go to the baby at once!" the woman told him. "He's smothering!"

"Yes, he *was*," said her son-in-law. "But we're up—we heard him!"

The grandmother, many miles away, had done more than hear the endangered child, she had *seen* him.

Despite the fact that reports of experiences like this one were being collected by researchers the world over, most scientists in the early part of the twentieth century refused to take them seriously. Some even insisted that the whole idea of ESP was impossible.

Although psychical research using scientific methods had been going on since the founding of the Society for Psychical Research in 1882, it was the work of J. B. Rhine at Duke University during the 1930s that marked the begin-ning of systematic, controlled laboratory experimentation to attempt to prove that ESP was real.

Rhine started with guessing games using local children and cards stamped with numbers or letters. Later the now well-known set of five ESP cards, with the symbols of circle, square, cross, star, and wavy lines, was developed.

Rhine's approach was to test large numbers of people, many of them university students. Occasionally, one would surface who displayed a consistent ability to guess the cards at above-chance rate. By this method, Rhine and his team eventually discovered seven students with extrachance ESP abilities. These subjects were extensively tested in experiments designed to examine differences between telepathy and clairvoyance, as well as the effects of physical distance between the subject and the test cards. Experimental controls to make sure that the results could not be due to sense perception or to procedural errors, such as incorrectly recording the ESP targets or the subjects' responses to them, were continually improved.

A much publicized example of these experiments was the Pearce-Pratt series. In these experiments, a graduate student named Gaither Pratt conducted the tests from one building, where, once each minute, he took a card from a preshuffled deck and, without looking at it, placed it face down onto a designated surface. At that same moment, determined by synchronized watches, Hubert

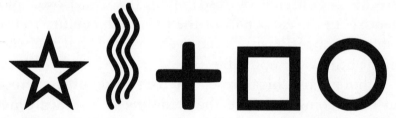

(copyright 1937 by J. B. Rhine)
The five ESP cards—star, wavy line, cross, square, and circle—were designed at the Parapsychology Laboratory at Duke University to test extrasensory perception. The card order was usually copied from series of random numbers in a room away from the subjects. A "run" consisted of twenty-five trials, and a test generally consisted of at least ten runs. For a telepathy test, the experimenter would look at each card and attempt to mentally project the image to the subject. For a clairvoyance test, the sender would not look at the card, to ensure that the subject's response would be to the card itself, rather than to information transmitted by the sender.

Pearce, a divinity student who was located in another building 250 yards away, tried to view the card clairvoyantly. Both men deposited sealed records with Rhine after each test, with Pearce recording his guesses and Pratt the sequence of the targets.

Four separate experiments were done involving 1,850 trials with 558 "hits" (meaning Pearce guessed correctly 558 times). Since only 370 hits should be scored by chance, the odds against chance being the explanation for this sort of success were overwhelming.

Rhine published the results of these tests and others in a 1934 book, *Extra-Sensory Perception*, which became a landmark in the history of psychical research.

In 1940, Rhine and his colleagues at the laboratory published a second book that was to become a classic, *Extra-Sensory Perception After Sixty Years*, in which all the parapsychology experiments of the preceding decade were reported and analyzed. The professional acceptance of this work was quite positive, and it looked like parapsychology was at last beginning to be accepted as legitimate scientific activity.

Rhine's experiments inspired others to try to repeat them. One such person was Gertrude Schmeidler, a young assistant in the psychology department at Harvard University. In her first tests, most of her subjects, who were undergraduates—plus anybody else she could corner and talk into helping her—scored a bit better on average than the chance score of five per twenty-five trials.

Then two subjects came along who did far *worse* than chance. Both were skeptical about ESP, one saying that even if it was true, he would not believe it. The other, a woman, was distressed that another woman, whom she respected, was now dabbling in "superstitions." They had agreed to the test so that Schmeidler could finish it up and return to things that mattered.

It didn't work out that way. The two subjects failed in scoring above chance, but in the process they scored so far below that they produced a negative deviation from chance. Schmeidler realized that in order to *avoid* getting a correct answer you have to *know what the correct answer is*. It seemed that her two subjects may have made a subconscious decision to disprove ESP by failing in the test, and in the process had actually shown evidence of ESP.

This effect was labeled *psi-missing*, the opposite of *psi-hitting*. If subjects achieve testing results that are far below chance, it is just as statistically significant as if they are above chance.

This discovery led Schmeidler into yet another area of exploration. In tests at Harvard and then at the City College of New York, she divided the people she tested into two categories—believers and nonbelievers. She called the believers *sheep* and the nonbelievers *goats*. Test results showed that sheep generally tended to score higher than goats, suggesting that people do better at tasks they feel positive about. Schmeidler's research further suggested that goats directed their attention away from extrasensory information and blocked its mental processing, because it went against their established belief system. In other words, they identified the actual ESP target and then wrote down a different one.

Schmeidler's sheep-goat experiments were important, because they showed that attitude and belief affect ESP results.

Some of the most significant telepathy experiments pertain to young people. Evidence of childhood ESP seems to peak at about the age of three or four and then decreases

110

rapidly, often disappearing entirely when the child starts school.

One such case in the Rhine collection involves Joan, who as a very young child seemed to have an uncanny knowledge of what was in people's minds. At age three, she started referring to unopened Christmas gifts as if they had already been unwrapped ("I love my little blue purse!") and began to inform her mother that unexpected visitors were coming before they arrived.

Joan's father had deserted the family and was not a part of the little girl's life, yet she seemed to know all about him. Once, when he became critically ill and was taken to the hospital unconscious, Joan assured her mother that he would recover. Although they had no contact with the father, she gave her mother accurate reports about when he was given his first foods and when he no longer needed blood transfusions.

When Joan was four, her mother contacted the Duke Parapsychology Laboratory and requested that the child be tested. The tests entailed having Joan look at the backs of twenty-five cards and guess which of the five ESP symbols were on the front. The expected score based upon chance in this test was five.

The testing was given to Joan in the form of a game. She started with great enthusiasm and scored fifteen on the first round, then eleven, and then twelve. These scores were so far above the norm that they could not be explained away as mere chance.

In a controlled ESP test today it is no longer permissible to let the subject see the backs of the cards, since there are sometimes slight irregularities whereby they can be told apart. On some of the old cards, the imprints of the symbols themselves could be discerned on the backs. But this is probably not the explanation for Joan's success, or she would have gotten better, not worse, with repeated guessing.

By the fourth round of testing, Joan had become bored and announced that she no longer wanted to "play." Her mother pressured her into participating just once more, at which time she scored at about chance, suggesting that a playful wish to succeed may be one of the elements in achieving high-ESP testing results.

Did the little psi whiz kid burn out? Not necessarily. Low ESP test scores do not always indicate how a person will perform outside the laboratory, and Joan's mother continued to relate instances of ESP for about another year. But after age five, Joan's ESP abilities quickly faded, and once she started school she stopped making predictions and was no longer demonstrating instances of spontaneous ESP.

It has been suggested that telepathy may be a young child's natural means of communication, making it possible to have his or her needs met by nurturing adults before becoming advanced enough to have the ability to speak out and ask for things. ESP tests conducted in classroom settings have shown much higher results with elementary-school children when the teacher was conducting the tests. But this did not carry over with tests involving middle-school and high-school students. This seems to indicate that the relationship between younger children and their teachers bears enough of a resemblance to the dependent child-parent relationship so that the young child's ingrained telepathic communication system is still in effect. On the other hand, teenagers, who are pulling away from family in an effort to establish their own identities, may respond to their teachers differently.

It's interesting to note, however, that teenagers did better on tests given by their teachers than on tests that were given by strangers or by fellow students. And they did even better when they liked their teachers. One study of 185 high-school students from seven classes who were asked to anonymously fill out a questionnaire that rated their teachers, showed that when student and teacher liked each other the student's scores on ESP tests were significantly higher than when they didn't.

It would seem, then, that telepathic communication may be strongly influenced by affection and emotional dependency.

Louisa Rhine speculated that the reason for the decline of ESP ability in school-age children might be that a child's developing socialization in school reduces the intensity of his or her emotional linkage to family members.

Bill Roll agrees, but thinks something else may be involved also. Bill believes that education itself may be a block to psychic awareness. As the child learns to speak, he or she acquires not only the basic and very important tool of human communication, but also a picture of the world as his or her parents and teachers believe it to be.

"Our language is a mirror of our reality," Bill says. "When a child learns to speak, it also learns that its acceptance by others depends upon its acceptance of their version of reality. In the average adult's view of reality, you cannot directly know what someone else is thinking; objects never move by themselves; you cannot know the future except by the logic of probability; it is impossible to see people who have died; and so on. If a child insists on talking about such experiences, most parents and teachers try to convince it that it's imagining things."

Bill says that in the process of learning, the brain itself changes, and as we learn to talk, the left side of the brain becomes dominant. Since most academic learning requires spoken or written input, the left side of the brain gets used most at school. Most formal schooling discourages the use of the right brain hemisphere, the intuitive side that is involved with creativity and intuition, so schoolchildren quickly lose their ESP abilities.

Noreen Renier, a psychic who worked on my daughter's murder case, knows about the two sides of the brain from her experience as a subject for brain research.

"That was one of the fascinating discoveries that came out of my five years of testing at Duke University and at the Psychical Research Foundation," she says. "The scientists hooked me up to an EEG machine and monitored my brain waves when I was just being my logical, everyday self. Then they monitored me while I worked with ESP. They discovered that when I switched from logical thinking to telepathy, I used the other side of my brain. Evidently the psychic comes from the intuitive right side."

Renier's theory is not a new one. More than one hundred years ago a British scientist named F.W.H. Myers thought that the right hemisphere of the brain might be involved in ESP communication. Myers observed that the automatic writing of trance mediums, with a tendency toward repetition, resembled the writings of patients who had lost the use of their left brain hemisphere.

Myers's idea has been supported by contemporary studies. In the United States, parapsychologist Richard Broughton, director of research at the Institute of Parapsychology, points to the tendency of ESP impressions to take the form of visual images rather than words as indicating that they originate in the right hemisphere, which is less word conscious.

Noreen Renier blames the exhaustion she experiences when doing police work on the effort required to keep switching back and forth between the two hemispheres of the brain.

"Basically, I'm a trance medium, and on the occasions when I go all the way under in a trance, I have no memory of anything that happens to me while I'm down there," she says. "When I work with the police, I have to keep jerking myself out of the trance to listen to their questions and edit what I'm saying, so I can give them the information they're looking for. It takes effort and concentration to keep switching sides of the brain like that, and it's terribly draining."

Psychic detective Nancy Myer-Czetli also uses her right brain hemisphere when she works on crime cases.

"My telepathic scope seems to be broader than is usual," she says. "It overlaps into all of my senses. I can smell scents that are relative to the scenes I am clairvoyantly seeing; I feel physical sensations; I hear sounds—it's as if I'm at a multidimensional movie, except it's running in my head. At other times it's as if I'm visualizing externally. The images form outside my mind, but they are as real to me as the furniture in my living room. I have even gotten bruises at times when what seemed to be a mental image somehow formed physically."

To test Myer-Czetli's abilities for myself, I asked her to establish mind-to-mind contact with somebody I knew but she didn't know and gave her the name of the troubled teenage son of a close friend. With nothing more to go on than the boy's name and geographical location, she correctly described his destructive behavior and gave me the depressing news that he was a cocaine addict.

I then gave her the name and geographic location of my own son Brett. Myer-Czetli gave me a detailed description of Brett—his personality, his personal relationships, and his career goals—and tacked on the fact that he had a slight distortion of hearing in his left ear from having worked for many years with a rock band.

The information was accurate.

Myer-Czetli not only works on cases for law enforcement agencies, she gives private readings for individuals with personal problems. There was one occasion on which these two facets of her work overlapped in an unusual way.

"Once I was working with the police on a serial burglary case, when a man showed up in my office wanting career advice," she says. "I had never seen him before, but I knew him mentally through telepathy. It was the burglar! To double-check what I sensed, I looked into his memory bank to see if the houses that had been burglarized were in there, and they were. In addition to that, I recognized the house he was casing, because the cops and I had driven past it when we were in the neighborhood of his last hit. So I knew where he was going to hit next, and I knew what night, and I also managed to extract his name and address.

"As soon as he left I phoned the head of the unit of the state police that I was working with and said, 'Guess what!' He thought I was pulling his leg, because it was too good to be true! I gave him a full description of what the guy looked like, and told him his name and address so they could have people following him. They staked out the house and caught him flatfooted in the act."

Like many psychics, Myer-Czetli describes herself as having been somewhat of a loner in childhood. Her father's foreign service career meant moving from country to country, and she had a hard time establishing long-term friendships. She also has dyslexia, a learning disability that affects visual perception and makes it difficult to learn to read.

"I firmly believe that everyone has psychic abilities," she says. "I think, though, that I worked to develop mine more than most people do in order to compensate for the fact that I am dyslexic and can't see things straight. When one of your senses doesn't work well, you start depending on others, and, in my case, the one I began relying on was ESP."

Formal experiments with the visually handicapped support this theory. In one experiment a group of sixty-six blind children were compared with a group of forty seeing subjects in an ESP test with 52,975 trials. The blind subjects showed consistently higher average scores than the sighted subjects.

People like Nancy Myer-Czetli and Eileen Garrett, who are forced by the circumstances of their lives to develop inner resources, seem to emerge into psychic awareness that extends beyond the ordinary and may last beyond childhood.

In the case of Garrett, her lonely childhood served to focus her attention upon the world of nature.

"Garrett's tremendous awareness of the beauty of the external world led to an increased awareness of the powers within her," Bill Roll says. "There were times, she said, when 'I felt I could reach out and touch the flowers, the trees, the horizon, and even the sky. I could sense the breath of a distant bush, the vitality in far-off flowers, the sap moving in a remote tree.' This sort of perception set her apart from other children even as a teenager. She said of her classmates in boarding school, 'They were content with what was indoctrinated or told them and seemed never to want to discover things for themselves. It soon became obvious that I saw things differently and knew things instinctively.' Garrett thought that her clairvoyant ability consisted in her capacity to connect with energy fields she saw around people and things."

The Canadian brain scientist Michael Persinger conducted a unique study in which he correlated successes and failures of ESP experiments with records of changes in the earth's magnetic field.

"Our planet is actually a big magnet with a north pole and south pole that is enveloped in a magnetic field," Bill explains. "This magnetic field is sometimes aroused, and sometimes calm and quiet. When there are sun spots or other activity from space, they rain down particles onto the earth and affect the stability of the magnet we live on by creating magnetic storms. These manifest themselves not only in northern lights in the northern hemisphere, but in interference with radio reception and, it seems, with ESP reception as well.

"What Dr. Persinger discovered when he started correlating these data with ESP was that the results of ESP experiments are markedly lower during periods of high magnetic disturbances. On the other hand, reports of physical instances of paranormal activity increase during those periods.

"This makes sense when you stop to think about it. The human body is an electric conductor and as such may produce electric current when surrounded by a magnetic field. So what seems to happen is that when a brain that's already aroused gets a little extra kick from the magnetic environment, you may have apparitions and other physical manifestations. But when you want to be in a receptive ESP-type mode, the brain needs to be as calm as possible. If the electromagnetic environment is too noisy, the brain cannot 'hear' the ESP messages."

Another dramatic correlation between weather and ESP is shown by people who have had a close encounter with lightning. They sometimes suddenly start reporting psi phenomena that they never before experienced or even believed in. And, like people who have been through a near-death experience, lightning victims often regard themselves as different from others and seem to perceive the world in an unusual way.

Greta Alexander of Delavan, Illinois, opened up to her psychic abilities in 1961, after being struck by lightning.

"It came through the window and set the bed on fire," she remembers. "Soon after that I started getting visions and sensing things. I didn't understand it at first, but now I realize the lightning must have heightened my magnetic energy and enabled me to focus better on the realm of vibrations."

Alexander, a down-to-earth housewife and mother of nine children, says she had no psychic abilities before being hit by lightning. She has since become a highly respected psychic detective.

"When lightning strikes and there's that kind of current induction, certain neurons in the brain are damaged," Dr. Persinger explains. "The regrowth basically restructures and rewires the brain, specifically in the deep temporal lobe which allows you to perceive things. The mental properties that lightning victims have may be quite different from what they were before they were injured."

ESP also appears to be affected by the time of day. Throughout history night has been considered a time of mystery, eeriness, and the supernatural, but parapsychologists believe this is more than just myth and think that we actually may be more susceptible to psychic experiences at night than we are in the daytime.

"There appears to be something different about the brain during the nighttime that allows psi phenomena," says Persinger. "Between midnight and four in the morning, there's the release of a hormone called nocturnal melatonin, which disinhibits the brain, leaving it open to ESP experiences. Telepathy and clairvoyance are more likely to occur during those hours than during any other. And, of course, those are the hours when most people dream."

One of the earliest attempts at ESP dream research was conducted in the 1960s by a New York psychiatrist named Montague Ullman. The technical development that made this research possible was the discovery that when people dream their closed eyes dart around following the happenings in the dream. Ullman decided to use these rapid eye movements (REMs) as a way to determine when a dream began and when it ended. By placing electrodes next to the eyes of the dreamer, he could know exactly when a dream started and when it was over. He could then wake the dreamer and record the dream, which would be fresh in memory.

Eileen Garrett invited Ullman to conduct his tests at the Parapsychology Foundation, a research center she had founded in New York. She also offered to be his first subject. On that occasion, Garrett dreamed she was watching horses furiously running uphill and was reminded of the chariot race in the movie *Ben-Hur*, which she had seen two weeks before.

As it turned out, one of the targets in the test was a color photo of the chariot race in *Ben-Hur*.

The next round of ESP dream experiments was conducted at Maimonides Hospital in Brooklyn and involved several other researchers, including Stanley Krippner and Charles Honorton. In a typical test, two volunteers—let's call the hypothetical subjects Ken and Barbie—would meet at the dream lab to get to know each other. Barbie would then be brought to one of the experimental rooms where she would lie down, and electrodes would be attached next to her eyes. The wires would be fed into a recorder in Krippner's room.

In the meantime, Honorton would have made a random selection of a picture from a group of art prints and placed it in a sealed envelope. The envelope containing this target picture would then be delivered to Ken, who was in a third room.

When Krippner received the signal that Barbie's REMs had started, signifying she was now in a dream state, he would signal Ken to open the envelope and try to transmit his visual and emotional impressions of its contents to Barbie. As soon as Barbie's REMs stopped, Krippner would wake her up, using an intercom, and she would describe her dream on a tape recorder. This procedure would be repeated several times a night. The taped descriptions of the dreams would then be transcribed, and the transcripts would be sent to a group of judges, who would compare the transcripts to a set of target pictures and rank the accuracy of the duplication.

An overview of all the 379 dream trials conducted by the Maimonides team gave 233 hits. This was an accuracy rate of 83.5 percent and gave odds against chance of more than a quarter of a million to one!

It had finally been done! Psychic dreams seemed to have been proved in the laboratory!

The research became even more exciting in 1969, when a friend of Bill Roll's, Malcolm Bessent, entered the program. This young British psychic, who was a protégé of Eileen Garrett and Douglas Johnson, said that he often dreamed about future events. To investigate this possibility, the team changed the testing procedure in a dramatic way—they didn't select the ESP targets until *after* Bessent's descriptions of his dreams had been recorded and placed in sealed envelopes.

In his first series of eight sessions, Bessent scored seven hits. His dreams were reflecting images that were going to be transmitted to him on a future occasion!

ESP dream tests were expensive because they required so many experimenters and so much space and equipment, and after some years the money at Maimonides ran out.

Researchers were then faced with having to find another way to induce the relaxed state of image-rich consciousness that had proved so helpful in facilitating ESP.

In 1973, Charles Honorton came up with a solution to that problem—the *ganzfeld*. *Ganzfeld* is a German word that means "whole field," and this procedure had previously been used by psychologists to induce a uniform field of sound and sight without sensory distractions in the minds of subjects.

In an ESP ganzfeld experiment, the receiver was placed in a relaxed position in a recliner and halved Ping-Pong balls were fitted over his or her eyes. A red light in the room, softened by the white spheres, created a uniform visual field. To mask distracting sounds, earphones produced a quiet hiss of white noise. As in the dream experiments, a telepathic sender in another room was asked to transmit a visual target. Sometimes stereoscopic View-Master slide sets were used or videotaped segments from movies and cartoons. The receiver was instructed not to make an effort to get the target, but to remain relaxed and to describe any images and other impressions that came to mind. Immediately after the session the receiver would be shown a set of four possible targets and asked to say how close his impressions had been to the actual targets.

For his first experiment Honorton tested thirty subjects one at a time. Close to half of these showed some indication of ESP, and in several instances the mental imagery of a ganzfeld receiver matched the mentally transmitted View-Master scenes almost exactly.

For example, one subject's target was a reel of U.S. Air Force Academy scenes. The report of the subject during part of her session was as follows:

"An airplane floating over clouds . . . planes passing overhead . . . airplanes . . . ultrasound . . . a five-

A subject in a ganzfeld experiment at the Institute of Parapsychology, Durham, North Carolina. (courtesy: Mort Engel)

pointed star . . . an airplane pointed down . . . a giant bird flying . . . six stripes on an army uniform . . . a mountain range, snowcapped . . . flying through the mountain . . . a sensation of going forward very fast."

Honorton established the Psychophysical Research Laboratories in Princeton, New Jersey, with the goal of accomplishing two things—developing an ESP experiment that other researchers could duplicate, and discovering what characteristics make a person a good ESP subject.

Honorton found that people who reported psychic experiences were better at the ganzfeld tasks than those who did not. The same was true of people who engaged in a mental discipline, such as meditation or relaxation exercises.

In looking for other factors that might be related to ESP, Honorton used a personality questionnaire, the Myers-Briggs Type Indicator. This test showed that extroverts (outgoing people) do better than introverts (self-contained people) at ESP tasks, and that intuitive (right-brain) people do better than logical (left-brain) people. It also showed that people who are guided by their feelings do better than people who make decisions primarily based on logic, and that perceiving types, who are open-minded and flexible, make better ESP subjects than judgmental types, who like everything to be planned and orderly.

Could Honorton's findings be repeated at another laboratory? Richard Broughton took up the challenge at the Institute of Parapsychology in Durham. Based on Honorton's research, Broughton and his colleagues predicted high scores from subjects who showed four characteristics: they reported previous ESP experiences; they practiced meditation; they were "feelers"; and they were "perceivers."

Out of a total of 102 ESP ganzfeld subjects, mostly students from Duke University, 28 showed all four features. When tested, these subjects scored an impressive 43 percent hits versus the expected 25 percent that could be attributed to chance.

Honorton's findings had been confirmed.

CHAPTER SEVEN

PRECOGNITION

Once you accept the concept that information may be obtained through mind-to-mind and mind-to-object contact, telepathy and clairvoyance no longer seem extraordinary.

But what about precognition, the ability to see into the future? The idea is as old as civilization itself, and prophecies abound in both religious and secular writings. Precognition would not seem to be caused by the linkage of minds with minds or by the linkage of minds with things. Yet precognitive experiences not only do take place, they are reported more frequently than any other instances of ESP.

After Kait's murder, in an effort to motivate informants, I wrote a book titled *Who Killed My Daughter?* Two months before its publication, trance medium Robert Petro did a prophetic reading for me. Petro, who had done over 15,000 taped and documented trance readings, met me for the first time when I walked into his office. He knew nothing about me, not even that I had lost a child.

Petro leaned back in a recliner, closed his eyes, and allowed himself to be put into a trance by his wife. The reading started as follows:

This person present in the year of 1992 is entering a process of change—change geographically and change emotionally. I feel that this year she must be cautious of personal health, particularly the heart, and that she must let go of her grief and move ahead with her life. This year she will be involved with attorneys, with moneys, and she may find herself standing completely alone with no help from anyone where she will have few if any people to turn to for guidance.

This all took place as predicted. By the end of 1992, I had moved from New Mexico to Florida; I had suffered a silent heart attack; I had been "involved with moneys" (unexpectedly large advances for foreign rights to my book). I had also found myself "standing completely alone, with few people to turn to for guidance" when I toured the country with *Who Killed My Daughter?* and defended controversial beliefs on national television talk shows such as *Larry King Live* and *Good Morning, America*. As the year drew to a close, I dared to hope that Petro had been wrong about my involvement with attorneys. Then, on December 15, I received a letter from an attorney representing a police artist who had done a composite drawing of Kait's killer, threatening me with a lawsuit for using the sketch in my book. Luckily I had my publisher's attorneys behind me, and the matter was eventually dropped, but it was an upsetting experience, and one that I had not anticipated.

Although the statements about standing alone and being involved with moneys were general enough to be applicable in some way to almost anybody, the other statements were not. When I listen today to the audiotape of that trance session, I am amazed by its accuracy.

One year later I visited Petro again, this time accompanied by my friend Paula, who volunteered to be the subject of a trance reading to test Petro's psychic abilities further.

Petro told her, "You seem to be concerned about your health, and the body seems to be warning. You are very sensitive to yourself and to your body. Because of this sensitivity you will now be taking steps necessary to make corrections and to create harmony within mind and body. . . . Also you're going to start to see things about your physical self that you don't like, and you're going to consider making changes physically."

"A facelift?" Paula suggested jokingly. Petro did not join in the laughter.

When Paula asked him about her relationship to her daughter Kristy, Petro responded, "This person entered into this lifetime as a means of stability for the mother and will help the mother to stabilize emotionally at the opportune time. When the mother will be at the weakest point in her life this particular child will be hope."

This past year, Paula discovered a malignant lump in her breast and had a mastectomy. Because the fast-growing cancer had already invaded six lymph nodes, she was given high-dose chemotherapy, which her doctor warned might kill rather than cure her.

Paula survived and is doing well.

"What gave me hope was the discovery that Kristy was pregnant with my first grandchild," she says. "That gave me something to live for."

The "physical change" she is considering making is reconstructive surgery.

* * *

127

It has been estimated that more than half of all ESP experiences have a precognitive aspect. Some impressive examples of these have been reported by Bill Roll's students:

"One night I had a dream that I was home with my family, and I was terribly upset," says Dotsy. "There was such an overwhelming feeling of sadness and loss! Everyone in my family was there except for my dad. Even though I don't remember it being revealed in the dream, I knew he was dead.

"The next day I called home to talk to him. I told him about my dream, and he said jokingly, 'Well, that's nice to know.' We ended the conversation by saying we loved each other, and that was the last time I ever heard my father's voice.

"The next day, in our backyard, he had a massive coronary and died instantly."

"As a young child I often seemed to know what was going to happen before it took place," says Holly. "One example of this occurred in April of the year that I was seven, when I told my mother that my grandmother was going to be buried on Halloween. My mother, of course, was extremely upset by this and told me never to say such a thing again.

"As it turned out, my grandmother died on October thirtieth. She was Jewish, and since tradition has it that all Jews must be buried within twenty-four hours of their demise, she was buried on Halloween."

"When I was a teenager I lived next door to a boy named Jay," says Dawn. "One night I dreamed about seeing him lying in a casket. I ran into Jay the next day and started to tell him about the dream and then thought better of it. We just talked about school, sports, and other trivial things.

"That night I had another scary dream about Jay. I dreamed that he was dead and his girlfriend was screaming. When I woke up I felt sort of sick at my stomach. Later that day, I was watching television, and the dream came back into my mind. At exactly that moment I heard a scream, and I knew immediately what it was. I ran outside, and Jay was lying on the ground in a pool of blood with his girlfriend standing over him, screaming. Later I learned that Jay had phoned his girlfriend, crying and threatening suicide. She rushed over to his house, and when she got there, he shot himself in the heart. The next day I went to the wake and saw Jay in a casket like the one he was in in my first dream."

Most of the reports of precognitive experiences on file at the Institute of Parapsychology involve violence to a member of a person's longbody. My own experience of having fragments of information pertaining to Kait's murder turn up in a book I wrote the year before she was killed supports the premise that the approaching death of a loved one can activate psychic abilities that were previously unrecognized. I was stunned when I read in the police report that the nickname of the man who was arrested for shooting Kait was Vamp, the same last name I had given the hired assassin in *Don't Look Behind You*.

But psychic Nancy Myer-Czetli does not find this surprising.

"I think most people have precognitive abilities," she says. "Most of the time, though, they don't take them seriously. I can't tell you the number of police cases I've worked on where the parents of a murdered or abducted child said they sensed it coming but didn't realize it was real. In the case of a writer, it's a natural part of the creative process to draw upon thoughts and feelings buried deep in the subconscious, so it's not surprising that premonitions about an impending tragedy might surface in a work of fiction that a writer happened to be working on prior to the disaster."

Myer-Czetli believes that precognition is an early warning mechanism that is there to help us protect our lives and the lives of those around us.

"If people can understand this, then maybe they'll pay more attention to their hunches," she says.

Robert Muller, the former assistant secretary general of the United Nations, accepts his many instances of precognition as a natural part of his life. He tells about one occasion on which, on his way home from the U.N. headquarters, he passed a white brick building and had a psychic vision of the bricks blowing out from an explosion. He waited half an hour to see if it would happen, and then told himself, "Wrong message," and went home. The following day, when he opened *The New York Times*, there was a banner headline about a gas explosion and a photo of the building with its white brick front blown off.

On another occasion, while at home having dinner with his family, he had a vision of "a big metal rope that was on fire." Excusing himself from the table, he checked the house from one end to the other and found nothing out of order.

"I sat back down at the table and said, 'There's no fire, but I saw a string of metal that was burning,'" he says. "Ten minutes later we heard an explosion, and the whole electric cable in front of the house came down. What was lying across our driveway? *A burning cable!* My children said, 'How did you know this?' I told them, 'I have no idea, I just saw it.'"

Although predictions of future events may take the form of hunches or materialize in works of fiction, most premonitions seem to come to people in dreams.

In 1927, J. W. Dunne published the first book that directed wide attention to precognitive dreaming. He claimed that nearly everyone has such dreams, but that most of us fail to recognize them. Sigmund Freud, the psychiatrist who brought dreams to the attention of science, believed that sleep creates favorable conditions for telepathy, and that dreams, with origins in the depths of the psyche, may be a residual form of ancient, prelanguage communication.

Some people argue that the fact that some dreams turn out to be prophetic may be nothing more than coincidence, and that, in light of the fact that each of us dreams several times every night, chance alone would account for an occasional instance in which a dream situation was later mirrored in real life. They also point out that even those dreams that appear to have precognitive elements aren't correct in all ways, and in most cases a slice of real information is surrounded by a mishmash of fantasy.

Both these arguments are indisputable.

It is true that knowledge from all our senses is stored in the subconscious and often becomes scrambled together when incorporated in dreams. For this reason, dreams are seldom totally realistic, and even precognitive dreams may be distorted. Along with this problem, there is the problem of memory. In the majority of cases, we don't remember our dreams unless something occurs in our waking state that triggers recollection. When we dream about an event and it later comes to pass, we may be jolted into recalling the dream because it has suddenly become significant.

Bill Roll says it is no coincidence that imagination is often mixed in with precognition and other forms of ESP, because imagination and ESP impressions are both made of the same material—memories. It is not possible to imagine something that is not constructed upon images that are already filed in your memory bank. As a test of this, try to imagine a brand new color that does not incorporate the primaries—red, yellow, and blue. You will find that impossible. The only colors we can visualize are shades and combinations of the colors that we have seen in real life. For this reason we cannot visualize ultraviolet light.

ESP impressions also are composed of memory material. When Dawn had her dream of seeing Jay in a casket, the images of what Jay looked like and what a casket looked like were already part of her stockpile of memories. It was the *combination* of Jay and casket that gave Dawn the message that Jay was going to die.

Which raises a bewildering question. If imagination and ESP are both composed of memories, how can we tell them apart?

Bill thinks we can't.

"There is usually no way to distinguish an ESP dream of a future event from a dream that is the product of simple imagination," he says. "If there had been something unique about Dawn's dream that identified it as precognitive and convinced her that Jay was in danger, she certainly would have told him or his girlfriend about the dream. She remembered the dream when she woke up because it was frightening, but she had no way of knowing it was prophetic until it came true. People are inclined to remember dreams about death and injury and to identify them after the fact as having been precognitive, not because they are basically different from other dreams, but because they are disturbing."

In the spring just before Kait's death, my friend Gwynne

had a terrifying dream while she was vacationing in Hawaii. She made the following entry in her journal:

In the dream I am driving a little red rental car and pull up at a traffic light, and a Polynesian-looking guy gets out and gets up next to me and puts four bullets into my head, and I hit a phone pole and am dead.

Gwynne was so unnerved by the dream that the following day she exchanged her small red rental car for a white one.

Four months later, when Kait pulled up to a traffic light in her red Ford Tempo, was shot in the head, crashed into a telephone pole, and died, Gwynne reread that journal entry with horror.

"I was given the message, but I couldn't interpret it," she told me.

People also are more likely to pay attention to dreams or hunches if they have had previous impressions that came true. Holly, who accurately predicted the date of her grandmother's burial, says she often knows what is going to happen before it takes place and for this reason pays special attention to her internal sensations.

It is common for people to have the feeling of being in a place or having something happen that seems so familiar that they feel they have already experienced it. This is called déjà vu (a French phrase meaning "already seen"). Much of the time déjà vu is caused by a mismatch between the left and right sides of the brain. This brain glitch occurs when visual information is processed a fraction of a second faster by the left hemisphere than by the right. Since the experience of recognition is provided by the left hemisphere, while the right processes the visual information, there is a sense of familiarity an instant before you perceive the scenery.

But déjà vu may also be due to precognition. This was the case with a Canadian teenager who described a dream in which she was sitting in a small room with posters on the wall:

"In one corner of the room there was an old-fashioned desk with an old, upright telephone on it," she said. "An old man was seated at the desk, writing. The phone rang and when he answered it he said, 'Yes, Emma, one pound onions and a dozen oranges—I'll bring them home.' In this same room with me were four other girls—I couldn't tell, however, who they were. Each girl seemed nervous, and so was I. One by one they went out and came back about ten minutes later. When my turn came I woke up."

The dream seemed of no importance, and the girl forgot all about it until two days later when she went to take her driver's test.

"There were three other girls who took driving lessons with me," she said. "We entered a small room where an old man was seated at a desk filling out forms. We were to go out one at a time to take the road test, and I was the last one to go. Of course, we were all nervous."

Without knowing why, the girl had a strong feeling of déjà vu, as if she were reliving an experience that had already taken place. Then the telephone rang, and the man at the desk answered it and said, "Yes, Emma, one pound onions and a dozen oranges—I'll bring them home."

The precisely worded statement jolted the girl's memory, and her dream came rushing back to her. In this case the déjà vu had been caused by a precognitive dream.

* * *

134

Startling as a story like this may be, it can't be considered real evidence of precognition, because, like most instances of precognitive dreaming, it cannot be verified.

But there have been some notable instances when precognitive dreams were documented.

Irene Hughes, who discovered her psychic gifts at the age of four, made a practice of recording her predictions in notebooks or on tape. Among these were the following:

That President John F. Kennedy would be assassinated (a prediction recorded in her notebook); *that three men would die in a space capsule* (a prediction recorded on tape in Washington, D.C., before the fire in the Apollo capsule that caused the death of three astronauts in 1965); and *that Bobby Kennedy would be shot through the head* (a prediction made to a newspaper reporter).

One of the most dramatic of all documented instances of precognition occurred in 1979, when, on May 15, David Booth, a rental car manager from Cincinnati, had a nightmare in which he saw a DC-10 jet airliner lose an engine, turn on its side, and fall out of the sky.

"It started to turn with the wing going up in the air, and it went on its back, and then went straight down into the ground and exploded," he said. "I can't even describe the kind of explosion it was and the instantaneous terror that struck me right then."

Booth continued to have that same dream night after night. Each time he saw the logo of one specific airline.

On the seventh day he contacted the FAA.

"We can't just arbitrarily ground an airline because somebody dreamed something," they told him.

On Friday, May 25, Booth had the dream for the tenth and last time.

"I woke up that morning, and all the emotions I had been having were still there, except that this time I knew that was *it*—it was the last time I was going to have that dream," he said.

That afternoon a DC-10 took off from Chicago's O'Hare Airport, flew half a mile, then suddenly turned on its side and slammed into the ground, exploding on impact. All 272 people on board were killed in one of the worst plane crashes in history.

Booth had correctly predicted the name of the airline, the model of the plane, the way it would turn on its side, and the fact that the engine would fall off as it plummeted to the ground.

The concept of precognition is disturbing to many because of the question it raises about the power of Fate. If we can know what is going to happen before it occurs, doesn't this mean that the future is predetermined? And if it does mean that, then what does that say about free will? Most of us are convinced that we can make choices in life and that those choices have an effect upon what later happens to us. Human society, including our legal system, is based upon the premise that we have options and are therefore responsible for our actions. We may not have the ability to affect *some* things, like the weather or the behavior of other people, but we do have the power to affect *other* things, and so have at least some control over shaping the future.

One thing that has been suggested is that there may be two kinds of future events—Type One, that are "set in concrete," and Type Two, that can be altered.

In the case of David Booth and the DC-10 crash, despite all Booth's best efforts, he was unable to avert the disaster he had predicted. Could it have been prevented, or was it inevitable? In other words, was his a Type One or Type Two precognition? Booth treated it as a Type Two and contacted the FAA, hoping that he could persuade them to ground the plane, but he did not succeed in doing so.

There have been instances, however, when a warning in a dream led someone to take an action that *did* avert a tragedy.

One such incident involves a young mother in Washington State, who woke from a nightmare in which the huge chandelier in her baby's bedroom fell into the crib. In the dream, she and her husband were standing in the wreckage, gazing down at their daughter's shattered body, and the clock on the baby's bureau said 4:35.

The dream upset her so much that she woke her husband and described it to him. He told her not to be silly and to go back to sleep, but she was too shaken to do so. Instead she got up, went into the baby's room, and brought her back to bed with them.

About two hours later, at exactly 4:35 A.M., she and her husband were awakened by a loud crash. The chandelier in the baby's room had fallen into the crib. Thanks to the mother's dream, the crib was empty and the baby was safely snuggled between her parents.

The future this woman foresaw was not the laid-in-concrete kind. She precognized the future that *would have been* if she had not taken her dream seriously and taken evasive action.

Hers was a Type Two precognitive experience.

There are also cases on record in which a premonition that might have prevented a tragedy was deliberately disregarded.

* * *

A woman in Utah was seeing her children off to school one morning when her ten-year-old son said, "Mom, I had a terrible dream last night! A car ran me down! It was so awful!"

The mother's first thought was to keep the boy home from school, but she talked herself out of it.

"I realized I had to be calm, although my heart was racing with fear," she said later. "I said that we can't live by dreams or we live a life of horror, but when the children left I uttered a silent prayer and told them to stay on the sidewalk. Some three minutes later, someone came running to me. A truck had run up on the sidewalk and struck my son down. He died seventy minutes later, never regaining consciousness."

Most people who have made a study of reports of precognition in everyday life believe they reveal the probable rather than the actual future. W. Edward Cox, a member of the Duke group of parapsychologists, had heard people claim their premonitions had saved them from train wrecks. If this was true, Cox reasoned, it would be logical for there to be more cancellations of reservations on trains that were going to crash than on trains that were going to arrive safely.

When Cox checked this out by comparing records of ticket cancellations before train wrecks with cancellations before uneventful journeys, his study showed significantly fewer passengers aboard twenty-eight railroad trains that were involved in accidents than on trains running at the same times of day a week before and a week after each event. Statistically, there was one chance in a hundred of this occurring by chance alone.

Bill Roll says that the more you study precognition, the more resemblance it seems to have to the normal kind of predictions we make based on logic. For instance, precognition is usually more accurate in regard to events in the near future than to those in the distant future.

"The same thing applies to predictions in everyday life," Bill says. "You'll probably be more successful in predicting what will happen during the next hour than in predicting what you will be doing at this time next week. With predictions governed by logic, as with precognition, it seems that the further you look into the future, the more likely it is that your prediction will not pan out, because there are more chances for things to intervene and make predictions go awry.

"There are exceptions to this, however, and occasionally events in the distant future are precognized with great accuracy. Dunne described a dream he had as a boy where the precognized events, including trivial details, took place when he was an adult twenty years later."

Nancy Myer-Czetli says that predictions of hers have prevented tragedies.

"There was one client I worked with who frequently drove through a dangerous intersection near where I live," Myer-Czetli remembers. "I had a feeling there was going to be a crash, and in my mind's eye I could see a school bus in front of her and an embankment going up the left side. I told her, 'You know, this sounds crazy, but if you go *up* the embankment, you'll survive and be fine. But if you go to the *right* of the school bus, which would be the logical thing to do, you're going to hit somebody coming around that bus head-on.' I described other details about the situation, so when the crash occurred, though it was quite a while after I did the reading, she realized right away that's what I was talking about and twisted the steering wheel so she went up the embankment. When she looked back she saw a Mack truck coming around the other side of the school bus."

Some psychics say that they are unable to use their psychic abilities to detect danger to themselves, but only to others. The Dutch psychic Peter Hurkos claimed that on several occasions he averted disaster for himself by sensing danger to those around him. Before boarding a plane, Hurkos made it a point to touch one of the other passengers to get a sense of whether that person's life was in danger, knowing that if it was, his probably was also.

According to Hurkos, once when he did this in Bangkok, the passenger he touched gave off such strong vibrations of impending doom that Hurkos suggested to him that they both cancel their reservations. The man refused to listen and boarded the plane anyway. The plane went down in the mountains.

So what do precognitive experiences most often reveal? Are they more inclined to be revelations of events that are destined to occur or warnings about what might happen if preventive steps aren't taken?

Louisa Rhine addressed this question in a paper entitled "Precognition and Intervention." From her vast collection of reports of precognitive experiences, she sorted out over 460 in which the events that were foreseen were of a kind people would want to prevent from happening. In about two-thirds of these cases there was no attempt made to intervene. When she eliminated those cases, she ended up with 191 cases in which some attempt was made to prevent the foreseen event from taking place. In 60 of those cases, the attempted intervention was not successful, usually because of a lack of enough specific information. In the remaining 131 cases, the attempted intervention was successful in the sense that the foretold undesirable consequences were avoided.

Robert Petro believes that the future is preordained, but

that we ourselves may be ordained to play a part in it, and our premonitions may direct us as to what that part should be.

"I believe there's a master plan and we're all assigned roles in it," he says. "We're not here to alter destiny, we're here to facilitate it. For instance, let's say you're at a party and notice that a friend has had too much to drink, so you take away his car keys. You may have been placed at that party as an instrument of destiny. Your friend's part in the master plan is to achieve certain things in his lifetime, and your part in the plan is to keep him from dying in a car wreck before he can accomplish his life's purpose."

The cases that have been discussed so far in this chapter provide anecdotal (or "word-of-mouth") evidence of precognition. But, as with other forms of ESP, the only evidence that is taken seriously by scientists is obtained during controlled testing in a laboratory setting.

The first subject to take part in a precognition experiment was Hubert Pearce, the ESP subject who had done so well in the clairvoyance card tests with Gaither Pratt. In precognition experiments at Duke University, Pearce was instructed to do what he was so good at—guess packs of ESP cards—but not in their present order. He was asked to predict the way they would turn up after they had been shuffled!

And he was successful!

Since there was no normal way to predict the order of a pack of cards that somebody else would shuffle, it appeared that precognition had now been proven in the laboratory.

But had it really? One of the experimenters suggested that the person who shuffled the cards used clairvoyance to sneak a psychic peek inside the sealed envelope that held

Dr. J. B. Rhine, at Duke University in about 1933, testing Hubert Pearce, the ESP subject who was able to predict the order in which ESP cards would turn up in a still-to-be-shuffled deck. (courtesy: Institute of Parapsychology)

Pearce's predictions and then arranged the cards accordingly. If so, this would not have been a test of Pearce's precognitive powers, but a test of the clairvoyant abilities of the card shuffler.

To make very sure this couldn't happen, the Duke researchers built a device to take the shuffling out of human hands—a mechanical card shuffler. The results of the precognition tests continued to be positive, and again it seemed that precognition had withstood the challenge.

But another research project that was under way at Duke threw a monkey wrench into the precognition works. Experiments in which people attempted to mentally influence the fall of dice showed evidence of a new psychic capacity—psychokinesis or PK (the power of mind over matter). If a person could mentally affect the fall of dice, why not also the cards in a mechanical shuffler? The supposed precognition results could be due to PK.

Ironically, the success of parapsychologists in proving clairvoyance and psychokinesis now made it almost impossible to prove precognition.

Precognition research was set back to square one.

Still, other areas of psi research continued to turn up unexpected discoveries to provide support for the validity of precognition.

One such discovery occurred at Stanford Research Institute as part of an ongoing experiment involving "remote viewing," in which the subject attempted to describe a randomly chosen scene being viewed by another person in a distant location. During this research a few trials were done in which the subject's description was recorded some half hour *before* the target scene was selected and viewed.

To the total amazement of the scientists, those sessions provided some of the best matches that were obtained.

Obviously a phenomenon like remote viewing, and especially before-the-fact remote viewing, has exciting practical applications. One laboratory working in this area is the Princeton Engineering Anomalies Research Laboratory at Princeton University. Scientists there have collected a sizable database from remote-viewing trials, including many that have confirmed the work at Stanford Research Institute.

So, given that precognition may be a reality, what does it tell us about ourselves and the world we live in?

"Precognition shows that our mind and brain may have access to a much wider database than is available to the familiar sensory system," says Bill Roll. "We may know things through the use of ESP that we didn't think we knew. The longbody has a big mind and a big brain with the capacity to see beyond the present.

"Precognition also tells us interesting things about our world. It suggests that a probable future may be laid out, but that in many cases it's possible to change. Precognition is longbody prediction, and as with ordinary prediction, information about events in the near future is more easily known than about events that are further down the road."

New York parapsychologist Nancy Sondow compares the structure of the future to a branching tree with its roots in the present. The farther up the tree (and into the future) we go, the more branchings (possibilities) there are, presenting more opportunities for precognitive impressions to go wrong.

Bill Roll uses a similar concept of the longbody (meaning the collective entity of ourselves and all the people and places to which we are connected), traveling along a road that divides at various points to provide us with an increasingly large selection of possible routes. The longbody may be able to survey all the possible destinations by means of ESP, but it is not omniscient and cannot know for certain which paths will actually be taken. That depends on circumstances in the future beyond the longbody's present knowledge and control. And because the road will have divided more often for the more distant events than for the events in the near future, near events are more easily foreseen than those further away.

Betty Muench has made predictions about events that she says will lead to the solving of Kait's murder:

7/22/89: There is one who will be as a kind of undercover person, and this will lead to the ultimate knowing in this case. . . . It will be that there will come the unveiling of the truth. It will be found out and then all the more sorrow at the seeming uselessness of it.

11/2/89: There will be those who will be caught and exposed, and it will be for this family to come to see and know what it is that Kait will have been dealing with in her final day.

4/26/92: There is a sense of some definiteness in Kait, and she will seem to know that there will be a resolution to her murder, and this pleases her.

5/29/92: The killers will not go unpunished. The mysteries will be cleared up. There will also come a kind of crackdown on certain activities that will lead to the capture of all those who will seem to have missed the loop in all this. Two people [she gave their names] will be brought forth. All will delight then in the destruction of the other. The stage is set!

Many of Betty Muench's other predictions have proven accurate.

We continue to hope and believe that these will also.

CHAPTER EIGHT

PSYCHOKINESIS

A university student was involved in an ESP testing program and found she was yielding some promising results. The professor was pleased and encouraged her to continue.

One evening she visited another member of the faculty and described how well she was performing on the ESP tests. He was concerned that she was wasting her time and, after several futile attempts to convince her to discontinue the testing, he became very upset.

"The only thing that could convince me that there is anything to this ESP business is if that picture on the wall fell down this very instant!" he bellowed.

He pointed his finger at the picture—and it fell to the floor.

This is seemingly an example of what is known as *spontaneous psychokinesis* (or *spontaneous PK*). The term *psychokinesis* means "movement by the psyche or mind." The more scientific definition used by parapsychologists is "a physical effect produced by a person without known intermediaries."

Apparent cases of spontaneous PK are not nearly as common as those of ESP. By 1963, when Louisa Rhine had received more than 10,000 letters about ESP, she had received only 178 accounts of apparent PK.

The largest number of PK incidents in Rhine's collection were involved with death. Those included unexplained instances of clocks stopping or starting; of things falling off walls and shelves; of objects breaking or exploding; of doors opening or closing; and of lights turning on or off for no apparent reason. In several cases the same object was involved in more than one separate incident of PK. In the case of one man, for example, a grandfather clock stopped at the death of his father and then again several years later after his mother's death.

Bill Roll's students present stories of their own PK experiences:

"My grandmother was diagnosed as having breast, bone, and lung cancer, and given only a short time to live," says Susie. "I flew to Miami to spend some time with her and say good-bye. On the day I left to fly home, she gave me her watch. She said, 'Later today when it [the watch] stops ticking, *I'll* stop ticking.'

"At the time I thought she just meant that the watch needed a new battery. However, at 3:44 that afternoon, the watch stopped ticking. At the same time, I had this feeling of peacefulness go through my body that is very hard to put into words. When I looked at the watch and saw that it had stopped, somehow I knew that my grandmother had just died.

"Later that night, I learned that the exact time my grandmother had died was three forty-four P.M."

*   *   *

Of course, there are cases of spontaneous PK that do not involve death, such as the case of the angry professor who apparently caused a picture to fall. But tension and stress are often triggers.

Here is another example from one of Bill's students:

"One afternoon after I returned from class, I was a little tired and lay down on my bed to have a rest," says Niles. "My mind was on math, which was a course I was taking that quarter. I was having a difficult time with the subject and was struggling very hard. I did not understand why I was doing so badly, because I would get A's on all my homework, but I just couldn't pass the tests. Even though I would study for hours and work all the problems within the chapter that we were being tested on, I'd blow the exam.

"While I rested and thought hard about this, I remember thinking that I needed some 'outside help,' so to speak. It was at this point that a book called *How to Study Math* flew off my bookcase. It was a thin paperback book and could not have fallen on its own, since it was literally crammed between two other books. I thought that this was a very interesting experience, and that book helped me a great deal in my struggle with math."

In cases of spontaneous PK, the selection of the object that is moved is usually significant and is tied in some way to the mind of a person who is in the vicinity of the object. Although he had not been thinking about it at the time, Niles had been aware of the existence of that volume in his bookcase. It seems probable that it was a subconscious memory of the book that caused that particular volume to become his PK target when he became upset about his performance on math tests.

148

In addition to spontaneous PK, there is another category of psychokinesis called *deliberate PK*. With deliberate PK, the subject consciously causes the physical effect to occur.

Teenage girls have described to me what seemed to be this type of PK as something they do at slumber parties.

"It's a game called Light as a Feather," explained Megan, age thirteen. "We turn out the lights, and one girl lies on the floor, and everybody else sticks just the tips of two fingers under her. Then we all start chanting, 'Light as a feather! Light as a feather! Light as a feather! Now, *up she goes!*'" and we pick her right up and lift her above our heads! We don't even feel the weight of her on our fingers!"

Although this experience might be attributed to PK, Bill Roll suggests a second possibility.

"It's more likely the girls have gotten into an altered state of consciousness in which they are unaware of the effort they actually exert," he says. "The same muscular rigidity and effortless strength is seen in demonstrations of hypnosis where a subject is placed between two chairs, heels resting on one and neck and shoulders on the other, and the hypnotist then stands on the subject's stomach. Another example is the mother who seems effortlessly to lift a car off her child who has just been run over."

But the conviction of Megan and her friends that they are using mind over matter may set the mood for another activity at their slumber parties in which *real* PK could be happening. The girls also play with a Ouija board and report that on several occasions they were able to get the marker to move without touching it with their hands.

"We just stare at it hard, and it starts spelling things out," one girl told me.

Deliberate PK is practiced by physical mediums (on those occasions when the effects at a séance aren't hoaxes).

One of the most respected of all physical mediums was a

man named D. D. Home. Born in Scotland in 1833, the orphaned Home was raised by an aunt who threw him out when poltergeist-type phenomena, including rapping sounds and movements of objects, took place in his presence. Eventually he was able to control the phenomena, and even as a teenager was holding séances during which furniture rose from the floor and floated in the air and musical instruments played melodies of their own accord. Occasionally Home himself was seen to levitate and hang suspended in space.

Unlike other physical mediums, such as the controversial Fox sisters, who were thought by many to be charlatans, Home conducted his séances in brightly lit rooms and invited inspection. Skeptics poured in to investigate, but no compelling evidence of trickery was ever found. During a series of controlled experiments conducted by the British physicist William Crooks, Home played a tune on an accordion that was enclosed in a wire cage so that he couldn't touch the keys. Crooks also conducted tests that showed that Home could mentally alter the weight of objects.

To the shock of the scientific community, who expected that their respected fellow scientist would expose fraud, Crooks laid himself open to professional ridicule by publicly stating that he believed Home's mediumship was genuine.

In the 1950s, Kenneth Batcheldor, a British clinical psychologist, took a renewed interest in the physical phenomena associated with séances. He believed that the psychological conditions that prevailed in the old séances could be recreated so that people with no known PK abilities would produce striking phenomena. Batcheldor startled his colleagues by suggesting that it was a mistake to introduce tight experimental controls at the outset of an experiment. He felt this was likely to inhibit the participants so that no phenomena would occur.

In Batcheldor's opinion something else was also crucial for success—the creation of a group that was willing to meet regularly for a joint purpose and establish the same sort of group consciousness that was generated by Megan and her friends. To test this theory, Batcheldor conducted a series of informal experiments in which he and two close friends, none of whom made any claim to PK ability, would attempt to move a table with the energy of their minds. During the first ten sessions, the table movements could be explained by normal pushing and tilting, but during the eleventh session the table rose from the floor. Batcheldor then installed switches, a battery, and a lamp on the table, and hooked them up so the lamp would light when all four legs of the table were off the floor.

As the sessions continued, the movements of the table became rowdier. Batcheldor described one occasion on which the table levitated and floated right across the room. "We had to leave our seats to follow it," he reported. "It appeared to be about five inches off the floor, and the signal lamp remained alight until we crashed into some other furniture near the wall and the table dropped to the floor. When we reseated ourselves in the center of the room, the table soon came to life again and took to rising up and then banging itself down with tremendous force, so that we feared it would break."

Although none of the three participants seemed to possess any PK abilities outside the group, it turned out that significant events only occurred when one of them, Mr. Chick, was present. The group met 200 times over a two-year period. Chick was there for eighty meetings, and in all of these but ten there was PK activity. When Chick was absent, the table did not perform, which strongly suggests that he was more responsible than the others for causing PK activity to take place.

Other groups in England and Canada conducted similar studies with similar results. One Canadian researcher, Iris Owen, reported on the positive PK experiences of a group composed of herself and seven other members of the Toronto Society for Psychical Research. When asked about the psychological relationship of this group, she described them as having "complete rapport."

"This is much more than a 'good friends' feeling," she elaborated. "The group members have come to regard themselves as a family, and they behave together very much like a closely knit family."

Bill Roll attributes the success of such PK groups to three PK-conducive factors: the formation of a closely knit group (a longbody); a strong common purpose; and an aroused, active mental state (contrary to ESP, which works better when the receiver is relaxed).

Once again at the forefront of parapsychological research, J. B. Rhine at Duke University was the first parapsychologist to conduct controlled research on PK effects. It began when a professional gambler, who was interested in ESP, visited the lab and claimed he could influence the fall of dice with his mind. Rhine, who had found from his ESP work that competition often increased success, proposed a dice throwing contest between the gambler and his star ESP subject, Hubert Pearce. Rhine challenged Pearce, a divinity student, saying he should easily win since he had access to a much stronger source of power than the gambler!

Rhine's initial experiment consisted of having his subjects throw two dice and attempt to will the sum of the spots turned up to be greater than seven. According to the laws of probability, the chance of this happening spontaneously is five out of twelve. This means that, in a run of twelve throws, the dice might be expected to come up five times with more than seven spots showing. The longer the testing continued and the more runs that were conducted, the more likely it would be to average out to about five hits out of twelve, if no element other than chance was affecting the results.

In Rhine's tests a group of twenty-five subjects who attempted to direct the dice with their minds completed 562 runs and averaged 5.35 hits per run, a highly significant result by scientific standards.

As might be expected, there were many criticisms of this experiment, ranging from the way that the throws were made to the precision of the balance of the dice themselves. In response to these criticisms, several dice throwing mechanisms were developed.

In 1943, Dr. Rhine published a cumulative report of his PK investigations, but it fell far short of quieting the critics and settling the issues.

Research on PK phenomena fell off considerably during the 1950s and 1960s due to a decrease in funding. However, in 1963, Russian parapsychologists discovered a truly amazing PK subject named Nina Kulagina. Not only was Kulagina studied extensively by parapsychologists from the Soviet Union, she was also investigated by many representatives of impartial scientific and medical institutes from other nations.

Unlike other countries during that time period, the Soviet Union was openly interested in finding practical uses for psychic energy, and was concentrating its efforts on trying to learn exactly how ESP and PK worked and how it might focus and control these energies to its national advantage.

Western parapsychologists had restricted access to Kulagina, but were sometimes allowed to observe her performance when she was tested by the Soviets. On one occasion in 1970, when Gaither Pratt and his associate Champe Ransom from the Division of Parapsychology at the University of Virginia were in Leningrad, several noted Soviet scientists agreed to hold a demonstration of Kulagina's abilities in the Americans' hotel room.

Following some experiments designed by the Soviets, Pratt and Ransom were allowed to set up and film the last demonstration themselves. They spread a patch of fine gravel on the table top and placed a nonmagnetic cylinder vertically in the gravel patch. Kulagina concentrated, and the cylinder moved and traced a path through the gravel. This feat was then repeated and also filmed.

This effect of psychokinesis upon ordinary or familiar objects has been labeled *macro-PK*.

Two other non–Soviet-bloc scientists were allowed to do laboratory experimentation with Kulagina. British physicist Benson Herbert and parapsychologist Manfred Cassirer were permitted one session with her in the spring of 1973.

Both came back convinced of her integrity.

As compared to ESP, which most often occurs when the subject is in a relaxed state, macro-PK effects tend to occur when the subject is not only wide awake but in a state of physical or emotional arousal.

Tests conducted on Nina Kulagina showed that when she was attempting to move an object, her pulse would show a marked increase, her breathing would quicken, and she would experience pain in her upper spine and the back of her neck. She also showed weight loss and a raised blood sugar level within one hour after her PK attempts.

One of the best known and most controversial practitioners of alleged macro-PK is an Israeli stage performer named Uri Geller, whose specialty is metal bending. Geller's colorful saga includes alleged confessions of fakery by members of his entourage and countercharges that the confessions were "bought and paid for" by his detractors.

The debate has centered primarily upon claims by competing entertainers that many of the effects Geller represents as authentic PK can be duplicated on stage by sleight-of-hand artists.

Researchers do not refute this, but scientists who have participated in experiments with Geller point out that their findings were not based upon his performances on stage. He has been tested in seventeen laboratories in eight different countries, where scientists have reported observing him bend solid steel rods without touching them, erase select information from computer tapes, defeat the shape-memory of the exotic metal alloy nitinol, and use his mental energy to activate Geiger counters. In an effort to guard against fraud, Geller has been routinely searched for such things as metals hidden under his fingernails and magnets in his clothing, and on one occasion his mouth was X-rayed in search of a miniature radio that a scientific journal had accused him of having implanted in a tooth. No such devices were discovered.

Geller's apparent PK abilities were also examined individually on three occasions by four highly respected stage magicians. All issued formal statements testifying to their belief that Geller did not use magic tricks to produce the events they witnessed.

One magician, Artur Zorka, stated in writing, "I was prepared to nail the guy, but the results were quite another story."

According to Zorka, he and another professional magician, Abb Dickson, descended upon Geller after one of his performances and challenged him to give them a lengthy

Alleged PK wonder-worker Uri Geller during an informal demonstration of metal bending. (courtesy: Uri Geller)

personal demonstration of telepathy and PK. The results of the ESP demonstrations were mixed; Geller got some strong hits but also some misses. The misses occurred primarily during the early stages of testing, when Geller was attempting to duplicate drawings made secretly by Dickson.

Zorka said that, in later tests, "Geller was able to duplicate on paper target designs of which I merely *thought.*"

When Zorka and Dickson dropped Geller off at his hotel, Zorka asked him to bend a key for him.

"He didn't even take it from me," Zorka later reported. "He told me to hold it between my thumb and forefinger. As

I did, he stroked it with his finger, and it started to bend. I placed the key into my palm and watched as it continued to bend. I cannot explain it. . . . I know of no way he could have used trickery. . . . The only way I will change my thoughts about this matter is when some magician comes along and duplicates what I saw Geller do, under the same rigid conditions."

As president of the Occult Investigations Committee of the Atlanta Society of Magicians, Zorka submitted the following statement: "It is the unanimous finding of this committee that although we, as magicians, can duplicate each of these test results using methods known by us, under proper conditions, there is no way, based on our present collective knowledge, that any method of trickery could have been used to produce these effects under the conditions to which Uri Geller was subjected."

Because of Geller's uneven record, which contains both evidence of extreme PK ability and evidence that suggests otherwise, and his increasing reluctance to participate in laboratory studies, he is not currently the focus of parapsychologists. Even so, his name is legendary as an alleged PK wonder-worker.

The development of computer-based automation of forced-choice experiments revolutionized PK and ESP research. Computers turned out to be ideal for controlling experiment methodology and doing all the record-keeping tasks that were often at the heart of the critical attacks on previous research efforts. Of equal importance, however, was the incorporation into these machines of *random event generators* (known as REGs), that were used to select targets. REGs were based on truly random physical processes such as the spontaneous emission of electrons during the radioactive decay of strontium-90. According to the accepted laws of quantum physics, the kind of physics that deals with subatomic energies and entities, it is impossible to predict the exact time that the next electron will pop out.

But some people could!

In 1969, Helmut Schmidt, a senior research scientist at Boeing Scientific Research Laboratory, developed the first automated forced-choice machine based on an REG. This machine presented four colored lights mounted in a row on a panel with a push button under each light. The subject's task was to predict which light would be triggered by the next electron in the REG and to register this guess by pressing the button below the lamp of choice. Complex electronic circuits within the REG then converted the next electron produced by radioactive decay into a signal that selected which light would turn on. In this four-choice machine the exact probability that each lamp would light was 25 percent. In early experiments containing more than 63,000 trials, certain subjects reached guessing rates of 27 percent for extended periods of time, although the overall average scoring rate was somewhat lower. A 2 percent deviation above the norm may seem small to those who are unfamiliar with statistics, but the odds against its being caused by chance are huge.

Thanks to the computer and the random event generator, this sort of result could be established by repeating the same mode of testing over and over and thereby could prove beyond reasonable doubt that something incredible was indeed happening. The versatility of Schmidt's computer-controlled machine allowed him to program precognitive ESP tests and PK tests into the same experiment. Highly significant scoring rates of between 30 and 33 percent (where 25 percent was expected by chance) were obtained for *both*, and Schmidt concluded that there was no difference in his subjects' ability to predict a future occurrence and to affect a natural physical process using mind power.

Apparently the subjects in these experiments were either able to affect or to predict a natural physical process that can be neither affected nor predicted according to the present theories of quantum physics.

The staunchest skeptics could not help but be impressed by Schmidt's meticulously conducted experiments. Psychologist Ray Hyman, a longtime critic of parapsychology and a prominent member of CSICOP, the Committee for the Scientific Investigation of Claims of the Paranormal, stated, "Schmidt's work is the most challenging ever to confront critics such as myself. His approach makes many of the earlier criticisms of parapsychological research obsolete."

Schmidt's more recent work has dealt with the subject of time-displaced PK. He is attempting to demonstrate that PK can go backward in time!

Basically, what this means is that, instead of working with the real-time output of the random event generator, these experiments use prerecorded REG outputs in an effort to answer the question: Can a subject's conscious efforts today influence the operation of an REG that was recorded yesterday?

Schmidt has developed some complex experiments to investigate this mind-boggling concept and is involving outside observers, including critics, in an attempt to make sure the tests are airtight. Since many experiments have shown that the experimenter as well as the designated subject may affect the results in parapsychological experiments, one of Schmidt's main concerns has been to eliminate the possibility that he himself might be unconsciously affecting the outcome of the tests by PK. For instance, if Schmidt could precognize on Monday, when he prepares the REG targets, what the subject's responses will be on Tuesday, the possibility exists that he might be able to use PK to influence the REG to correspond to these responses.

The time-displaced PK experiments are beginning to provide Schmidt and the other physicists who explore micro-PK with data from which understanding of this phenomenon may emerge.

Richard S. Broughton states in his book, *Parapsychology: The Controversial Science*, "The role that consciousness plays in quantum physics is one of the burning issues in physics today, and Schmidt's time-displacement PK experiments bring parapsychology face to face with that issue."

The history of parapsychology, as of science in general, is full of ideas that seemed right at the time and that later were rejected in favor of others. Will this be the fate of time-displaced PK? There are indications that time-displaced PK happens, but the evidence is circumstantial and the jury is still out.

PK effects on REGs have been labeled *micro-PK*. Is it the same thing as macro-PK? Scientists don't know yet.

On a personal note, I have had only one experience with macro-PK, but I have had that experience many times.

About five weeks after Kait's death, I was awakened at two A.M. by the ring of the telephone. The phone was next to the bed, and I quickly snatched up the receiver so it would not wake my husband.

I was greeted by the dial tone.

Night after night the same thing happened—at close to two A.M. the telephone would ring one time, and when I answered there would be no one on the line. If I didn't pick up the receiver, there was no second ring. I finally decided that the calls must be coming from a sadist who had read about Kait's murder in the paper and thought it would be fun to harass her grieving family.

Eventually the calls tapered off to an average of two or three a week, with occasional blocks of time when there wouldn't be any.

Then I wrote *Who Killed My Daughter?* and my publisher sent me on a national tour with the book. On my first night on the road, in a hotel room in New York City, the phone rang at two A.M. I lifted the receiver, and there was no one on the line. The phone rang almost every night throughout the three-week tour, despite the fact that I was in a different city every night and no one knew my schedule except my publisher and my husband.

I felt as if I had stumbled into the Twilight Zone.

When I got home from the tour there was a pile of mail on my desk that included the latest issue of *The Inpsider*, the newsletter published by the Parapsychological Services Institute.

The reader mail column contained the following letter from a girl named Shari:

I am an only child and was very close to my father, who was a professional musician. When I left home to attend college, he called a great deal. Even when we were both living in the same city, he called frequently. He seemed to have a strong need to communicate.

My father passed away recently. Since his passing, my "piano phone," a little white telephone in the shape of a grand piano with keys for a dial, emits a distinctive ring on the average of a few times a week, often later in the evenings between 11 and 11:45. The first time that I heard it, it awakened me near the hour of his passing. Now the ring goes out often right before I fall asleep, or when I'm feeling sad and missing him.

I have picked up the receiver after it has made its

161

unique ring to find only a dial tone. However, recently I intercepted the call between the initial high-toned ring and the ones that followed it and the phone was totally "dead," as though it were unplugged, and then I heard a break in power after I queried, "Daddy? Daddy?"

I get a very good and loving feeling from the calls and am wondering if my experience is unique.

Bill Roll, who serves as an editorial consultant for the newsletter, answered as follows:

Phone calls from the dead are a relatively common experience. Many report a ring that may sound flat and abnormal, the connection is often bad, and the call is frequently concluded with the caller either hanging up or the line going dead. D. Scott Rogo, the late parapsychologist, wrote a book, Phone Calls from the Dead, containing several such cases. In one a woman reported speaking to her deceased father who told her where to find some important papers regarding his estate.

There are several theories. On one extreme it has been suggested that the spirit of the deceased is manipulating the telephone equipment. On the other extreme some suggest that the person receiving the call actually causes it through psychokinesis. Whatever the explanation, I would encourage you to pay attention to this phenomenon, to document your experience, and to draw continued comfort from the contacts.

When I reviewed my own situation, I realized how much my own experiences resembled Shari's. Kait, a typical teenager, had been a telephone addict and, like Shari's father,

had felt a strong need to communicate. When she gradu-
ated from high school and got her own apartment, she
called every night to touch base with me, even though we
saw each other almost every day.

Because of my terrible longing to be in touch with my
child again, was I unconsciously activating the phone by
spontaneous PK?

Or was *Kait*, in a desperate effort to identify her killers,
attempting to use PK to communicate with the living?

As Bill suggested, I am documenting my phone calls.

CHAPTER NINE

PSYCHOKINETIC TEEN—OR POLTERGEIST?

On the night of Friday, March 2, 1984, a poltergeist outbreak began in the home of fourteen-year-old Tina Resch of Columbus, Ohio.

Poltergeist is a German word that means "noisy or rowdy ghost," which seemed an apt explanation for the havoc that was being wrought upon the horrified Resch family.

There was little to indicate the turmoil that lay ahead for them when Tina's mother, Joan, went into the family room to send Tina and three young foster children to bed.

"I'm older than the little kids!" Tina objected. "I should be able to stay up a little bit later and not be treated like two-to-three-year-old kids!"

But Joan, who was exhausted after a long, hard day, refused to give in. Tina had been getting more and more rebellious lately, putting up an argument about anything and everything and refusing to do even the simplest chores around the house. Joan needed a break from her as well as from the foster children.

Tina went to her room, but she was furious. This was one more example of how unfair her parents were! Over the years Joan had taken in over 250 foster children, and the household revolved around their needs. Tina felt as if she were living in a round-the-clock day care center in which she had no more rights than one of the toddlers.

Fuming, she got undressed and crawled under the covers. Then she glanced at her digital clock and saw that something strange was happening. The numbers had begun to race as if someone were hurriedly setting the time ahead to a more appropriate bedtime.

Then the radio came on of its own accord. Tina turned it off, and it came back on, so she decided it must be broken. "That's okay," she told herself. "I have another radio."

The following day the clock radio was working perfectly.

On Saturday morning the foster children hogged the television set watching cartoons, while Joan took advantage of the unaccustomed peace and quiet to go into the bathroom and set her hair. Suddenly the television switched itself off. The oldest of the foster children went to get Joan to ask her to come fix it, but before she could do so the set went back on—then off, then on—flicking back and forth as if an invisible hand were at the controls.

Then to add to the confusion, the ceiling lights in the family room came on and the stereo in the living room turned on by itself. Joan went in and turned it off, and it came back on again. She unplugged it, and it still came on. Then she heard the sound of something slamming in the kitchen, followed by a whirring noise. The clothes dryer in the corner of the room had burst into action. Joan turned it off by opening the door of the unit, but as soon as she was back in the bathroom the door slammed shut and the motor started up again. She opened the door again.

Joan at once suspected Tina of the mischief. She knew that Tina was irritated at her and at the children and thought she had been meddling with the television and the dryer in order to annoy them.

Deciding that enough was enough, she left the door to the bathroom open and told Tina to sit in the hallway where she could watch her. While Tina was there and the children were playing in the family room, the dryer door slammed shut and the machine started up again. Then the garbage disposal in the kitchen began to grind, and Joan started to wonder if she had gone crazy.

By the time Tina's father, John, came home from doing errands the electrical disturbances were so severe that he called a family friend, Bruce Claggett, who owned an electrical firm, and asked him to come over and check things out.

Claggett examined the electrical system and found nothing wrong with it.

When he was ready to leave, Claggett switched off the kitchen lights, and to his amazement, they popped on again. He turned them back off and once again started to leave, and they came back on. This bizarre scenario was repeated over and over and involved all the lights downstairs. The moment he extinguished the lights and turned away, the switches flipped up again all by themselves! Even when Claggett fastened them down with adhesive tape and Band-Aids they continued to jump back up of their own accord, and in most cases the tape totally vanished.

"I don't believe generally in supernatural forces or strange powers," he told people later. "On the other hand, I know for a fact that those things happened and that switches untouched by hands were moved and tape disappeared. There was some sort of force doing things that I couldn't account for."

After Claggett gave up and went home, the electrical occurrences were replaced by another phenomenon. The water in the upstairs bathroom suddenly started running.

When John went up to check on it, he found that the faucets were open and the drains had been closed in both the tub and the sink in the children's bathroom. Assuming that one of the children was responsible, he turned off the spigots, opened the drains, and went downstairs, determined to catch the person who was playing games with him.

Although nobody went up the stairs, the water started running. Again the spigots were opened and the drains were closed.

"The second time I knew there hadn't been anybody upstairs except myself," he said later.

This was just the beginning.

In the days that followed, the Resches' normally orderly world turned into a chaotic nightmare as the objects around them seemed to take on a life of their own. Glasses, dishes, and candles started flying around in the house, and pieces of furniture zipped out from the walls as if they were on coasters. When the family gathered at the dinner table, the foster children's chairs kept jerking out as if they didn't want to be sat on; glasses flew off the table and smashed against the walls; and a toy cradle that belonged to one of the children flipped two feet into the air, fell to the floor, and broke.

Things became so violent that, fearing for the safety of the children, Joan felt that she had no choice but to return them to Children's Services.

To escape the turmoil, the Resch family spent two nights

in a motel, but when they returned to their home the polter-geist activity started up again. It seemed that everything that could be broken was being broken, and household objects were behaving like untrained animals. Heavy couches and chairs kept moving or turning over; the kitchen chairs followed people about or bumped into them; and food and fruit juice were splashed on the walls and ceiling.

One of the most dramatic incidents occurred when Tina was fixing breakfast and eggs flew out of the carton and smashed against the wall.

Joyce Beumont, a friend who was visiting, gave a graphic description of the incident:

"The eggs were sitting beside the stove, and they just started flying," she said. "Tina wasn't anywhere near there. One hit over by the window, and there were eggs on the floor. It was very messy."

She said that although she saw the eggs hit the walls, she didn't see them in flight because they went too fast.

Word soon got out that strange things were happening at the Resches', and newspaper and television reporters rushed over with their cameras. When Fred Shannon, one of the top news photographers in the country, arrived on the scene, he was greeted by a disaster area. Glasses, coasters, and a lamp went crashing to the floor; a couch slid out from the wall; and a telephone receiver went flying across the room and landed next to a visitor, who was cowering on the sofa.

The telephone receiver flew several times, and Shannon was able to photograph it in flight on three occasions. One of the pictures was picked up by the wire services and sent to newspapers worldwide, making the Resches instant and unwilling celebrities.

Joan and John Resch began to be worried that their house had been infested by evil spirits. In the hope that

168

Phone caught on film by photographer Fred Shannon as it flies past Tina Resch during an outbreak of poltergeist activity in her home. (courtesy: Fred Shannon)

their minister might be able to perform an exorcism, they requested that he come over and bless their home. When the minister entered the living room, he was shocked to see the couch come scooting out from the wall all by itself.

This upset him so much that he folded his hands and told the family, "There are things in this world we just do not understand." He left as quickly as he could and did not come back.

No sooner had the minister gone than Tina was hit from behind by a brass candleholder that flew in from the kitchen. Then a candle from a holder on the wall above the love seat where she was sitting sailed over to crash against the wall across from her, and a wall clock hurtled down to strike her on the head.

Tina herself was now under attack, and she was terrified.

A newspaper columnist who knew that Bill Roll had investigated a number of poltergeist cases phoned to ask him to come to Columbus to see if he could figure out what was happening. By the time Bill arrived at the Resches' home on March 11, their nicely furnished living room looked as if it had been struck by a tornado.

John confided to Bill that he felt that Tina was responsible, because the incidents occurred only when she was at home. At the same time, he was certain that she wasn't causing them in any normal way.

"I blame a lot of it on her," he admitted. "I keep trying to tell myself that she doesn't have control over it, but when you see what things are happening, you've got to believe that some of the turmoil she is going through is causing our problems. All the things that have been happening in some way reflect her feelings toward the house or toward us. She's just revolting against everything!"

In Bill's opinion this was not only possible but probable. This was far from his first experience with poltergeist activity, more commonly referred to by parapsychologists as *recurrent, spontaneous psychokinesis* (shortened to *RSPK*). These sudden movements of objects, flashes of light, appearances of water, and other physical occurrences had been recorded in all cultures and through all ages. In one study Bill conducted of 116 reported cases of RSPK, outside witnesses to the PK activity had included police officers, government officials, psychologists, scientists, teachers, lawyers, and members of the clergy, as well as the families themselves and their relatives and friends.

Having visited many homes that had been plagued by poltergeist outbreaks, Bill was familiar with the theories that had been offered to explain them. One, the "tricky teen" theory, held that what appeared to be supernatural phenomena were actually nothing more than instances of cleverly orchestrated fraud by mischievous youngsters.

Bill knew for a fact that this was sometimes the case, and that teenagers did on occasion fake poltergeist activity. His first encounter with such a teen had been with Ernie, a thirteen-year-old boy who lived with his grandmother. The grandmother, an uncle, and two friends of the family were certain that a poltergeist had invaded the apartment. They reported that ashtrays, table lamps, and bottles of medicine were soaring through the air of their own volition at times when it was impossible for Ernie to have thrown them.

But Bill was suspicious, because no one had been watching Ernie at the time that the things near him were sailing around. He invited the boy and his grandmother to visit the Duke Parapsychology Laboratory, where he was working at the time, and placed them in a room with a one-way mirror. That mirror was actually a window through which one of Bill's colleagues could observe the pair without their knowing they were being watched.

Ernie's grandmother left the room on two occasions. As soon as she was gone the first time, Ernie picked up two measuring tapes and hid them under his shirt. When his grandmother left the room the second time, Ernie hurled the tapes after her, and then pretended that they had been thrown by a poltergeist.

Ernie was a "tricky teen" who was looking for attention.

A second theory that Bill had more difficulty accepting was the one that had occurred to the Resches—demon possession. None of the poltergeist occurrences that he personally had been involved with had shown any evidence of having been caused by demons. It was natural for religious people to turn to the clergy in an effort to rid their homes of evil spirits, but Bill, who had worked on many cases where exorcisms were attempted, had never seen one accomplish its purpose.

On one occasion the result had actually been humorous.

In this case the poltergeist activity had included "bottle poppings." Medicine, laundry detergent, and wine bottles—always the type with screwed-on caps—would suddenly pop open with loud explosions and then fall over and dump their contents onto the floor. The people who lived in the home were Catholic and asked their priest to bring them bottles of holy water to place in the areas of the house where the poppings were taking place. What they didn't expect was that the bottles would have screwed-on tops.

By the time the ritual had been completed, the carpets felt like lawns after a shower, and the poltergeist activity was just as violent as it had ever been.

It was Bill's opinion that in the majority of cases poltergeist infestations were caused by recurrent, spontaneous PK. He based this belief on the fact that, in every case he personally had observed, there had been a living person, not a ghost, at the center of the disturbances, and most of the time that person had been a teenager who was experiencing a difficult adolescence.

As Bill soon came to realize, Tina Resch was such a teenager. Abandoned by her biological mother when she was ten months old, she had been taken in by the Resches, first as a foster child and later as their adopted daughter. Although Tina was bright, she'd had social problems in school and was tutored at home, seldom getting out of the house except to attend church and Girl Scout meetings. This unnatural situation would have been depressing to almost any young adult, but Tina had other problems to deal with as well. She had been traumatized by the sudden death of her best friend; by a breakup with her first boyfriend; by the fact that her birth mother didn't want anything to do with her; and by the need to compete for attention with a constant stream of foster children.

Five hundred eighty-five RSPK occurrences were reported in the Resch home and other places where Tina went. These included 125 episodes where people were watching Tina at the time the object moved and another 34 when she wasn't even in the room where the incident took place. In addition to the Resch family, thirteen people had witnessed the incidents, including Bill himself and four psychologists and parapsychologists who helped him in the investigation.

Other than one blatant instance in which Tina, in response to accelerating pressure to "prove herself" to cameramen, defiantly reached out and tipped over a lamp, Bill didn't think the girl could have caused these occurrences by trickery. Instead, he believed that the energy that was hurling objects about the house came from Tina's psyche and was created by her intense feelings of unhappiness and frustration. She longed to be the center of her parents' attention; she wanted her rivals, the foster children, out of the house; and she needed to vent the anger she felt toward her parents for being, in her opinion, too strict and domineering.

To understand Tina better and to help her with her psychological problems, Bill invited her to accompany him back to North Carolina, for laboratory testing and psychological counseling. This was fine with both Tina and her parents. Tina was eager to learn what was behind the weird things that were happening around her, and her parents hoped that, with Tina out of the house, the destruction would stop.

To their great relief, it did. There were no more disturbing incidents after Tina left.

Tina's first trip to North Carolina had to be cut short. The testing had hardly been started when she broke her leg riding a trail bike, and after ten days in bed in the hospital

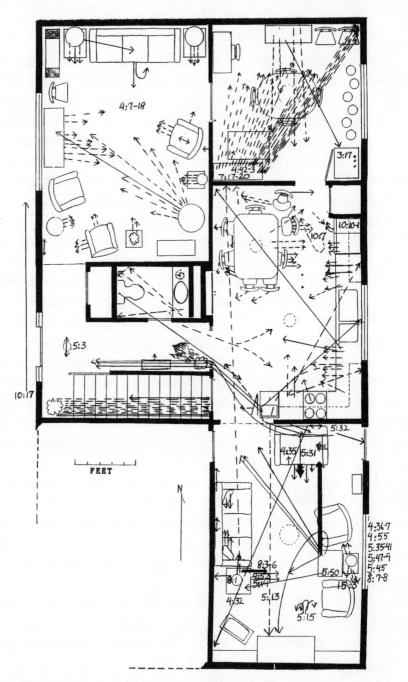

Diagram of the first floor of the Resch home, showing the movements of objects. This shows how a case of this type is researched. (courtesy: William Roll)

and in Bill's home, she returned to her home in Ohio to recuperate.

The testing was rescheduled for the following October.

Bill didn't attempt to conduct these experiments alone. His team of coworkers consisted of Jeannie Lagle Stewart, a psychotherapist, and Steve Baumann, a neuroscientist, who had recently built two new PK detection devices at Spring Creek Institute. What these scientists wanted most to discover was whether Tina could voluntarily use her PK abilities to affect materials similar to tissues in the human body.

But there was one thing that worried them. Seven months had passed since the episodes in Ohio, and the turmoil at the Resch home had pretty much stopped. Because outbursts of RSPK activity seldom last long, it was possible that Tina might by now have outgrown her abilities.

In preparation for her first test at the institute, she was asked to select eight items to be RSPK "target" objects. She chose four eating utensils—three spoons and a fork—her deodorant stick, her toothbrush, her hairbrush, and a lipstick.

While Jeannie Lagle Stewart watched carefully to make sure there could be no trickery, Tina was asked to concentrate on those objects and try to cause them to move. The deodorant stick flew off a table and landed six feet away under a chair. A spoon went sailing off also and landed three feet away.

Then the fork took off as if it had wings and flew fifteen feet to strike Tina in the back of the head.

Tina grabbed the fork and hurled it away from her.

"Stop hurting me!" she screamed.

Lagle Stewart, who was standing beside her, was so startled by the attack of the fork that she found herself yelling at it, "Leave Tina alone!"

Obviously, Tina still had it when it came to moving objects.

But the most important testing took place in the laboratory where Baumann had installed his PK detectors. Over four days' time Tina participated in a series of experiments with pacemaker nerve cells and with piezoelectric crystals. The word *piezoelectric* comes from the Greek word *piezo*, which means "to press," and these crystals are called "piezoelectric" because if pressure is applied to them they generate electricity. Bones, teeth, intestines, and tendons contain tissue largely composed of piezoelectric crystals.

The scientists felt that if Tina could cause a physical effect on the crystals by the use of PK, it was possible that PK might someday play a role in healing.

During the tests, Tina was seated in front of a transparent cylinder that contained two piezoelectric crystals and was told to try to affect just one of them by PK. Significant disturbances were recorded in *both* the crystals, which showed that Tina's PK energy was powerful, but she did not have the ability to control it precisely.

She also proved able to produce a dramatic effect upon the nerve cells, which were similar to those that maintain rhythmic activity in the heart. When she worked on the nerve cells she would stand with her palms extended toward them and try to imagine energy streaming out of her hands. Under normal circumstances the nerve cells fired at regular intervals, and Tina's task was to speed them up or slow them down.

To the amazement of the scientists, she was able to stop a cell from firing for twenty-three seconds and then start it up again at its normal rate of speed.

During Tina's rest breaks, her PK continued to be in evidence, as objects in the laboratory kept moving about.

At one point Lagle Stewart warned her, "Don't break any

of the expensive computer equipment, because we can't afford to pay for it."

Tina said, "I'll try not to," and kept her promise.

All in all, there were fifty-eight occurrences of what appeared to be PK or RSPK during Tina's short stay in North Carolina. Twenty-four of these took place when Tina was not closely supervised, so the possibility of "tricky teen" behavior could not be totally ruled out. In each of the remaining thirty-four instances, however, she was in the company of people who were watching her closely and could guarantee that she had done nothing physical to cause the occurrences. Besides that, many of the objects that were moved were beyond Tina's reach, so there was no way she could have sneakily thrown them.

After working with Tina, Bill and his colleagues were convinced that she had the ability to influence matter with her mind and that the RSPK outbreak in her home had been a product of her unhappiness. Tina was a troubled teenager, and was projecting her anger in an unusual manner that extended to the people and objects that surrounded her.

"It's my belief that it was Tina's resentment of the foster children that caused her psychic attack upon the things those children were involved with," Bill says. "The furniture in the family room where they played, the television set on which they watched cartoons, the chairs they sat on while eating, their toy cradle, were the very first objects to be sent flying. And the disturbed relationship Tina had with her parents seemed to be reflected in attacks on the home furnishings and personal possessions that they were most proud of.

"In contrast, the playful flicking up and down of the light switches when the electrician, Bruce Claggett, attempted to leave the house might have been brought on by Tina's posi-

177

tive feelings. Claggett was a longtime friend, and Tina liked him. The use of her psychokinetic energy to provide a light show for him to investigate might have been her subconscious method of keeping him from going home.

"The concept of good and evil also may have had a place in this drama, since Tina had never been hit by any of the objects that flew about the house until the arrival of the minister. When he came to bless the house and rid it of evil spirits, Tina, who had begun to suspect that she was at the heart of the disturbances, suddenly viewed herself as evil. Subconsciously she may have decided she deserved to be punished and from then on directed many of the attacks against herself."

To Bill and his colleagues all this strongly suggested that human beings have an unrecognized capacity to interact directly with their physical environment and that this ability may be activated in particular individuals at times of extreme stress.

But why should these individuals become poltergeist agents when hundreds of thousands of equally stressed people do not? Tina Resch may not have had a picture-perfect home situation, but how many people do? If the anger and frustration of every teenager who felt he or she didn't get enough attention from parents or resented being grounded or ordered to do chores brought on a poltergeist outbreak, there wouldn't be a high school in this country that didn't have windows shattered by zooming books, pencils, blackboard erasers, and food-laden cafeteria dishes.

Bill believes it's possible that there may be a link between RSPK and epilepticlike disturbances in the brain of the person who triggers it. When he surveyed ninety-two cases of poltergeist activity, he found that nearly 25 percent of the "agents" were on record as having experienced trances or mild seizures.

But what about the 75 percent who had normal brain activity? And what about the many thousands of people who experience seizures, yet live in conventional homes in which the furniture stays in place and electrical appliances don't go crazy?

There's a lot of room for further investigation of poltergeists.

CHAPTER TEN

PSYCHIC DETECTIVES

When Mary Cousette of Alton, Illinois, mysteriously vanished, her boyfriend, Stanley Holliday, Jr., was charged with her murder. But without a body there was little chance of conviction.

In desperation, police brought in psychic detective Greta Alexander, who ran her hand over a map and directed them to an area they had already searched. She also described the circumstances under which Mary's body would be found. Not only did a second search turn up Mary's remains, but twenty-two of Greta's twenty-four predictions proved accurate, including the fact that the person who found the body would have a deformed hand.

Owen Etheridge, a teenager in Lompoc, California, begged psychic Dixie Yeterian to find his missing father. After psychometrizing the father's watch and ring, Dixie made a private call to the police to report that the man was buried east of town, wrapped in a green sheet, and had been shot in the head by the very same son who had contacted her. When confronted with this, the startled boy made a full confession and led detectives to the grave, where his father's body was found just as Dixie had described it.

These stories may seem incredible, but they are documented. Despite the fact that ESP research is not fully accepted as a science and there still are a number of skeptics who doubt its validity, in recent years the use of psychics in investigations of homicide, kidnapping, and missing persons cases has become almost routine for many law enforcement agencies around the country. In fact, their use extends to the international level. The Carter administration employed psychics from the Stanford Research Institute's remote-viewing program to pinpoint the location of captives during the Iran hostage crisis, and the Reagan administration utilized psychics to try to detect the terrorists responsible for the bombing in Lebanon.

Are the psychics who do this type of work some kind of superbeings?

The ones I know personally are adamant in their insistence that they are not.

Nancy Myer-Czetli, Robert Petro, and Noreen Renier, three of the psychics who worked with our family in the investigation of Kait's murder, don't think of themselves as extraordinary, but as ordinary people who were born with a surplus of one particular kind of talent and have taught themselves to use it to benefit humanity.

Here, in their own words, are the stories behind their unusual careers.

181

NANCY MYER-CZETLI OF GREENSBURG, PENNSYLVANIA

The last thing I ever wanted was to work on murder cases, and I never set out to be a psychic. Both things just happened.

I don't think psychic ability is uncommon. It's a survival ability that we all have to some extent, but it's more pronounced in some people than in others. It's present in most young children, but once they start school the socialization process tends to destroy it.

As a child I assumed that everyone else saw the world in the same way I did, just as people who are color blind assume other people see colors the way they do. I took my gift for granted as children will and used it to my advantage. I could always predict what my punishment would be if I misbehaved, and I'd decide if the mischief I was contemplating was going to be worth the consequences.

It wasn't until I was almost thirty years old and the mother of three children that I started to realize that I knew things other people didn't.

In 1975, a houseboat overturned on the Delaware River, leaving two of the passengers missing. When I read about it in the paper, I felt certain that the older man had been hit on the head and killed when the boat went over, but I had a feeling that the teenager, Lee Cilimburg, had not been seriously injured in the accident and had strong survival instincts that might have carried him through.

The boat turned over in a section of the river where the shores are swampy, and people have been known to get lost in there for weeks. I didn't want to barge in where I wasn't wanted, but I kept thinking, "What if this was *my* kid, and there was a psychic who could help find him and she didn't come forward because she wasn't invited?"

So I called the police, and when I got off the phone with the trooper, I knew exactly what he'd done with the notes he'd made. He'd decided I was a nut and thrown them in the trash can. So I called the newspaper, and they sent a reporter out to the house to find out if I was a wacko. He asked me a lot of questions and then called his editor to say he thought I was on the up-and-up, because I knew a lot of facts that hadn't been in the paper. He knew I hadn't had any contact with the family, because he'd talked with them right before he came to see me, so he suggested to the editor that this was worth pursuing.

The reporter drove me down to the river in the area where the boat had flipped, and I stood on the shore and psychometrized the water. When I did that, I realized at once that Lee Cilimburg was dead, but I also knew that he had come very close to saving himself. He'd been swimming toward shore and had gotten tangled up in something. And I also had a feeling about where the body would turn up, which turned out to be accurate. That was interesting too, because the people who were experts on the currents of the Delaware River swore up and down that there was no way the body could be taken there.

The reporter repeated my predictions to the police, who didn't take them seriously. When everything I'd said proved correct, right down to the fact that Lee Cilimburg had been qualified to survive in difficult situations because he'd worked on Great Lakes tankers and had had survival training, it made front page headlines.

I started doing police work after giving a seminar on psychic phenomena that was attended by Colonel Irvin Smith, who was at that time head of the Delaware State Police. He set me up in order to test my abilities. I was psychometrizing objects, and Colonel Smith tried to trick me by giving his ring to another trooper to hand to me. I could sense the ring wasn't his, and when I gave my reading, I turned and spoke directly to Smith instead of his accomplice. There was personal stuff in the reading, and Smith started getting uncomfortable and told me to stop.

At lunch break, Colonel Smith arranged to have me seated next to him and immediately asked me, "When are you going to go to work for me?" He started talking about all these hideous murder cases, and I said, "No way! Absolutely not! I don't think the information I get is detailed enough for police work."

Smith wouldn't take no for an answer. He badgered me for months, until I finally went out on a case with him just to show him it wouldn't work. I was wrong. It worked so well he was tickled pink, and the next thing I knew, like it or not, I was a detective.

When I work on a case, I specifically ask not to be told much about it, because that makes it harder for me to concentrate on getting new information. I want only the victim's name, date of death or disappearance, and photographs of the crime scene.

The photos are extremely important to me, because the cells of the environment store knowledge. I can't explain how they do it, but I know that they do. The environment carries a record of what takes place in it, and that's what I work with on homicides. When police photographers are working, they circle the body, moving around and getting all the angles, and at some point they will stand quite accidentally in exactly the same spot in which the killer stood. That's the photo that gives me the most information, because I'm able to see the victim as the killer saw him in those final seconds right before the crime took place.

When I begin to work on a murder case, I'm not able to

Nancy Myer-Czetli identifying photos of suspects. (courtesy: Steve Czetli)

start by linking minds with the killer, because I have no feel for him. I have the victim's name and a picture of the victim's remains, and I have usually requested a snapshot of the victim as close to the time of death as the family can provide, so I can start by how that victim thought. I get a sense of the victim's personality, and then when I look at the photos of the murder scene I can start by observing the changes that are occurring in the thinking of the victim as things start happening. How is this situation affecting him or her? At what point does the victim realize that he or she is in terrible danger?

When I reach that point I deliberately separate myself from the victim, because if I didn't do that I would experience, not only all of his or her anger, frustration, and terror, but the physical pain that accompanied the death. So, now, I adopt the point of view of an immediate witness. I mentally stand beside the victim and try to observe what's going on while the crime is occurring. It's like a movie running in my head that gives me better emotional distance and better control. It also functions kind of like a VCR in my head, so if there's something I catch off to the side that I think needs more attention, I can back that thing up and rerun it any number of times. If I'm working directly with police officers and they have a question like, "You're looking in *this* direction, but what's happening *behind* you?" I can back the image up and turn around and look in another direction and see what's going on there. It gives me a lot of flexibility, and I'm not so tied up in the victim's emotions. When you experience the victim's terror, you can become immobilized.

I also avoid going into the mind of the killer. I observe the activity, and I can sense things about him, but I keep a very strong distance between my mind and his. Because this person, who has destroyed the life of another person, is definitely not normal, and, if I link minds with him, his distorted point of view is going to have a negative effect on me.

I've had some interesting cases. On one occasion I was asked to help find the killer of Leonetta Schilling, a woman from Maryland who was stabbed eleven times. I felt the assailant was related to Mrs. Schilling and that she hadn't been afraid of him because she'd been his babysitter. I described the killer to the police and picked the photo of Allen

Finke out of a stack of thirty-two suspects. He was arrested and later convicted. Finke was Mrs. Schilling's nephew, and when he was a child she had been his babysitter.

I don't think there's anything spooky about psychic ability. It's no more mysterious than any other talent—writing, painting, singing, or my teenage daughter's gift for figure skating. It frustrates me terribly to see psychics portrayed in the movies, because they're all so weird.

When people meet me, they're floored by the fact that I'm disgustingly average. A photographer once said, "Please, do something that looks psychic, because I want you to look psychic in the picture." I told him, "No, that's the whole point. I want people to know that what I do for a living is normal."

ROBERT PETRO OF SEDONA, ARIZONA

You'll find that many psychics have had blemished childhoods. In my own case, I was born with a learning disability and did not learn how to read and write until I was in my thirties. Needless to say, I was a misfit at school and a target for ridicule.

And I was different in another way also that was just as debilitating. When I was four years old, I saw my grandfather stagger out of the bathroom and drop dead right in front of me. When I ran to my mother to tell her what had happened, she reassured me that Grandpa was fine. She led me back to the bathroom, and the body wasn't there; Grandpa *was* fine—at least, for the moment.

Three months later, the event I'd described took place. My grandfather came out of the bathroom, collapsed, and died. What I'd seen was a vision of the future, but it had been so real that I had thought I was actually witnessing it.

That kind of experience has persisted throughout my lifetime.

When I was about thirteen, I kept having visions of my mother crying, and she was covered with blood. It was all over her—her face, her hands—it was a terrifying picture. The vision upset me to such a degree that I was a basket case and they sent me to the school psychiatrist. Several weeks later, I was in the wrong place at the wrong time and got shot in the head. The scene I had witnessed in visions became horrible reality—my mother was standing there, covered with blood and crying. The thing I had not foreseen was it would be *my* blood.

My ability became even stronger after I had a near-death experience at age thirty-two. I was a professional diver, and in a dive off the coast of Massachusetts, my equipment malfunctioned, and I couldn't get air. Everything turned black, I heard voices and singing, and I seemed to be floating in darkness. Then I saw a pinhole of light and as I started to go toward it, it got bigger and bigger. When the other divers fished me out of the ocean, I appeared to be dead.

Of course, I was resuscitated, or I wouldn't be here, but I was never the same again. Almost immediately I began to have visions of things that were going to happen, not just to the people I was close to, but to absolute strangers. I saw a well-known congressman go down in a plane crash in Alaska and reported it to the government. I predicted that the Strategic Search Command was going to find the wreckage of a plane that they would think was the congressman's, but that they would be mistaken, and that that particular plane would be one that crashed a year before. When they did find the congressman's plane, it would be in a pine-wooded area about twenty miles from a town, and there would be no survivors.

That was exactly what happened. There were front-page

headlines proclaiming that the congressman's plane had been found, and then the story was retracted. His plane was found days later in the location I described, and he and his companions were dead.

The next major turning point in my development as a psychic occurred because of a prediction I made very casually. I was looking for a house to buy and in the process asked one young couple why they were selling their home. They told me it was too large for them. They had bought it because they hoped to have a family, but the wife had had three miscarriages, and they now felt they would never have children.

I said, "I'd feel guilty buying this place, because you're going to be pregnant by Easter. You're going to have a healthy baby girl, and you'll be sorry if you get rid of this house."

In the spring the man arrived on my doorstep.

He said, "My wife has just found out that she's pregnant, and her doctor wants to talk to you. He's fascinated by this psychic stuff and wants to know if you'll let him try to hypnotize you."

I agreed to the experiment and allowed the doctor to put me under. He did it in his office with a tape recorder running, and my wife was there taking shorthand. While under hypnosis, I was taken to a level of consciousness I had never experienced before, and it was then that it was discovered that I had multiple talents. In trance I started spouting all kinds of information about topics that I knew nothing about.

The doctor was very impressed and told his colleagues, "Here is an eighth grade dropout who can't even read, but when he's in a trance he seems to have access to data regarding such things as psychology, history, science, and healing! He can even do medical diagnosing!"

They got very excited and conducted all kinds of experiments on me. A medical research team hooked me up to equipment to monitor my brain and had me doing psychokinesis, telepathy, psychometry, everything they could think of. Then they brought in a government agent who wanted me to supply information about MIAs and downed Air Force pilots. It was pretty overwhelming, and I was as excited as they were. By letting these people discover me, I was discovering myself and was finally beginning to understand why I had always been so different.

Before long law enforcement agencies throughout the country began to solicit my talents to help investigate murders, missing persons, and bank robberies. I pushed myself to the limit and was growing psychically by leaps and bounds. The problem was that I couldn't cope with it emotionally. What none of us realized was that I was absorbing the negative energy from everything I was investigating. When they took me out to murder sites, I took the pain and terror from the things that had happened there home with me. It built up inside me like a sickness, and I finally reached a point where I had a breakdown.

One night I was sitting at the dinner table with my wife and children, and something cracked. I started crying and couldn't stop. I excused myself, went upstairs and got my gun. Then I went to a hotel, rented a room, and tried to kill myself. But when I attempted to pull the trigger, something Divine intervened. I heard an explosion and saw a bright light; then I opened my eyes and I was lying on the floor with the gun still in my hand. Something had stopped me from committing suicide. Evidently it wasn't my time to go yet—there were things I was supposed to accomplish before I checked out of this world.

I realized then that I couldn't take on all the pain of the world. I'm just one mortal man, and I don't have the strength for it. So I've made a very strong effort to get my life into balance. And I've come to understand better how my abilities work.

What seems to happen when I go into trance is that I plug into the person I'm doing the reading for. I *become* that person and seem to know everything about him, including his past and his future. I don't feel that this information comes from an outside source; I think it springs from that person himself. The information is already inside him, but he doesn't know how to access it. What I do is connect with him telepathically to draw out knowledge that he already has but is unaware of.

In the past twenty years I've done over 15,000 documented trance readings, and another 5,000 that weren't taped because the subject matter was too sensitive. I've also done a lot of work for government agencies from many different countries. One of the proudest moments in my career was when the United Nations Parapsychology Society awarded me the United Nations Silver Peace Medal for "service to humanity."

There's nothing unique about being a psychic. There are lots of us around. I wish I had realized that sooner. If I'd known, as a child, that other people like me existed, I wouldn't have been so lonely.

NOREEN RENIER OF MAITLAND, FLORIDA

People ask me, "Do you ever remember doing things when you were young that were considered psychic?" I've racked my brain, and I can't come up with a thing.

I didn't like school and particularly hated math. The things I excelled in were public speaking, drama, and sports, which I now realize come from the right side of the brain. The left brain is the logical, rational, thinking mind, and people tend to forget the intuitive right brain is there. That's the side of the brain children utilize so naturally. When they start school, lots of children are classified as slow learners because they haven't yet learned to switch the hemispheres for learning.

I married young, and by the time I was twenty-one I had two children. Nine years later my husband and I were divorced, and I eventually became a public relations director for Hyatt Hotels. While I was working at that job, I was asked to book a room and do some promotion for a lecturing psychic. Either she was very powerful or I was very sensitive, because just being around that psychic had a strange effect on me. My whole body felt like it was vibrating when I was around her for a while. That's when I became interested in the subject of parapsychology and started reading up on it.

I had two close women friends who were also interested, and occasionally we would get together to meditate. One afternoon we were sitting around a table, meditating with our eyes closed, when all of a sudden my body felt as if somebody had plugged it into a wall socket. I was terrified and cried out, and I heard a voice that wasn't mine! That voice kept saying strange things that I had nothing to do with, and I thought I was going crazy! I somehow forced myself to open my eyes, and one friend was sipping my coffee to see if it was spiked, and the other was crying because, without realizing it, I had just given her a message from her deceased mother.

After that I was hooked! It was just so astonishing that I wanted to experiment with it all the time. I became so obsessed that I couldn't concentrate on my work. I kept wanting to touch rings and watches and do readings for people. Eventually, of course, I got fired, and probably deserved it.

I had to continue to earn money, because I was support-
ing two teenagers who liked to eat, so I went to a rival hotel
and gave a psychic demonstration, and they gave me permission to do fortune telling in their lounge. I charged five
dollars a session, and it was wonderful, because I got so
much practice and was paid for doing it.

But I didn't just want to perform, I wanted to find out
how this worked! To me it didn't make sense that I could
touch an object and see a picture in my mind. At first I
thought I might be reading the minds of my clients, and
then something happened that proved that wasn't the
answer.

A lady came in, very upset because her nephew, who
lived in another part of the country, had been in an accident, and she wanted me to home in on him to see how he
was doing. So I touched her ring—it was hers, not the
nephew's—and saw a man in a coma. He had curly brown
hair and two scars on one side of his head. I also gave the
woman the number "14" twice.

"You're a fake!" she told me. "My nephew has straight,
shoulder-length blond hair and no scars at all!"

The next day she came back to apologize. She'd discovered that her nephew had cut his bleached hair, which had
grown in brown and was curling, and the scars were from
the surgery. He recovered from the coma exactly fourteen
days and fourteen hours after my reading.

So I said to myself, "Okay, I'm not reading minds, something else is going on. What *is* it?"

That's when I contacted Dr. Bill Roll of the Psychical
Research Foundation and put myself through five years of
laboratory testing. I acted as their guinea pig and scored
high on almost every task they gave me.

My first police case happened accidentally. I was lecturing at a college and somebody asked me if I would do a

public service. It seemed there was a rapist terrorizing this little town of Staunton, Virginia. He'd strike, and they'd just barely get the ink dry on the news story when he'd strike again. His victims ranged in age from sixteen to sixty, and half the people in the audience had friends or relatives who had been raped by him.

They had a small police force and no clues to follow up on, because the man wore a mask. I tuned in to the rapist and started describing some things about him, and a rape victim in the audience told the police about it. They were open-minded enough to say, "Let's give her a shot at this."

We got permission from two rape victims to go into their homes so I could get a feel for the rapist's presence there. I immediately knew he had a scar on his right knee, drove something that went round and round, wore a green uniform with his name on it, was very mechanical, had been in prison, and stuttered when he got nervous. I told the police they would catch him before Christmas.

They arrested him a few days before Christmas and thanked me for my "present." Everything I'd said turned out to be right. The "thing that went round and round" was a cement truck.

When I work a case, I get into the heads of the victims. With the 1986 murder of Jake and Dora Cohn, for instance, I went into Jake's mind as he was sitting, reading, in his living room, and stayed with him as he heard a noise, picked up a baseball bat, and walked down the hallway to the room where he was killed. Then I went into the mind of his wife Dora and told police "the killer ate with us and was doing some work for my husband." When I was Jake, I said, "I am shot in the face," and when I switched to Dora, I said, "I'm talking to a woman on the phone and I'm shot in the head." I was also able to give the killer's initials as R.S.

My reading led to the 1989 arrest of a man named Robert Skinner who had had dinner at the house and was fixing the floor for Jake.

When I started doing this stuff, my daughters were still in high school and thought I had flipped. They were embarrassed and stayed away from me a lot during that period. Then, when I started doing police work and took them to a few lectures to show them I was respected, they developed more tolerance for my work.

Actually, one of my daughters would be a much better psychic than I am. She's done a few readings, and she was excellent. The first time she did one, it shocked me. I was holding a woman's cross and doing a reading for her, and she was fighting me all the way. That can really affect me. If the people I read for are hostile and doubt my authenticity, I pick up on those feelings and can't concentrate.

My seventeen-year-old daughter was with me and got so irritated she reached over and grabbed the cross and closed her eyes. Then she described a scene of a young boy drowning.

The woman whispered, "Yes, that boy was my son."

My daughter handed back the cross and said, "See, it works! Now, leave my mother alone."

Later I said to her, "Honey, that proves you're psychic!" and she said, "Absolutely not," and refused to talk about it. The last thing she wants is to follow in her weird mother's footsteps. She always had dreams about the future when she was young, though, and everything she would dream about would come true.

I am the first to admit that there are plenty of charlatans out there who pretend to have much more psychic ability than they do and prey on vulnerable people made desperate by tragedy. But those of us who are legitimate aren't afraid to be challenged.

In 1986 I actually took a man named John Merrell to

court for labeling me a fake, and I had unimpeachable witnesses to testify in my behalf. FBI agent Mark Babyak testified that I helped locate a crashed airplane, pinpointing the fact that it came down at the intersection of three counties and naming the letters they started with. And Robert Ressler, a seventeen-year veteran of the bureau, confirmed that I had worked successfully on a number of his cases. He also corroborated the fact that I predicted the assassination attempt on former President Reagan during a lecture at the FBI Academy in January 1981, months before that event took place.

The jury found that Merrell had committed libel and awarded me $25,000, which I really appreciated. Believe me, a career as a psychic isn't going to make you rich.

When people like these, who have proven track records in psychic detective work, are willing to contribute time and energy to help with criminal investigations, why are some law enforcement agencies still unwilling to utilize their services?

There are several reasons.

1. Psychics are sometimes dead wrong.
"I'm a human being, and I make mistakes," says Nancy Myer-Czetli, who claims an 80 to 90 percent success rate. "In order to do a psychic reading I have to function from the intuitive part of my mind only. If the logical part takes over, the accuracy rate drops. To some degree I can analyze what I'm getting, but I can't stop the chain of impressions, or I interfere with the transmission.

"The other thing that can throw me off is emotion. Certain cases affect me emotionally more than others, and giving in to those feelings can skew what's happening and block the flow of information. It's a constant struggle when I am working murder and missing persons cases, particularly those that involve children, to keep the emotion out of there and not let it distort my perception of what's coming through to me."

Bill Roll believes that the reason for this is that emotion may cause a psychic to dredge up personal matter from the psychic's unconscious instead of material that pertains to the case.

"Then, there is the fine line between being relaxed and attentive (ESP-conducive conditions), and being sleepy and unengaged (ESP impediments)," Bill says. "And you can't expect much from a psychic who has a cold or is not feeling up to par.

"Also, because of background and personal memories, some psychics may be better at solving one kind of crime than another. Gerard Croiset, a famous Dutch psychic, was good at finding missing children—he identified with them because of his own stressful childhood—but he was less successful in working on burglaries, because his family had been poor and he felt sorry for the thieves."

2. Information from psychics is often inexact.

For one thing, psychics are seldom able to provide names.

"Names are associated with the logical left side of the brain," explains Myer-Czetli. "When you identify people psychically, you are working out of the right brain hemisphere, and you identify them by how they feel mentally, not by what their names are."

Psychics also often have a problem with time.

"The past, present, and future may get jumbled together," says Robert Petro. "You get an impression of an event, but you don't know if it's already happened or if it's going to happen at some future date. Or you may get the number six and interpret it incorrectly—you think it means six weeks, and it's actually six months or six years."

3. Psychics may not be able to connect with the target.

Most psychic detectives use psychometry and attempt to establish connection with the victim by touching something that was on the body at the time of the attack.

This works best for Noreen Renier if the object is metal.

"I especially like watches," she says, "because people wear them all the time, not just on special occasions, so they tend to absorb a lot of a person's energy. Sometimes, however, such objects are not available, particularly in missing persons cases. And if the object has been in the possession of more than one person, I may displace, and get information about people other than the victim."

4. Information from psychics is sometimes distorted.

"It seems that a lot of things can go wrong during a psychic's processing of information," says Bill. "Psychics are impressionable—that's why they're psychics—but the impressions they receive are not necessarily restricted to the target. They can also come from the spoken or even unexpressed opinions of the police and family members who are involved in the case. For instance, if a woman has been murdered, but her family hopes desperately she is alive, the psychic may unconsciously repress the murder scene and, instead, see the woman alive, as the family is trying to visualize her.

"There's also a processing problem if the appropriate memory images aren't present in the psychic's mind. The psychic may receive true impressions, but not be able to interpret them, because they don't relate to anything that he or she has ever experienced. The brain is like a computer. You can type a request on the keyboard, but if the program is not in the computer, you won't get the right answer."

In fact, Bill feels the computer analogy is a useful one for trying to understand how a psychic detective works.

"To get started, you need to turn the current on," he says. "For the psychic, that current is motivation to do the job. But there mustn't be too much current, so you need a surge control, otherwise a power surge (for the psychic, too much emotion) may wipe the memory clean and you will get only gibberish.

"Second, you need to be hooked up through phone lines with the other computer you want information from (for the psychic, the link is usually a psychometric object, a photograph, a map, or being in the location in which the victim was killed or last seen).

"Third, when you seek information from the other computer, you have to be sure that your own computer has enough available memory to receive the message. Psychics often have very good memories for the type of information they receive, but they need to be sure these memories are available. This usually means getting into a dissociated state, such as a light trance. Technically, it means working in the right-hemispheric mode and utilizing the side of the brain that is intuitive and image-rich.

"Fourth, you must be able to interpret the message. If you have a Japanese computer with Japanese characters, and you know only English, you won't get very far. Psychic information rarely comes in photographic exactness, but often in symbols, and psychics don't all interpret these in the same way. To Douglas Johnson, a British psychic I often worked with, the vision of an open book with a blank right-hand page meant that his client was beginning a new page in his or her life. To another psychic, that same image might mean that the client is going to flunk and needs to start studying."

Douglas Johnson expressed this same concept in more poetic terms in a message he claimed to have channeled from his spirit guide, Chiang.

"Transmitting information psychically is like pouring water into a mind," Chiang allegedly told Johnson. "If you pour water into a vessel that is shaped round, the water will be round-shaped in that vessel. Therefore the words that we pour through human instruments are certain to take the shape of the mind of that instrument, although the essence of that message may well remain. That is our difficulty. Some instruments are better than others. We make use of what material is available."

5. Law enforcement officers may be worried about their professional image.

In her book, *Silent Witness: The Story of a Psychic Detective*, Nancy Myer-Czetli describes the sort of harassment the police officers who first used her services were subjected to.

"Many were constantly serenaded with the theme to *The Twilight Zone* or the song 'Can You Read My Mind?' from the movie *Superman*," she says. "Others were subjected to such pranks as finding crystal balls or dead bats left on their desks. Some officers were even officially reprimanded by their superiors for working with me."

Marcello Truzzi, director of the Center for Scientific Anomalies Research and coauthor of *The Blue Sense: Psychic Detectives and Crime*, attributes such behavior to the nervousness many officials in law enforcement have about "the giggle factor."

"News of a psychic's failure usually results not only in criticism of the police, but also in public ridicule," he says.

"Knowing this, many police departments have tried to keep their attempts at using psychics secret from the media, sometimes even when the psychic proved successful. Though it is perhaps understandable that police may be likely to deny having used a psychic if the psychic failed, there is also evidence that they may want to avoid giving public credit to a psychic even when there are private admissions of the psychic's usefulness. Police who use psychics need to come out of the closet and provide scientific evaluators with the needed score sheets."

Truzzi goes on to observe that, while information from psychics may be limited, even incomplete knowledge is better than no knowledge.

"When confronted with a fifty-fifty decision choice, even if our theory gives us only a fifty-one percent chance of being right, we have an edge," he says.

That edge could mean the difference between bringing a criminal to justice and letting him roam free.

CHAPTER ELEVEN

PSYCHIC HEALING

In the trance reading Robert Petro did for me in the spring of 1991, he warned me that I was going to have health problems. I shrugged this off, because I didn't want to believe it. My health had always been excellent, and I needed a full quota of energy to meet the deadline for the final revisions on *Who Killed My Daughter?*

I completed my work in good health, but as soon as the book was finished, something terrifying happened. My husband and I were visiting our married daughter, Kerry, and her family, and I was leaning over to take a pan of chicken out of the oven, when my hand wouldn't close on the door handle. Then my arm went limp, and I felt the left side of my face contort. I tried to call out to Kerry that something was wrong with me, but the words came out so slurred that they were impossible to understand.

I'd had a stroke, and a battery of medical tests could turn up no cause for it.

Luckily, the stroke was a minor one, and most of the effects proved temporary. By the time I got out of the hospital I was pretty much okay, except for some residual weakness in my left arm and leg, a smile that was a little bit lopsided, and a left hand that didn't type quite as fast as the right one.

The problem was that the stroke had triggered seizures.

To reduce the risk of another stroke, I had been placed on a blood thinner, and to control the seizures I was placed on an antiseizure drug. The first medication doubled the side effects of the second one, and I was so doped up that I couldn't get out of bed.

To make things worse, in a very short while I was scheduled to go on a national tour for *Who Killed My Daughter?* It was going to be a marathon. For three weeks I was to spend each day in a different city doing radio and television appearances and newspaper interviews, and then fly to the next city, check into a hotel, and grab a few hours' sleep before the next round started. There was no way I could handle such a schedule in the condition I was in, and I was getting worse instead of better.

When the day finally came that I couldn't sit up to eat, I told my husband, "You'd better phone my publisher and cancel the tour."

"You wrote Kait's story to motivate informants," he reminded me. "If you don't promote the book, it won't reach those people. Why don't we ask Betty Muench if she does healings?"

I thought that idea was ridiculous but was too weak to argue.

"If you'll dial the number and hand me the receiver, I'll talk to her," I said.

When I explained the situation to Betty, she said, "I don't do the laying-on-of-hands kind of stuff, but I can ask the Friends in Source what's wrong with you and how to fix it."

"Go for it," I told her.

I didn't expect the reading to achieve anything. I was convinced that the stroke had done serious damage to my brain and that I was doomed to spend the rest of my life as a zombie.

Betty called me back and read me the message from her spirit guides:

What is the true source of Lois's minor stroke and seizures and how best to heal her? There is a sense of resistance within the mental head level of Lois and it would seem to be the source of her manifested distresses in the seizures and stroke. She can release this resistance by accepting that for a time longer she will have to work with her anger about the violent situation which surrounded Kait. Therefore there has to come a compromise with herself.

There is a need in her for choline and this can be had in a very healthy form in supplements and this will strengthen the brain. A work-up by an endocrinologist would also show depletion of amino acids in her due to stress and overwork. Mental work is as depleting as physical work and she will thus be depleted of connections both within and without. There will be in the use of chemical medication that which will not seem to respond well within and this inner self will not require this.

There is in Lois fire and determination. There should be no concerns and worry over whether she can meet the heavy schedule that lies ahead for her. In doing this schedule she will know a completion of the resistance energy within her.

This disharmony and disease are not something which would seem to be permanent in her. There is more work for her in this lifetime.

"What's choline?" I asked.

"I don't have any idea," Betty said.

My husband phoned a health-food store and was told that choline is a nutrient that enhances brain function. He bought me choline and a variety of amino acids, and I started chugging them down.

By the date of the tour, I had pretty much weaned myself off the antiseizure medication. I completed the tour as scheduled without experiencing any seizures and have experienced none since.

I continue to take choline.

The term for what Betty Muench did for me is a *psychic diagnosis*. Without any medical knowledge or training of her own, she apparently was able to tap into some sort of universal pool of such knowledge and to extract from it information pertaining to my health.

Although for hundreds of years there have been medical doctors who have been interested in psi phenomena, the first well-known case of psychic diagnosis in medical practice occurred in 1903, when Drs. Wesley Ketchum and Thomas House made a trip to Bowling Green, Kentucky, to seek the advice of one last specialist on behalf of one of Ketchum's patients. This patient was a young college student from a wealthy Kentucky family who had collapsed during football practice and when he regained consciousness appeared to be completely out of his mind. He could not speak, his eyes were glazed, and he alternated between having violent seizures and sitting for hours staring into space.

The family had consulted medical specialists all over the country, and they all agreed it was an incurable case of dementia praecox.

As a last resort, Ketchum and House had decided to do something outrageous and consult a diagnostician who not only had no medical degree but had only a sixth-grade education.

This "specialist" was a clairvoyant named Edgar Cayce.

Dr. Ketchum did not bring his patient for examination. Instead, he and House went alone to visit Cayce and perched nervously on chairs in the psychic's office while Cayce loosened his starched shirt collar and lay down on a couch to "sleep."

Once Cayce was in a light trance, House said to him, "You have before you the body of 'John Smith' from Hopkinsville, Kentucky. Go over this body and tell us what you find."

Although there was no "body" present, Cayce appeared to be aware of one and to be examining it.

"His brain is on fire," he reported. "The convolutions in his brain are all red, as red as fire. His mind is distorted. In a very short time, unless something is done for him, he's going to be a raving maniac."

"What treatment do you suggest?" Ketchum asked eagerly.

"Specific treatment put to the limit," Cayce answered. He then named a little-known drug.

"Anything else?"

"That's enough."

And it was, for Ketchum knew exactly what the procedure was. However, it was Ketchum's faith in Cayce that was put to the limit. After more than three weeks of treatment there was no sign of change in the boy's condition.

Then one morning the phone rang. It was the boy's mother.

"Dr. Ketchum?"

"Yes." Dr. Ketchum held his breath in anticipation.

"Good morning, miracle man!" the woman exclaimed joyfully.

She went on to say that her son was greatly improved and she now believed he would recover.

Thus began an amazing era of psychic diagnosis of medical cases by one of the United States' most famous mystics. During the next thirty years Edgar Cayce did almost 9,000 readings on health problems, all carefully documented. In all, over 6,000 individuals were diagnosed by Cayce, many with a succession of readings. Since many of the cases referred to him were extreme, some having been "given up" by the medical doctors, instances of miracle cures (as with the young football player) abound. Fortunately, Cayce had follow-up correspondence in many cases, and this too is part of the archives that are preserved in the Cayce Library in Virginia Beach.

Dr. Harold Reilly, a well-known physiotherapist in New York City, who initially treated some of Cayce's referred clients and later made an extensive study of his readings, coined the acronym CARE, which stands for Circulation, Assimilation, Rest, and Elimination—factors that Cayce thought were necessary for physical health. "Circulation" included exercise, massage, and skeletal adjustment; "assimilation" involved a healthy, well-balanced diet; "rest" meant allowing time for relaxation, recreation, and recuperation; and "elimination" centered on paying attention to the four body systems that rid the body of wastes: the lungs, the skin, the kidneys, and the bowels.

Like Dr. Ketchum, Dr. Reilly at first didn't talk openly about his work with Cayce patients or about using Cayce's readings to prescribe treatments for his own patients.

"I felt foolish telling people that a sleeping prophet was telling me how to run my business," he admitted later.

A time came, however, when Reilly had become such a strong believer in Cayce's teachings that he no longer cared what people thought just as long as the treatments worked.

"I know more about Cayce now, for I understand the concept behind his work," he said. "You get everything working right, body and mind, and illness hasn't got a chance."

Years before psychosomatic medicine came on the scene, Cayce stated that tension and stress were responsible for stomach ulcers. He also claimed to see an energy body surrounding and interpenetrating the physical body and suggested that this might be able to provide information about a person's emotional and physical condition.

Cayce was generally scorned by the conservative medical profession while he was alive. Later, however, his readings on disease became a resource for medical researchers. One authority said, "Cayce was a hundred years ahead of his time with his concept of health flowing out of perfect harmony among blood, glands, nerves, and mind."

At about the same time that Edgar Cayce was starting his career, Thomas Hudson began writing about the nature of the human mind. He reached the conclusion that people have two minds, one practical, to deal with the world around them, and the other nonpractical, to cope with their inner problems. Hudson called these the *objective* and *subjective* minds. Hudson's theory was that the subjective mind is especially powerful, because it is attuned to and in harmony with nature and the universe. He believed that illness results from loss of contact with this fundamental harmony and suggested that the best way to prove this theory would be through attempts at mental healing. Scientists now realize that people do, indeed, have two minds. The left brain in many ways resembles what Hudson termed the objective mind, and the right brain, the subjective mind.

Roughly a hundred years later, Lawrence LeShan, a psychologist and author of the book, *The Medium, the Mystic, and the Physicist*, decided to test this theory by first teaching himself how to achieve an altered state of consciousness and then attempting to perform psychic healing. His experiments involved mentally connecting with a person who had health problems (usually without that person's knowledge), and attempting to revitalize him by making him the focus of healing energy.

These experiments proved so successful that LeShan became convinced that if a healer can establish psychic connection with a patient it is possible for him to activate the sick person's self-repair and self-recuperative abilities.

He also believed that even greater success could be achieved if the healer could go one step further and draw upon the vast energy of the universe to help the patient heal.

Radical as this seemed, it was not a new concept. People had been doing it for centuries and calling it prayer.

In 1984, Dr. Randy Byrd, a cardiologist at San Francisco General Hospital, conducted a unique experiment in therapeutic prayer. This carefully controlled and extensive research project centered upon cardiac patients in the hospital's coronary care unit. Byrd used a computer to select 192 patients to serve as test subjects and an additional 201 patients to use as controls. The groups were matched for age and the severity of their conditions.

Byrd then recruited the help of clergy from an assortment of different faiths throughout the nation. Each was given the names and diagnoses of particular patients and asked to pray each day for their "beneficial healing and quick recovery." Five to seven people prayed for each patient, and none of the patients was aware that he or she was being prayed for.

When Dr. Byrd reported on his yearlong experiment at the 1985 meeting of the American Heart Association, the results were startling to everyone:

Sixteen of the control patients had required antibiotic

treatment, as compared to only three of the prayed-for patients.

Eighteen of the control patients had suffered pulmonary edema (a dangerous condition involving water in the lungs), as compared to only six of the prayed-for patients.

And twelve of the control patients had required artificial help with breathing, while none of the prayed-for patients had required it.

It was difficult for anyone not to be impressed by these findings.

In fact, Dr. William Nolen, a notorious skeptic about psychic healing, stated to newspaper reporters, "It sounds like this study will stand up to scrutiny. Perhaps doctors should write on their order sheets, 'Pray three times a day along with their regular treatment.' If it works, it works."

Another method of psychic healing that dates back to Biblical days is the *laying on of hands* (healing by touch). In more recent times investigators have attempted to bring psychic healing under laboratory scrutiny. Dr. Bernard Grad, of McGill University in Montreal, Canada, spent more than three decades researching the biochemical and biophysical effects of touch and conducted pioneering experiments involving the laying on of hands in a laboratory setting. Grad's first experiences were with a healer named Estebany, who believed that planet Earth was surrounded by a life-supporting energy field that under normal circumstances was available to everyone, and that sickness resulted from a breakdown of the assimilation process. Estebany believed that when he touched a sick person this energy moved down his arms and hands to the patient and that he could facilitate healing by reestablishing the normal link to this energy. Grad's studies of the bioenergetic effects of the laying on of hands in healing skin wounds in mice, in preventing goiters from developing in mice, and in facilitating the growth of plants under a variety of conditions, provided strong evidence that something positive does, indeed, happen as a direct result of such "treatments."

Nancy Myer-Czetli, who devotes part of her time to psychic healing, feels that the laying on of hands is a natural response to injury.

"We do that all the time," she says. "When you hit your funny bone, what do you do? You yell, 'Ouch! That hurts!' and grab hold of your elbow. The minute you have an injury, you're moved instinctively to cover it with your hands. That's your automatic reaction to stop the pain. If you pay attention when you do that, you'll realize that there's a warmth that develops almost immediately between your hand and the injured part of you. There's an energy flow. If you open yourself up to it and project that energy out through your hands, you're quite capable of stopping the pain. And you can use that same system to heal others. We're all built to do that; we've just lost touch with the process."

My friend Mona, who went to a healer for relief from the excruciating pain of rheumatoid arthritis, describes the energy flow she experienced as far more than "warm."

"It was like the heat of a stove," she says. "And the amazing thing is that he never actually touched me. He asked me to lay my arms on the table, and he passed his hands about three inches above my hands and held them there. If someone puts his hand next to yours, it's natural to feel some sensation of warmth, but what I felt from the healer was very intense heat that passed through my hands, up my arms, and into my body. Not only did this heat relieve the pain, but it also seemed to energize me."

Bernard Grad is not the only scientist who has been

conducting research on the possible effect of consciousness on biochemical and biophysical processes.

William Braud, at the Mind Science Foundation in San Antonio, Texas, has studied the rate of self-destruction of human red blood cells in vials containing a saline solution with and without a psychic trying to influence the process. In a 1990 report on his findings, Braud concluded that positive psychic energy can have a significant effect upon the reduction of the self-destruction process.

Daniel Wirth, at Healing Sciences International, has been conducting research on noncontact therapeutic touch. In one of his experiments, forty-four university students were given surgical wounds through the skin on their arms with a biopsy instrument. Then the surface areas of the wounds were precisely measured. From a separate room, a therapeutic touch practitioner administered psychic healing treatments to half the subjects for five minutes every second day, without the subjects knowing they were being treated. The other half of the subjects were used as controls and did not receive treatment. When, at the end of eight days, the wound sizes were again measured, the psychically treated wounds were found to be healing 50 percent faster than the others. At the end of sixteen days, thirteen of the twenty-two treated wounds were completely healed, while none of the nontreated wounds was healed.

In a speech to a group of parapsychologists, Dr. Larry Dossey, a physician of internal medicine, described experiments in three different laboratories in which people who were hooked up to EEG machines in separate rooms attempted to get in touch with each other mentally in an effort to synchronize their brain wave patterns.

"They were told to establish some kind of empathic connection with each other and come together on an emotional level," Dossey said. "When they felt they had achieved sort of a heart bond, they were to press a button. When these people pressed the button—at about the same time—the EEGs began to cycle with each other and track each other!"

Dossey feels the medical community should pay more attention to such findings.

"Parapsychologists have demonstrated beyond a doubt, in my judgment, that the intentions of one mind can exert physiological changes on another distant body," he said. "They have shown that distant mental efforts can bring about positive healing effects. Anytime anything begins to affect physiological functions—whether a toxin, a bacterium, or another mind—this becomes the business of medicine! Why, then, cannot physicians and parapsychologists join hands in examining the medical relevance of this information to real life situations?"

One ancient mystical belief is that the human body is surrounded by light called an *aura*. People who claim to see auras describe them as energy fields composed of one or more colors, surrounding the human body. The colors are said to vary according to the health, emotions, or thoughts of the subject. Many psychics see energy not only emanating from the body, but also pouring into the body from the outside.

Nancy Myer-Czetli says she sees auras all the time around everybody.

"It's like looking at people with rainbows around them," she says. "The aura provides a lot of information about what is going on with a person physiologically. I see energy loss patterns defined by different shadings of red. If somebody has a sinus infection, for instance, I'll see what appears to be a red badger's mask right across his face. I'm not a doctor, and I'd never prescribe treatment, but after look-

ing at a sick person's aura, I can usually tell what the problem is and can guide him or her to the right kind of medical
professional.

"The color I hate worst to see in an aura is gray. When I
see a person with an aura that is totally gray, it's almost
always because that person has a terminal illness and is not
going to live very long."

Many psychics seem to be able to detect illness from
auras.

Greta Alexander says, "Cancer is easy for me to recognize, and so is heart disease, but I'm not in a position to
diagnose people because I'm not a physician. I consult with
a physician, and it's up to him to do the testing. I feel that
what the mind can conceive the body will achieve, and the
mind is in a constant process of growing. We have not
scratched the surface of what the mind can do."

Two scientific means for studying the aura have been
developed. One is called *Kirlian photography* or *radiation-
field photography*, and the other uses highly sensitive light
amplifiers to map very faint natural light that seems to be
radiated by the body. This effect is called *bioluminescence*.

In the 1970s the Psychical Research Foundation (PRF)
investigated these two areas at the Department of Electrical
Engineering at Duke. The original focus was not psychic
diagnosis but the existence of the soul. A deceased gold
miner in Arizona, James Kidd, had left his estate for soul
research, saying he thought it possible to photograph the
soul, and the PRF received some of the funds. Since the
aura and the soul might be the same, and since Kirlian
photographs might show the aura, Bill Roll asked Dr. William Joines, who had worked with the PRF before, to build
a Kirlian camera and head a research team. Joines and his
graduate students made important discoveries. They found
that the Kirlian aura, shown as areas of color around a

214

person's hand, is due to an interaction between electromagnetic radiation from the camera, the air surrounding the hand, and perspiration from it.

"Since some diseases affect perspiration and thereby produce distinctive colors, a Kirlian photograph may have a diagnostic use," Bill says. "But it turns out to be a picture of sweat, not the soul, and therefore is not a form of psychic diagnosis."

The PRF team then acquired a photomultiplier, hoping to detect light from the body in the absence of the electric field from the Kirlian camera. The device was installed in a darkroom and its output amplified ten billion times so that a single quantum of light could be detected.

"Several subjects tried but couldn't influence the detector," Bill says. "We then asked Karen Getsla, a psychic I had worked with before, to see what she could do. During sessions when she administered psychic healing to two subjects, the recorder registered light. It was also interesting that in each case the subject reported a region of visible light in the darkroom. Then the money ran out, and we had to stop before we could repeat the test and know for sure whether the effect was real or due to electronic noise in the system.

"If real, the most likely candidates for bioluminescence are fluorescence of the skin, electrical corona from the body, and infrared radiation from nerve or blood cells. Since Karen was working in her healing mode and since healing is often associated with a feeling of warmth by the client, I go with the last choice. Of course, this still does not tell us if we are dealing with PK."

Russian scientists believe Kirlian photographs and bioluminescence are evidence of what they call the *bioplasmic body*. Dr. Viktor Inyushin, of the State University of Kazakhstan, believes that bioluminescence is the same as the aura and that it reflects a person's emotions and state of mind. He also believes that it receives and broadcasts psi information.

Recently, there has been a significant shift from the traditional drugs and surgery approach of medicine to an approach that recognizes the role of the mind in healing.

This approach is called *mind-body medicine* or the *holistic health movement*.

Stanley Krippner, professor of psychology and director of the Center for Consciousness Studies at Saybrook Institute in San Francisco, says that over many years, involving travel on six continents, he has observed a great deal of successful healing by native practitioners. Effective treatment, he continues, always involves a positive mental attitude on the part of both the patient and the healer.

In a 1989 anthology, *Healers on Healing*, thirty-seven healing practitioners—many of them physicians and psychologists—share their joint belief that an emotional, caring connection between doctor and patient facilitates healing. They also stress that, in the final analysis, all healing is *self-actualized*, meaning that, in the long run, all patients heal themselves.

These practitioners believe that, although drugs and surgery may be extremely important in removing barriers to self-healing, they are not, of themselves, sufficient to heal the person who is injured or ill. We hear of cases in which the surgery was successful, but the patient still died. We also hear of cases in which the medical therapy was not effective and the doctor said there was nothing more that could be done. Then "nature" took over, and there was a case of "spontaneous remission," which simply means that the patient somehow managed to recover on his or her own.

Dr. Bernard Siegel, a pediatric and general surgeon in New Haven, Connecticut, would like to replace the word *patient* with a new term—*respent*—meaning "responsible participant" in the healing process.

"We're going to have to confront this thing we call 'the mind,'" Siegel says, "because the mind is a reality, and your thoughts become physical. You communicate with your body in several ways—through your thoughts and feelings, through images you form in your head of illness or wellness, and, literally, even through talking to your body. You can tell your hand to get warm or cool, and things happen. When my patients come into the operating room, I tell them, 'Don't leave yourself out of what's going on here. Use all the tools you have to make yourself well!'"

Bill Roll divides psychic healing into two categories, one of which involves psychic diagnosing and prescribing, such as what Betty Muench did for me when she told me I needed choline.

"That's also what Edgar Cayce did," Bill says. "He didn't use ESP to actually cure people, he joined his patient's longbody with the store of medical information in his own subconscious and in this way knew what was wrong with his patients and what treatments would cure them.

"The other form of psychic healing is *direct healing*. Direct healing seems to be accomplished in one of two ways. One way is through the use of a form of PK where the healer focuses a stream of healing energy on the afflicted parts of the patient's body and directly influences them. Tina Resch, the teenage girl who was the subject of the highly publicized poltergeist outbreak, showed evidence of having that kind of ability when she used her mind energy in the laboratory to produce physical changes in material that was very similar to tissues in the human body.

"The second type of psychic healing involves the healer's sharing his or her own state of wholeness with the patient. This type of healing is based on the premise that the pa-

Tina Resch during tests in which she attempts to affect a nerve cell by psychokinesis. (courtesy: William Roll)

tient's ill health is caused by a conflict or imbalance within the patient. The healer gets into a meditative state of inner harmony and psychically extends himself to unite with the patient and make him part of his longbody. In this way, his own inner harmony is extended to the patient, and the wholeness of the healer brings the patient into balance."

Bill, who was instructed in the two types of healing by Lawrence LeShan, routinely combines them to treat the minor health problems of his family and friends. When his sons hurt themselves playing soccer, Bill would hold his hand on the places of injury and will the hurt to go away. Usually it did.

"We are all healers," he says. "It's natural for us to provide this sort of help to others. But people should not consider attempting to cure serious disorders in this manner without also obtaining medical treatment. Each is important, and the two can work together with each strengthening the positive effect of the other."

The concept that there may be more to healing than surgery and medicine has opened new vistas for scientists working in the health field, and while some physicians find it threatening, others are excited by it.

"In the next decade or so, if the medical profession opens up, consciousness will be a subject for research," says Dr. Siegel. "Then we'll really begin to look at the effect your thoughts have on me, and mine on you, and how we can interact in healing each other."

CHAPTER TWELVE

CRITICS OF FRAUD—AND
FRAUDULENT CRITICS

Parapsychology is understandably a controversial science.

Although surveys repeatedly have indicated that 50 to 75 percent of the population have had experiences that they believe were psychic, this is not the same as scientific evidence obtained under controlled conditions.

By its very nature, psi is difficult to study in a laboratory. Most reported instances of telepathy and clairvoyance, out-of-body experiences, and apparitional sightings occur spontaneously during crises, which are impossible to induce artificially. Another thing that makes it hard to test psychic ability is that the strongest psychic connections seem to have an emotional aspect and take place between members of a longbody, such as husbands and wives, parents and children, and siblings. Because the typical research subject does not have a deep emotional bond with the experimenter, it is surprising that scientists have achieved as many positive results as they have with experiments involving such things as card guessing and dice throwing.

Despite the impressive body of experimental evidence for the reality of ESP, the idea that information can be transferred from one mind to another without passing through the channels of sense, and that mental and emotional energy can affect the physical environment in ways that are not yet explainable, has met with tremendous resistance. To confirmed unbelievers the only acceptable explanation for the psychical experiences reported by hundreds of thousands of people is that all these people are either hallucinating or lying, and the only explanation for the evidence of ESP obtained through scientific experiments is that those experiments must have been fraudulent.

And some of them have been.

One such case occurred in the summer of 1974, when Dr. Walter J. Levy, a researcher at the Institute of Parapsychology, was discovered cheating. Levy, who was conducting research on *anpsi* (the possible existence of psi in animals), was caught faking his research by two of his colleagues, who reported him to J. B. Rhine. Levy confessed to the fraud and was fired.

Opponents of ESP research used this opportunity to cast doubt upon the validity of *all* psi experiments, although Levy was only one researcher at one laboratory and the fraud was uncovered by parapsychologists themselves. Experimenter fraud is a problem in every area of science. In fact, that same summer, a researcher at the Sloan-Kettering Institute for Cancer Research was also caught falsifying research with animals. Although a solid body of successful research in anpsi had been conducted at other universities, the Levy scandal had the effect of undermining that whole area of research. Because he was Levy's superior, Rhine's reputation was damaged by the incident, although he didn't

221

try to cover it up and there was never any indication that he personally ever tampered with data.

There also have been occasions when the subjects of laboratory experiments have committed fraud. In one highly publicized case, a stage magician who calls himself The Amazing Randi arranged for two young magicians to pose as psychics in order to trick researchers at the McDonnell Laboratory for Psychical Research at Washington University in St. Louis, Missouri. The experiments with these subjects were classed as exploratory and conducted under relaxed conditions, and, as might be expected, the results showed what appeared to be psychic phenomena. When the weaknesses in the experiments were brought to the attention of the researchers by their colleagues, they increased the controls. The two magicians were then no longer able to produce apparent psychic effects through trickery, and were ultimately dismissed as subjects. When Randi realized the game was over, he called a press conference to unveil his "sociological experiment" and to ridicule the researchers for having been temporarily hoodwinked. The McDonnell Laboratory was closed, perhaps because of the negative publicity.

Until 1992, when he resigned from the group to protect them from the libel suits that were being launched against him by Uri Geller after Randi challenged Geller's abilities, Randi was referred to by many, including his colleagues, as the unofficial "hit man" for the Committee for the Scientific Investigation of Claims of the Paranormal, commonly known as CSICOP. This organization was founded in 1976 by several scientists and scholars, including Dr. Paul Kurtz, a philosopher at the State University of New York at Buffalo and editor of *The Humanist*, a philosophical journal known for its attacks on religion, and Dr. Marcello Truzzi, a sociologist of science at Eastern Michigan University and director of the Center for Scientific Anomalies Research. The praiseworthy goals of CSICOP, as stated by its founders, were "the critical investigation of paranormal and fringe-science claims from a responsible, scientific point of view and distribution of factual information about the results of such inquiries to the scientific community and the public."

It soon became apparent, however, that certain key members of the group were less interested in investigating the field of parapsychology than in abolishing it. After only one year, Truzzi, an open-minded skeptic who is opposed to inquisitional techniques, became disillusioned by the attitudes and actions of his colleagues and resigned from the committee.

"Traditionally, skeptics doubt and debunkers deny," Truzzi says. "In other words, skeptics practice *nonbelief*, while debunkers practice *disbelief*. It's my opinion that the first obligation of any investigator or scientist is to do nothing to block inquiry. A skeptic's role should not be to close down research, but to challenge and investigate. I'm not opposed to the allegation of anomalies and the idea of keeping the door open to new phenomena. It's been my experience that most of the people who are working in the field of parapsychology are honest and sincere and are trying to do the best job possible. There is certainly bunk out there that needs to be debunked, but I think we have to be very careful not to throw the baby out with the bath water."

Truzzi feels that one major problem with the executive committee of CSICOP is that they make no distinction between the paranormal and the supernatural.

"Those terms have totally different meanings," Truzzi says. "The term *supernatural* refers to God and the occult. A miracle within the church is supernatural, because it's assumed that it has been caused by God's intrusion into the world by stopping the laws of nature, such as parting the

Red Sea or raising someone from the dead. *Paranormal* has a different meaning entirely. That term was coined by people involved in technical research to refer to natural phenomena that we don't yet fully understand, but which, in the future, may be explained by science."

In 1981, CSICOP was embarrassed by what has come to be known as the Starbaby Scandal. This fiasco involved an investigation of a study conducted by French psychologist Michel Gauquelin, whose research had disclosed significant correlations between the achievements and occupations of individuals and the positions of the planets under which they were born. One particularly interesting finding was that a statistically impressive number of champion athletes were born under the sign of Mars.

A team of investigators from CSICOP attempted to discredit Gauquelin's research by conducting their own experiment. When, instead of disproving the "Mars effect," the team of investigators inadvertently confirmed it, one of CSICOP's founding members, Dennis Rawlins, claimed that the team misrepresented their findings. Public exposure by Rawlins produced such a furor that CSICOP announced their decision to attempt no more scientific investigation.

Rawlins, who was unceremoniously ejected from the committee, announced his disillusionment at the discovery that "the science establishment would cover up evidence for the occult."

Some critics are so dedicated to their mission of convincing the public that ESP is impossible that they will reject the positive results of the most impeccably conducted experiments by alleging fraud, simply because the findings support something they don't wish to believe.

The Amazing Randi built his career as a psychic debunker upon attempts to discredit the alleged PK wonderworker, Uri Geller. Randi has been accused on numerous occasions of distorting facts as part of an ongoing campaign to discredit psi in general.

Bill Roll's experience with Randi during his investigation of the Tina Resch poltergeist case supports those allegations.

"James Randi made sure that the Resches would not welcome him into their home by turning up at their door in a long black cape and publicly ridiculing them by comparing them to children who believe in Santa Claus and the Tooth Fairy," Bill says. "Since the RSPK effects reported by family members, visitors, investigators, clergymen, and members of the press were, to his mind, 'impossible,' he simply insisted that this body of witnesses had not seen what they said they saw. Without even having been inside the house where the phenomena were taking place or talking with the eyewitnesses, Randi distributed a statement to reporters that said: 'Examination of available material indicated fraudulent means or perfectly explainable methods have been employed to provide the media with sensational details about an otherwise trivial matter.' He dismissed my own firsthand observations of the phenomena with the flippant comment, 'Roll is myopic and wears thick glasses; he is a poor observer.' Admittedly, I wear glasses, but I'm not myopic, and the kinds of events I reported were independently witnessed by visitors to the home and, later, by other parapsychologists in North Carolina."

Randi has been accused of disregard for the facts and having a propensity to misquote people. In a major lawsuit in the spring of 1993 a jury determined that he had libeled a scientist, although the jury refused to award any monetary damages.

Indisputably, fraud is possible in any area of science. Still, some critics extend themselves to the point of absurdity in their efforts to discredit experiments.

On one such occasion, C.E.M. Hansel, a British psychologist and a member of CSICOP, visited Duke University for the express purpose of examining the two locations in which the Pearce-Pratt card-guessing experiments had been conducted twenty years earlier. After checking things out, Hansel triumphantly announced that Pearce must have sneaked across from his station at the University Library in order to spy on Pratt while he was sitting at a desk in another building, recording the target cards. He speculated that Pearce accomplished this without detection on thirty occasions, either by peeking over two different transoms or by creeping up into the attic and peering down through a trapdoor. It made no difference to Hansel that there was no evidence to indicate cheating or that the well-crafted experiment had gone unchallenged for two decades. Even when confronted with blueprints that showed that the layout of the rooms had been significantly changed since the time of the experiments and the scenario he had concocted would have been physically impossible, Hansel stuck by his guns and published his "exposé."

In reality, fraud by members of the scientific community is far less likely than by professional psychics, particularly those under pressure to perform before an audience. Even legitimate psychics may occasionally find themselves in a position in which they are tempted to cheat.

British medium Doris Stokes explained how this might occur.

"Occasionally in the middle of a séance, when the voices have been coming through loud and clear, they'll suddenly stop," she said. "I'll simply lose contact. The audience will be staring up at me expectantly, waiting for me to speak, and nothing will happen. When you're standing up in front of hundreds of people who are expecting to hear you perform miracles, it's terribly difficult to say, 'Sorry, I can't do it at the moment,' and sit down again. If you fail to produce the goods on just one evening, several hundred people will go away and tell their friends you're a fake. So much is at stake that it's not surprising that even the most genuine of mediums are occasionally tempted to 'fill in' with bits of information they've overheard in the lobby or in the lavatory."

Stokes admitted that she had done this twice, but each time had been stricken with guilt and apologized to the audience.

It is easy for the average person to be fooled by a con artist, especially by one who says what that person wants to hear. It is easy, too, for honest researchers to misinterpret data, especially if it seems to support their hypotheses. There also are people with a small amount of psychic ability who mislead the public by portraying themselves as more gifted than they actually are. Every area of science needs to be subject to critical inspection, and some psychic detectives, such as Noreen Renier and Nancy Myer-Czetli, go so far as to suggest that there ought to be government licensing of psychics who are involved in police work.

Skeptics who challenge claims of psychic phenomena provide an invaluable service to the field of parapsychology by exposing quackery and pinpointing the weaknesses in flawed experiments. But in order to do this important job effectively, it is imperative that critics approach it intellectually rather than emotionally, with open minds and an attitude of conservative objectivity that allows them to make an honest appraisal of the evidence.

CHAPTER THIRTEEN

A PERSONAL JOURNEY INTO THE WORLD OF PSI

My own belief in the validity of psychic phenomena is not based upon the results of laboratory research or upon the anecdotal evidence presented by others. It's the result of a series of personal experiences—terrible, bizarre, yet indisputable—that have forced me to change my mind about what is and is not possible and to realize how shallow my view of reality has been.

This started with the discovery that a number of details relating to the murder of my daughter Kait—including the name of the man who would be arrested for shooting her—were things I had written about in my teenage suspense novel, *Don't Look Behind You*, published one month before her death.

Kait was an organ donor, and after the transplant surgery the young man who received her heart and lungs asked his mother to get a pencil and paper and take notes. He then described a vivid dream he'd had while under anesthesia in which a young, blond girl was being chased in her car by slightly built, black-haired, dark-complected men who wanted to kill her. He also described a previous occasion on which these same men had threatened her. This man had no way of knowing the identity of the organ donor. It seemed that Kait's memories had been transferred along with her heart.

But this was just the beginning.

The day after Kait's funeral, my oldest daughter, Robin, went to a psychic. She did this on her own, without consulting the rest of us, and my husband and I were not happy about it. We were a conservative, middle-class family who had always regarded psychics as shameless opportunists who took advantage of people made vulnerable by tragedy, and we were horrified by the thought that our precious memories of Kait might be degraded by a fraudulent medium who was out to make money from our grief.

Yet the psychic, Betty Muench, although she usually charged for her readings, had refused to accept payment because of the tragic circumstances, and much of what she told Robin proved to be accurate. This included the statements that Kait's killers had been driving a low-rider; that there were two men in front and one in back; and that, although there were no eyewitnesses, arrests would be made because the men would be heard bragging.

Six months after the shooting, tipsters phoned Crime Stoppers and named three young Hispanic men whom they had heard boasting about having killed Kait. The informants identified the driver of the low-rider that chased Kait down as Juve Escobedo; the triggerman who fired from the passenger seat as Mike "Vamp" Garcia; and the passenger in the backseat as Dennis "Marty" Martinez.

Betty also told Robin that there would be "an intimidated police force with no one willing to make the effort to get the whole truth," and said our best help would come from a newspaper reporter named Mike Gallagher. She said Gallagher would "keep Kait's story from becoming buried and intimidated," that he would cause the police "a great headache," and that he would be "instrumental in getting it onto media shows that will appeal from the national level."

All those predictions proved accurate. Not only did Mike Gallagher write a series of provocative articles that embarrassed the police by pointing out the flaws in their investigation, but he appeared on *Unsolved Mysteries* to tell a national television audience that he believed Kait had been assassinated.

Betty also told Robin that Kait's Vietnamese boyfriend and his friends were involved in illegal activities that Kait had found out about and had been planning to expose. She said that Kait's boyfriend was "in a sense the instigator of this event, but it is not that he will have been the one to have done this. It is as if he will seem to know who will have done this. There will have been the hiring of what the Vietnamese consider the lesser ones, the Hispanics, and they will simply use the Hispanics to do their work."

As if to give credence to that reading, we received a phone call from an anonymous tipster who told us the men who had been arrested for Kait's murder had killed before and did so for pay.

We relayed all this to the police, but they didn't want to hear it, possibly because the random-shooting case was a simple one to prosecute.

Since Betty Muench did not like working on crime cases, I asked Bill Roll how to find a good psychic detective who had experience investigating murders. He suggested that I contact Marcello Truzzi, the sociologist who had helped found (and had later resigned from) CSICOP. Bill told me that Truzzi was a skeptic about people who claimed psychic abilities and that anybody he steered us to was likely to be authentic.

"I went to high school with a boy by that name!" I exclaimed.

Incredibly, it turned out to be the same person. Several decades had passed since we had seen each other, but Marcello remembered me and sent me the names and addresses of the nation's top psychic detectives.

I wrote to the ones with the most impressive track records, and the first to respond was Noreen Renier, who volunteered to work on Kait's case using psychometry. Noreen told me that if she held something that belonged to the victim, she could describe the killer to a police artist, who would then make a sketch.

I sent her the cross Kait was wearing when she was shot and then started having misgivings. The idea of psychometry seemed so farfetched to me that I was afraid I might be setting myself up for extortion.

It didn't take long for me to realize that Noreen was not a fake. She phoned before starting the drawing to make sure she was "reading" Kait correctly and asked me to verify some things about her. She said she felt Kait had suffered a lot of abdominal pain (her intestines had been damaged by celiac disease, and she had experienced terrible cramping all her life); that she had recently moved (she had just gotten her own apartment); that there was "a little school around her, but she didn't go all that much" (she had been taking two college classes in summer school); that she was mad at her boyfriend (she was breaking up with him); and that she had been killed at night while she was driving her car.

When I confirmed those facts, Noreen said, "Well, good, then I've homed in on her. Now I'll go into a trance and see if I can get a face for you."

I had never believed in mediumship and wasn't even sure that I believed in an afterlife. Still, I felt there was nothing to lose by trying to reach out to Kait on the chance that I might be wrong and her spirit still existed. So, while Noreen and the police artist were "getting a face" in Florida, I sat in our home in New Mexico and tried to communicate with my daughter. Since the alleged shooter, Mike "Vamp" Garcia, was already in custody, we didn't need a picture to see what he looked like, so I asked her to try to find some way of using this opportunity to let us know the motive for her murder. Were the police correct when they insisted the shooting was random, or was our family right in our suspicion that the killing had been murder-for-hire?

Noreen mailed me two sketches. The first was of a man she felt might be in some way responsible for Kait's murder, perhaps because Kait had seen him purchasing drugs. But

Lois Duncan examines sketches of faces described during a trance reading by psychic detective Noreen Renier. (courtesy: Lois Duncan)

232

it was the other picture that caused my knees to buckle. It was a detailed portrait of "Mike Vamp," the drug-runner's hit man in my suspense novel, *Don't Look Behind You*, exactly as he appeared on the jacket of the British edition. The edition with this jacket was not available in the United States, so neither Noreen nor her police artist could possibly have seen it. Only Kait and I had seen that picture. I had shown her the proofs of the artwork just days before her death, and she had commented on how "scary" the hit man was.

When I told Noreen what she had sent me, she was stunned. This kind of thing had never happened to her before; normally she produced a picture of a real person. The only explanation she could come up with was that Kait was using this method to symbolically get across the message, "This wasn't a random shooting! *I was killed by a professional hit man like the one in Mother's book!*"

Along with the sketches, Noreen sent me a tape on which she went into a trance and actually seemed to *become* Kait.

"The night I'm killed, I meet a man in a shopping center with a 'C' in it," I heard my dead daughter say in Noreen's husky voice. (The shopping mall closest to our house was Coronado Center.) "We drive up the hill toward the north to that big place up there—stucco walls, flat roof, a lot of land around it—I want to call it the Desert Castle. I shouldn't have gone! There was a very important man there that I wasn't supposed to see. They had to make sure I wouldn't talk. The crime committed against me was to silence me. *I will never be silenced!* I'm *not* a bad person! I *was* a good daughter to you, Mother! I told you *almost* everything! Almost.

"I promise I won't tell, and they let me go. I pick up my car and drive to my girlfriend's house. When I leave there I'm shot. The police have fear. This is a very powerful man.

They have somebody to convict, and they want to let it go at that."

The voice was Noreen's, but the wording was Kait's. She had called me "Mother," not "Mom," as her friends did their mothers. Even the flowery term "Desert Castle" rang true to me, as Kait had always had a tendency to be overdramatic.

This experience left me so shaken I could barely function. Then another psychic, Nancy Myer-Czetli, checked in. Nancy told me she obtained her information through telepathy and could zero in on the thought patterns of victims and killers by viewing photos of crime scenes.

"When people get frightened they leak information," she explained to me. "Somehow that energy gets stuck in the cells of the environment. It's like there are memory scars engraved on the scenery."

Nancy asked for a video of the television coverage of Kait's murder. After she watched it, she phoned me.

"The killing was a setup," she said. "I don't buy 'random' at all, because the killers were checking out numbers on license plates to make sure that they got the right car. Money changed hands, that came across very strong to me. Your daughter was playing Nancy Drew. She'd stumbled onto information about organized crime, one element of which was an interstate drug network, and she was trying to learn more about it. She saw a VIP buy cocaine. The drug dealers had her killed because they were afraid she would talk."

The similarity between the two readings was mind-boggling. But might it be mere coincidence? My daughter Robin begged me to get a third opinion, so, at her urging, I decided to get more input from Betty Muench, who acquired information through automatic writing. There was a time when I would have regarded this idea as preposterous, but I had now reached a point where I no longer scoffed at anything.

While Betty sat at the typewriter, I sat in a chair across from her and asked, "What may we know about the Desert Castle?"

I gave no explanation for that question. For all Betty knew the "Desert Castle" might have been a restaurant.

Betty's fingers started to fly across the keyboard. There was no way she had time to compose what she was writing; it was as if she were taking dictation from voices I couldn't hear:

The Desert Castle is a place in which those will be found who will work with death and who will do so for money. There is one who claims to be the possessor of this place, but that is a lie. The ownership is in question, and it has a sense of having been abandoned out of fear of this group of illegitimate occupants.

"If Kait saw a drug transaction, who was involved in it?" I asked.

The typewriter rattled off an answer:

This one in question is an important person, one who has the podium and is in charge of such a position. He covets his reputation and is usually very careful about his actions, yet there will have been an instance in which a certain urgency will have overcome him, and so there will not have been the usual caution. There is a dread of discovery that borders on paranoia, and this will be part of his fear about his observation by Kait. He will not have had anything to

do with the actions after that, but his followers will be
involved, and this is what must be considered in the
death of Kait.

"This man didn't order Kait's murder, but the fact that
she saw him buy drugs may have been what triggered it,"
Betty told me. "At least, that seems to be what Kait now
believes."

Noreen had described the Desert Castle as set against a
mountain backdrop, twelve miles northeast in a two-thirty
o'clock position from where Kait was shot. I didn't expect
my husband, an electrical engineer with a scientific mind-
set, to be receptive to information from such unorthodox
sources, but he surprised me.

"When you give the same problem to three different consultants and get the same answer from all of them, you have
to pay attention," he said.

We bought a map of the city, drew a clock around Kait's
murder site, and drove twelve miles in the direction of the
two-thirty mark, ending up in an elite subdivision composed of large, expensive homes in the foothills. After pho-
tographing all the houses that fit Noreen's description, we
sent a package of pictures to Nancy Myer-Czetli, so she
could inspect them for "emotional scars on the scenery."

Nancy told us she reacted strongly to two of the photos.
At first we thought she was hedging her bets, but when we
examined the negatives, we discovered that the pictures she
had selected were two very different views of the same
house, one taken from the front and the other from the side.

"I can't believe you've actually found it!" she exclaimed,
unaware that another psychic had directed us to the site.
"After looking at the photos, I think Kait had been in the
area of this house and possibly in it and was aware that

drug activities were going on there. This was a part of the activity she was going to expose. Intruders were using this place as a drug exchange point. I feel the owner of the house was out of town at the time. The VIP who was making the purchase was stocky, square-faced, dark-haired, and middle-aged."

Her description matched the man in Noreen's first sketch, although Nancy had not seen that picture. None of the psychics knew we were working with the others.

In April 1991, fifteen months after the arrest of Mike "Vamp" Garcia, his lawyers produced evidence gleaned by private investigators that Kait's boyfriend and his friends were involved in criminal activity that overlapped five states. This made the case for assassination now appear stronger than the case for random shooting. Since the police had made no attempt to establish murder-for-hire as a motive, the district attorney withdrew the charges and let Garcia and the other suspect walk.

Several months later, Dennis "Marty" Martinez, the man in the backseat of the Camaro, phoned the police and confessed to the murder, saying that he and his friends had been hired by the Vietnamese to kill Kait. The police wouldn't take a statement until fifteen days later, when Dennis recanted, saying he had been drunk when he confessed. He was not arrested and has never been given a polygraph test.

As of this writing, Kait's death is once again an unsolved mystery, but our family continues to have faith that justice will be done. This belief is reinforced by the psychics whose abilities we have come to respect.

Noreen Renier tells us, "Kait says she will never be silenced."

Nancy Myer-Czetli assures us, "The fat lady hasn't sung

yet." She feels that new information is going to surface. There are people who know what happened, and we only need one of them.

But our strongest reason for believing that Kait's killers will be apprehended is a message that Betty Muench received through automatic writing:

There is an assurance in Kait that there will come this which will seem to put the collar on the wolf who will have been after her. There is an image of a kind of wild wolf with something on its neck as it howls with its neck up in the air. There is in this a sense of message that there is knowing in Kait that the lone wolf will come into forms of justice which Lois and all her family and friends will bear witness to.

Betty could not have known by any "normal" means that the original title of the book that my editor retitled *Who Killed My Daughter?* was *One to the Wolves.*

For anyone reading this book, the natural next question to ask is, "What if the psychics' predictions turn out to be wrong?"

I don't want to believe that, of course, but I realize it's possible. I know that precognitive readings can be affected by telepathy, and our family's driving desire for a closure to Kait's case may be affecting the psychic readings without any of us realizing it.

But even if that's the case, my quest for answers will not have gone totally unrewarded, because in the process of searching for the truth about my life's worst tragedy, I have inadvertently stumbled upon truths that have given my life new meaning. I have become convinced that I am still connected to Kait, despite the fact that her body is no longer living. I also have come to accept that I am connected psychically to other people and things on this earth. There is too much evidence of that to be able to deny it.

My picture of reality has changed, and in a way that's scary, because it has forced me to change the image I've had of myself and of my relationship to others. Before, I always thought of people as islands, separate from each other except when they were in physical contact or were linked by a mechanical device such as a telephone or radio. I've now come to realize that there are invisible bridges between these islands and that every entity is connected to every other. As with islands, our closest and strongest connections are with those nearby, the family and friends who are dear to us, but the bridges continue beyond that to everybody and everything.

I have begun to regard even people I don't know as part of myself, and that seems strange. But it's a good feeling too, because it gives me a sense of belonging and makes me more compassionate toward others. I have also come to believe that we are connected psychically with physical objects, as evidenced by clairvoyance, psychometry and psychokinesis. If more people could realize that our longbody includes the physical environment—not only our homes and possessions, but also the distant forest and ocean—they might become more protective of the world we live in.

There are practical benefits of knowing about psychic connections, such as psychic healing, psychic archaeology, crime solving, and finding missing persons. It may be, however, that the most important thing that parapsychology can do for us is to help us to find ourselves in other people and in the physical environment. Parapsychology teaches us that we don't exist for ourselves alone, but are part of the all—that psyche is connected to psyche, and longbody to longbody. If we hurt others, we hurt ourselves; and if we hurt ourselves—by abusing our minds and bodies, by not learning and growing and becoming the most that we can be—we hurt, as well, everyone and everything that is part of us, which means *everyone* and *everything*.

Parapsychology is an exciting and enriching journey of ongoing discovery into one's own self, which is also the universe around us.

How startling this is to know—and how wonderful!

POSTSCRIPT

by William Roll

There is a story from ancient Greece about a princess who was so lovely that words couldn't describe her. Her name was Psyche. On a scale from 1 to 10, Psyche would have rated a 20. The god of love, Eros, became enamored of her, and they had a child named Joy. Not coincidentally, *psyche* is the Greek word for mind, soul, and self. This myth tells us that to know yourself—to unite mind, soul, self, and eros—is an exciting and joyful experience.

But what is the self? And if the self is so wonderful, why haven't we all discovered it and begun living happily ever after? It's not difficult to understand why. The self is like the air we breathe—it's around us all the time, and we depend on it, but it's invisible, so people may not even know it exists. The self is like the unseen bonds that hold a flock of birds together. The birds don't necessarily need to understand the bonds to fly in formation. In the same way, we don't have to understand or even believe in psi phenomena to reap their benefits in our lives.

Psychic bonds are not limited to people and things that are close to us in space and time, but include people and places far distant. To the psyche, out of sight does not mean out of mind. You are psychically closer to a close family member in a distant town than to the neighbor you hardly know. This is what telepathy, mind-to-mind ESP, reveals. Clairvoyance, object-to-mind ESP, shows that we are also psychically connected to material objects; things talk to us, though we may not listen. Things may also hold place memories, as in local apparitions and psychometry. If we enter a home or hold someone's possession, we may recall events connected with it, especially if the events carry strong emotions. In psychokinesis you may directly affect things in a similar way as you make your hands and feet move. You could say that inanimate objects are actually animated, not by spirits, as people once thought, but by people like yourself.

In the same way that your familiar mind belongs to a physical body, your psyche belongs to a *longbody* (a word suggested by psychologist

241

Christopher Aanstoos). This is considered a real physical body that encompasses other people and things, somewhat the way a human body includes its organs. But the longbody is not confined to the visible universe; it reaches into space and time to embrace departed loved ones. To become aware of the psyche is exciting and enriching because the psyche stretches so far.

Many cells make a human body, and many selves make a longbody. Beyond the longbody there is an even larger body, the physical universe of stars and galaxies. Much as you can experience the psyche, the soul of the longbody, you can become aware of the spirit of the universe. Some people who have been near death describe it as a Being of Love and Light. If you don't have strong attachments to others, either negative or positive, your little soul may unite with the universal spirit at death, without stopping at the longbody. But you don't have to wait until death before knowing the Being of Love and Light. Like the psyche, it's around all the time and open to experience.

How can you open yourself to your psyche and to the Being of Love and Light? It's as natural as breathing. In fact, if you let yourself become aware of your breathing, you are halfway there. The word for breath in Latin is *spiritus*, and conscious breathing is a psychic and spiritual exercise. If you sit quietly, exhale from the bottom of your lungs, and follow the breath as you send it out and then take in fresh air, this increases your "gut feeling" and intuitive sense.

To be psychically and spiritually aware, people need to be educated about their psychic and spiritual connections. This is the main purpose of this book. The Three Rs, reading, writing, and arithmetic, are not enough. A fourth R is needed. The fourth R stands for the right brain hemisphere, the site of imagination and intuition. If you know the three Rs, but not the fourth, you are like a car with a flat tire—you won't get very far and you may not have a good time getting there. Conscious breathing is a starting point in developing your capacity for imagination and intuition—a capacity that makes you aware of your psychic and spiritual connections.

GLOSSARY

Apparition: The visual appearance of a person whose physical body is not present

Astral body: The body a person seems to occupy during an out-of-body experience

Astral plane: A world some people believe exists above the physical world

Astral projection: An out-of-body experience

Aura: A field that some psychics see surrounding the living body

Automatic writing: Writing without being aware of the contents, as when a medium apparently transcribes written messages from disembodied spirits

Channeling: The process by which a medium apparently allows a spirit to communicate through his or her person

Clairvoyance: The viewing of distant scenes not apparent to the eye

Crisis apparition: An apparition seen when the subject is at the point of death or is the victim of a serious illness or injury

Déjà vu: The feeling of having experienced something before

ESP: Extrasensory perception—the ability to gain knowledge through means other than the five physical senses or logical inference

ESP cards: Cards with the five symbols—star, circle, square, cross, and wavy lines—usually in packs of twenty-five

EVP: Electronic voice phenomena—voices and other sounds, often attributed to the dead, imprinted on audio-recording tape

Forced choice experiment: An experiment in which the subject is forced to choose among an assortment of possible targets, such as the five ESP cards

Free response experiment: An experiment in which the subject knows only the general nature of the target—for instance, that it is a picture—but not anything else

Ganzfeld experiment: An experiment where input from the outside world is reduced by placing halved Ping-Pong balls over the eyes and by masking external sounds

Goat: A subject in an experiment who does not believe in the ability for which he or she is being tested

Haunting: Recurrent sounds of human activity, sightings of apparitions, and other psychic phenomena, in a location when no one is there

Hit: A choice that proves correct

Laying on of hands: A process by which certain healers profess to be able to heal patients by touch

Levitation: The lifting of physical objects by psychokinesis (PK)

Longbody: A web of living connections among people, places, and objects

Medium: A person who professes to be able to communicate with spirits (also referred to as a "mental medium")

Medium (direct voice): A trance medium who apparently acts as a transmitter for the voices of disembodied spirits

Medium (materialization): A medium who seems to be able to give physical form to the deceased from a substance called "ectoplasm"

Medium (physical): A medium who is the center of moving objects and other physical incidents supposedly caused by spirits

Miss: A choice that proves incorrect

Motor automatism: Bodily movement of an intelligent and purposeful kind of which the person is not aware, as with automatic writing

NDE: Near-death experience—the out-of-body and other experiences people report having when they are close to death

OBE: Out-of-body experience—the experience that the self is in a different location than the physical body

Paranormal: Above or outside the natural order of things as presently understood

Parapsychology: The branch of science that studies psychic phenomena

PK: Psychokinesis—the power of the mind to affect matter without physical contact

PK (deliberate): Psychokinesis that occurs as a result of conscious effort by the person causing it

PK (macro): The effect of psychokinesis on objects in general

PK (micro): The effect of psychokinesis on random events such as random event generators (REGs)

PK (spontaneous): Psychokinesis that occurs without conscious effort by the person who causes it

PK (time-displaced): The concept of psychokinesis going backward in time to affect events that have already taken place

Place memory: Information about past events that apparently is stored in the physical environment

Poltergeist: A German word meaning "rowdy ghost" (see also RSPK)

Precognition: The ability to predict things beyond present knowledge

Psi: A letter in the Greek alphabet that denotes psychic phenomena

Psi hitting: A test performance significantly higher than expected by chance

Psi missing: A test performance significantly lower than expected by chance

Psyche: The Greek word for "self," "mind," or "soul"

Psychic: A person with above average ESP abilities

Psychic healing: A mode of healing affected by the psychic abilities of the healer

Psychometry: ESP of events associated with inanimate objects

REG: Random event generator—a target selection machine that operates in a way that should be impossible to predict

Remote viewing: Another term for clairvoyance

REMs: Rapid eye movements during sleep that indicate dreaming

RSPK: Recurrent spontaneous psychokinesis—a possible cause of apparent poltergeist activity

Séance: A group of people who gather in an effort to communicate with the dead

Sheep: A subject in an experiment who believes in the ability for which he or she is being tested

Target object: In ESP, the object or event the subject attempts to perceive; in PK, the object or event the subject attempts to influence

Telepathy: The direct passing of information from one mind to another

Thought form: An apparition produced by the power of the human mind

Trance: A sleeplike state in which there is a change of consciousness

Sources

EDUCATIONAL OPPORTUNITIES

PSI Home Study Course: Psychic Research: Old Superstitions or New Science? This twelve-lesson overview of the issues and facts surrounding psi phenomena is a thorough introduction to modern psychic research. Upon completion of the course, including lessons in ESP, hauntings, and apparitions, the student receives a certificate signifying completion of a basic course in psychic research. For more information contact: Judy Winters, Psi Home Study Course, Parapsychological Services Institute, 1506 Holly Bank Circle, Dunwoody, GA 30338.

FRNM Summer Study Program, offered annually at the Foundation for Research on the Nature of Man. This series of lectures and classes by some of the field's most noted researchers covers a variety of current psi issues. Included are discussions on mediumship, hypnosis, psychic detectives, psi ethics, and psychophysiology. For more information contact: FRNM, 402 North Buchanan Boulevard, Durham, NC 27701-1728.

For information about colleges and universities that offer courses in parapsychology, write Education Department, American Society for Psychical Research, 5 West 73rd Street, New York, NY 10023.

RECOMMENDED BOOKS
Basic books are marked with an asterisk.

By and About Psychics
Brinkley, Dannion
Saved by the Light Brinkley was hit by lightning and twice had a near-death experience. He encountered a being of love and light and saw future events. When Brinkley recovered he found he had developed psychic abilities. (Villard Books, 1994)

Garrett, Eileen
Many Voices, The Autobiography of a Medium Escaping from a harsh childhood in Ireland, Eileen delved into the psychic world for healing and understanding. She became a trance medium and went to the United States, including Duke University, where she showed strong evidence for ESP. Garrett established the Parapsychology Foundation, which still supports work in the field. (Putnam, 1968)

Harribance, Sean, The Christian Psychic (as told to the Reverend H. Richard Neff)
This Man Knows You Tells of Sean's colorful but troubled childhood in Trinidad, the emergence of his psychic skills, and his conversion to Christianity from Hinduism. To seek scientific validation of his abilities, Harribance went to the Institute of Parapsychology and the Psychical Research Foundation in North Carolina, where he was one of the most successful ESP subjects on record. (Naylor, 1976; available from the author at P.O. Box 908, Sugarland, TX 77487)

Hastings, Arthur
*With the Tongues of Men and Angels: A Study of Channeling Covers the phenomenon of channeling from early time to the present, with special emphasis on its "New Age" manifestations. Discusses psychics throughout history who were believed to channel spirits. (Holt, Rinehart & Winston, 1991)

Jaegers, Bevy C.
Psychometry: The Science of Touch The author discusses her use of psychometry to help law enforcement professionals solve crimes and describes how readers can develop this skill. (Aries Productions, 1980)

Monroe, Robert A.
Journeys out of the Body Based on the journal recordings of the author's OBEs, which include trips to other dimensions. Includes analyses of the various elements of his OBEs and contains instructions for having OBEs. (Bantam Doubleday Dell, 1977)

Myer-Czetli, Nancy and Steve Czetli
Silent Witness: The Story of a Psychic Detective Nancy Myer-Czetli discusses her growth as a psychic from her earliest years and describes her career as a psychic detective. Her story is corroborated in detail by detectives and law enforcement professionals with whom she worked. (Carol, 1993)

Puryear, Herbert B.
The Edgar Cayce Primer An introduction to the philosophy of the nation's best-known trance medium, including his views on health,

dreams, reincarnation, and Karma. (Association for Research and Enlightenment, Virginia Beach, VA)

Stearn, Jess
Edgar Cayce: The Sleeping Prophet. The life, the Prophesies and Readings of America's Most Famous Mystic Stories about Cayce's medical diagnoses and cures (involving patients he had never met), his views on Atlantis and reincarnation, and the "Cayce babies," who had life-readings by Cayce. (1968, Bantam)

Swann, Ingo
Natural ESP: The ESP Core and Its Raw Characteristics The author, who has successfully participated in many psi experiments, discusses unlocking the extrasensory powers of your mind. He develops his ideas from the literature of parapsychology and his own experiences. (Bantam, 1987)

Wilson, Colin
The Geller Phenomenon An overview of the life, and laboratory testing of the psychokinetic abilities of, the famous and controversial "metal-bender," Uri Geller. (Aldus, 1976)

Healing and the Body

Dossey, Larry, M.D.
Healing Words: The Power of Prayer and the Practice of Medicine Larry Dossey, a physician, examines the role of prayer in the practice of medicine. Reviewing case histories and PK research on living systems, Dossey attempts to show how prayer could complement but not replace good medicine. (HarperCollins, 1993)

Krieger, Dolores
Accepting Your Power to Heal: The Personal Practice of Therapeutic Touch The author encourages everyone to recognize his or her ability to heal through manipulation of the human energy field. Her techniques reportedly have benefited sufferers from cancer, burns, AIDS, and other serious conditions. (Bear and Company, 1993)

Murphy, Michael
The Future of the Body: Explorations into the Further Evolution of Human Nature Murphy, founder of Esalen Institute, outlines the capacities of the human body and psyche and argues that because body and spirit are inseparable, it is likely that the body will be the vehicle of our evolution as a species. (Jeremy P. Tarcher/Perigee, 1992)

249

Introductions and Overviews

Broughton, Richard S.
Parapsychology: The Controversial Science An overview and history of parapsychology with a discussion on why the field remains controversial. Emphasizes laboratory findings but includes psi in real life, including poltergeist research. Shows how psi abilities may have practical uses. (Ballantine, 1991)

Edge, Hoyt L., Robert L. Morris, John Palmer, and Joseph H. Rush
Foundations of Parapsychology: Exploring the Boundaries of Human Capability An examination of the field's methods, findings, and theories. The authors address the scientific, philosophical, and social implications of psi research and discuss skeptical viewpoints. (Routledge & Kegan Paul, 1986)

Eysenck, Hans J. and Carl Sargent
Explaining the Unexplained: Mysteries of the Paranormal An introduction that covers most aspects of the field, from the gifted psychics of early research to the concepts of modern physics, that may throw light on recent research findings. (Prion, 1993)

Irwin, H. J.
An Introduction to Parapsychology, 2nd Edition This textbook outlines the origins of parapsychological research and critically reviews investigations of extrasensory perception, psychokinesis, poltergeist phenomena, near-death and out-of-body experiences, apparitions, and reincarnation. Also, criticisms by the skeptical are presented, and the status of parapsychology as a scientific enterprise is assessed. (McFarland, 1989)

Rhine, Louisa
Hidden Channels of the Mind A renowned researcher analyzes cases of spontaneous ESP on file at the parapsychology laboratory at Duke University and draws some fascinating conclusions based upon this large collection of anecdotal evidence of telepathy, clairvoyance, and precognition. (William Morrow, 1961)

Robinson, Diana
To Stretch a Plank: A Survey of Psychokinesis A survey of the facts, fallacies, and theories of psychokinesis, including research in medical science and an introduction to psychics in the field. (Nelson-Hall, 1981)

Targ, Russell and Keith Harary
The Mind Race An exploration of the many facets of psychic functioning, with an emphasis on remote viewing, telepathy, and precognition. Includes techniques to increase the reader's psychic ability. (Villard, 1984)

Ullman, Montague, Stanley Krippner, and Alan Vaughan
Dream Telepathy: Experiments in Nocturnal ESP A report on the ESP experiments with dreaming subjects conducted at Maimonides Hospital, Brooklyn, New York. Includes precognitive dreams and a discussion of the psychological aspects of ESP dreams. (McFarland, 1988)

White, Rhea A.
Parapsychology: New Sources of Information, 1973–1989 A classification of 483 parapsychological works, including books on mediumship, psychokinesis, and altered states of consciousness. Also reviews the history and criticism of parapsychology. (Scarecrow, 1990)

Wolman, Benjamin B., Editor
Handbook of Parapsychology Thirty-two contributors provide a detailed account of parapsychological research and its implications for science and society. Topics include poltergeists, telepathic dreams, discarnate survival, and Soviet research in parapsychology. (McFarland, 1986)

Near-Death Experiences
Greyson, Bruce and Charles P. Flynn
The Near-Death Experience: Problems, Prospects, Perspectives An anthology of scientifically oriented papers on near-death experiences, with an in-depth review of current theories of the phenomenon. Contributors include Michael Grosso, Raymond Moody, and Kenneth Ring. (Thomas, 1984)

Moody, Raymond A.
Life After Life Documents well over a hundred cases of individuals who described out-of-body experiences, meetings with a being of love and light, and other psychical and spiritual experiences when the person was near death. (Mockingbird, 1975)
The Light Beyond Reviews of case histories of near-death experiences and discussions of common factors such as out-of-body experiences, life reviews, and profound personality changes. (With Paul Perry, Bantam, 1988)

Ring, Kenneth
Heading Toward Omega: In Search of the Meaning of the Near-Death Experience The author's study of more than one hundred persons who have had near-death experiences. Examines the significance of the NDE and its implications for humankind's evolution to a higher consciousness. (Morrow, 1984)
The Omega Project: Near-Death Experiences, UFO Encounters, and Mind at Large Combining scientific analysis and case histories, the author shows that UFO abductees share similarities with NDE survivors. He

posits the existence of an "encounter-prone personality" that may represent a new stage in the evolution of the human mind. (Morrow, 1992)

Sabom, Michael
Recollections of Death: A Medical Investigation A study by a physician of patients who were near death and had near-death experiences, with a discussion of common factors. Compares medical research with parapsychological studies. (Harper & Row, 1982)

Out-of-Body Experiences

Harary, Keith and Pamela Weintraub
Have an Out-of-Body Experience in 30 Days: The Free Flight Program A guide to facilitate out-of-body experiences. Topics covered include sensitivity awareness, shifting attention, and overcoming fear. (St. Martin's Press, 1989)

Irwin, H. J.
Flight of Mind: A Psychological Study of the Out-of-Body Experience The author explains out-of-body experiences on the basis of psychological and physiological studies and provides a summary of OBE research. (Scarecrow, 1985)

Mitchell, Janet Lee
Out-of-Body Experiences An approach to OBEs as personal experiences as well as from a historical perspective. Descriptions of OBEs elicited by surgery, drugs, sensory deprivation, and real-life situations. (Ballantine, 1981)

Muldoon, Sylvan and Hereward Carrington
The Projection of the Astral Body An early study of OBEs, the book describes Muldoon's experiences, discusses the "laws" of the projection of the "astral body," and gives instructions on how to induce OBEs. (Samuel Weiser, 1929)

Poltergeists and Hauntings

Auerbach, Lloyd
ESP, Hauntings and Poltergeists: A Parapsychologist's Handbook An examination of poltergeist cases, hauntings, techniques used by parapsychologists, and a parapsychological research center directory. (Warner Books, 1986)

Gauld, Alan and Cornell, A. D.
Poltergeists A study of poltergeist cases from around the world, with an analysis of leading characteristics of these events and tentative conclu-

sions about the "clusters" into which the cases fall. (Routledge & Kegan Paul, 1979)

Rogo, Scott D. and Raymond Bayless
On the Track of the Poltergeist The author tells about his poltergeist investigations, outlines the major theories of the phenomena, and gives recommendations for people having such experiences. (Prentice-Hall, 1986)

Roll, William G.
The Poltergeist Early poltergeist cases are summarized and the author's own investigations are described in detail. Roll compares the demon theory with the view that the incidents are due to psychokinesis, and provides a guide for investigating cases. (Signet, 1974)

Precognition

Ebon, Martin
Prophecy in Our Time An exploration of prophetic experiences, both real and fraudulent, including a report on investigations in this area by Freud and Jung. (New American Library, 1968)

Hearne, Keith
Visions of the Future: An Investigation of Premonitions The author reviews anecdotes and studies of precognitive dreams, and details the type of person most likely to have these dreams. (Aquarian/HarperCollins, 1989)

Ryback, David and Letitia Sweitzer
Dreams That Come True: Their Psychic and Transforming Powers Reviews precognitive dreams from the point of view of psychological counseling. Includes a discussion on learning to make use of information in precognitive dreams. (Doubleday, 1988)

Psychic Detectives

Duncan, Lois
Who Killed My Daughter? Duncan documents her search for her daughter's killer. Faced with insufficient evidence provided by the police, she turns to psychics. With their help she uncovers information that proves to her that her daughter's death is anything but random. (Delacorte, 1992)

Lyons, Arthur and Marcello Truzzi
The Blue Sense: Psychic Detectives and Crime The authors investigate how psychics are helping law enforcement agencies across the country.

Also surveyed is the use of psychics by intelligence services and the military. (Mysterious Press, 1991)

Wilson, Colin
The Psychic Detectives Exceptional psychic performances outside the mainstream of experimental research are discussed, including crime detection, psychometry, and psychic archaeology. (Pan Books, 1984)

Psychic Experiences of Children

Drewes, Athena A. and Sally Ann Drucker
Parapsychological Research with Children: An Annotated Bibliography Summaries of research with children from 1881 through 1990 along with an introduction and overview of present work. (Scarecrow, 1991)

Morse, Melvin
*Closer to the Light Descriptions of children's near-death experiences, and their similarities to and differences from adult NDEs. The author discusses whether you must be near death to have a classic NDE. (With Paul Perry, Villard, 1990)

Stevenson, Ian
Children Who Remember Previous Lives A description of the author's research of children who seem to remember a previous life. Stevenson explains the way he conducted his research, the results obtained, and his conclusions. (University Press of Virginia, 1987)

Relation of Parapsychology to Other Fields

Capra, Fritjof
The Turning Point: Science, Society & the Rising Culture An examination by a physicist of the dynamics underlying the major problems of our time, and a new vision of reality that allows the forces transforming our world to flow together as a positive movement for social change. (Simon & Schuster, 1982)

Evans, Hilary
Alternate States of Consciousness: Unself, Otherself, and Superself A discussion of altered states of consciousness, including dreams, religious ecstasy, hypnosis, near-death experiences, and encounters with extra-terrestrials. (Aquarian Press, 1989)

Grof, Stanislav, M.D.
Beyond the Brain In a serious challenge to the existing neurophysiological models of the brain, Dr. Grof examines nonordinary states of consciousness induced by psychedelic drugs and other means, and pro-

poses a new model of the human psyche. (State University of New York Press, 1985)

Grosso, Michael

The Final Choice: Playing the Survival Game Grosso examines the dangerous split between our high technological intelligence and our underdeveloped moral consciousness. Based on reports of ESP, psychokinesis, near-death experiences, and other "miracles," this book outlines a portrait of human potential. (Stillpoint, 1985)

Frontiers of the Soul An overview of religious psychic experiences, with a chapter about the Virgin Mary. The author believes paranormal religious experiences, including Marian visions, are evolutionary steps in the transformation of human consciousness. (Quest, 1992)

Soulmaker An investigation of extraordinary encounters with UFOs, ghosts, angels, and goddesses, this book invites the reader to reexamine the self, death, and relations with others and to begin the journey of soulmaking. (Hampton Roads, 1992)

Jahn, Robert G. and Brenda J. Dunne

Margins of Reality: The Role of Consciousness in the Physical World Two researchers draw upon a decade of psi research at Princeton University to bridge the gulf between physics and psi. The result is a fundamental reevaluation of the role of consciousness in the establishment of physical reality. (Harcourt Brace Jovanovich, 1987)

LeShan, Lawrence and Henry Margenau

Einstein's Space and Van Gogh's Sky A psychologist and a physicist investigate the relationships between consciousness and reality. The book is divided into three parts, The Meanings of Reality, The Search for Scientific Truth, and Domains of the Social Sciences. (Macmillan, 1982)

Murphy, Lois Barclay

There Is More Beyond: Selected Papers of Gardner Murphy Gardner Murphy (1895–1979) was a well-known psychologist and a leader in psychical research as well. This collection includes selections on the history of psychology, parapsychology, science, and humanity. (McFarland, 1989)

Rao, K. Ramakrishna, Editor

Case Studies in Parapsychology This book contains a collection of papers in honor of Dr. Louisa E. Rhine's contributions to the field of parapsychology. Included are a biographical sketch by her daughter and new perspectives on her work. (McFarland, 1986)

Cultivating Consciousness: Enhancing Human Potential, Wellness, and Healing The birth centenary of Dr. Louisa E. Rhine was the occasion for the publication of this book which incorporates papers presented at a conference held in Durham, N.C., in 1991. The book discusses consciousness from a variety of nonmechanistic perspectives. (Praeger, 1993)

Tart, Charles
Open Mind, Discriminating Mind: Reflections on Human Possibilities Essays and reflections on topics in parapsychology, spiritual practices, dreams, psychological growth, and survival after death. (Harper & Row, 1989)

Survival After Death

Becker, Carl B.
Paranormal Experience and Survival of Death Becker reviews substantiated accounts of reincarnation, apparitions, and demon possession, and analyzes what such experiences imply about survival after death. (State University of New York Press, 1993)

Berger, Arthur S.
Evidence of Life After Death: A Casebook for the Tough-Minded Berger summarizes thirty cases in light of their evidence of survival after death. The book is divided into three sections: spontaneous mental phenomena, the mental phenomena of mediumship, and spontaneous and mediumistic physical phenomena. (Thomas, 1988)

Gauld, Alan
Mediumship and Survival The author spans a century to gather evidence of mediumship, reincarnation, possession, ghosts, and out-of-body experiences, and discusses whether these phenomena are evidence of life after death. (Granada, 1983)

Gershom, Rabbi Yonassan
Beyond the Ashes: Cases of Reincarnation from the Holocaust Gershom has based this book upon the past-life memories of people he has counseled over a period of ten years who, as young children, seem to have had vivid and detailed recollections of former lives as Jews who were executed during the Holocaust. (A.R.E. Press, Virginia Beach, VA, n.d.)

Moody, Raymond A.
Elvis After Life Apparitions of Elvis Presley and other unexplained phenomena that followed his death, such as the meltings of his records and breakage of memorabilia. (Peachtree, 1987)
Reunions: Visionary Encounters with Departed Loved Ones Discusses the historical background of mirror-gazing, and the author's recent re-

search in the use of this ancient technique to facilitate apparitions of the dead. (With Paul Perry, Villard, 1993)

Rogo, Scott D. and Raymond Bayless
Life After Death: The Case for Survival of Bodily Death A review of the survival literature, including historical background and accounts of mediumship, apparitions, reincarnation, and other phenomena. (Aquarian Press, 1986)
Phone Calls from the Dead Case studies of people who claim to have received phone calls from deceased loved ones, sometimes with important information, and the interpretations of this phenomenon. (Prentice-Hall, 1979)

Stevenson, Ian
Twenty Cases Suggestive of Reincarnation
Cases of the Reincarnation Type, Vol. 1: Ten Cases in India
Cases of the Reincarnation Type, Vol. 2: Ten Cases in Sri Lanka
Cases of the Reincarnation Type, Vol. 3: Twelve Cases in Lebanon and Turkey
Case histories from different cultures of children who seem to remember previous lives are presented and explanations offered, including the theory that the information about the deceased was acquired normally by the children, and the author's own view that the deceased were reborn in their bodies. (University Press of Virginia, 1974, 1975, 1977, and 1980)

Weiss, Brian L.
Many Lives, Many Masters The true story of a traditional psychotherapist whose patient began recalling past-life traumas that seemed to hold the key to her recurring nightmares and anxiety attacks. (Simon & Schuster, 1988)
Through Time into Healing An exploration of the use of past-life regression therapy to erase trauma and transform mind, body, and relationships. (Simon & Schuster, 1992)

ANNUAL AND QUARTERLY PUBLICATIONS

Advances in Parapsychological Research Krippner, Stanley, Series Editor. Published annually, each volume contains articles by leading researchers and scholars in parapsychology. The series is a source of information about present-day research and thinking. (Harcourt Brace Jovanovich)

Journal of the Society for Psychical Research (49 Marloes Road, London, England, W8 6LA), *The Journal of the American Society for Psychical Research* (5 West 73rd Street, New York, NY 10023), and *The Journal of Parapsychology* (P.O. Box 6847, College Station, Durham, NC) are quarterly journals that publish research and theoretical papers in parapsychology as well as book reviews.

*Proceedings of an International Conference Parapsychology Foundation. Each volume, usually published annually, contains papers by experts on a specific subject, such as the relationship of parapsychology to education, creativity, anthropology, and physics. (Parapsychology Foundation, 228 East 71st Street, New York, NY 10021)

Research in Parapsychology Parapsychological Association. The annual proceedings of the Parapsychological Association contains summaries of current research from PA conventions, as well as the unabridged presidential and invited papers. (Scarecrow)

TAPES

Psychics in Action A series of audiocassettes in which Lois Duncan interviews some of the nation's most renowned psychics and has them demonstrate their abilities in telepathy, psychometry, and mediumship. The psychics in this series include Nancy Myer-Czetli (psychic detective); Betty Muench (channel); Robert Petro (channel); and Bevy Jaegers (psychic detective and investment counselor). For more information contact: RDA Enterprises, 6110 Pleasant Ridge Road, Suite 3431, Arlington, TX 76016.

TEST MATERIAL

ESP Testing Cards Standard twenty-five-card deck with basic testing instructions, and pad of twenty-five *ESP Record Sheets,* can be ordered from the Foundation for Research on the Nature of Man, 402 North Buchanan Boulevard, Durham, NC 27701-1728.

ABOUT THE AUTHORS

Lois Duncan is the author of forty books, most of them young adult suspense novels involving psychic phenomena. She has received fifteen young readers' awards worldwide; six of her books have been Junior Literary Guild selections, and three have received Parents' Choice awards. She has received five Special Awards from the Mystery Writers of America, as well as the Margaret A. Edwards Award, presented by *School Library Journal* and the Young Adult Library Services Association to honor a living author for a distinguished body of adolescent literature.

William Roll, Ph.D., is project director for the Psychical Research Foundation and chairman of the Parapsychological Services Institute. He is a former research associate at the Parapsychology Laboratory of Duke University, past president of the Oxford University Society for Psychical Research, and past president of the Parapsychological Association. He has published more than a hundred papers in professional journals and has been featured several times on the television series *Unsolved Mysteries*, on *Sightings*, and on other programs as an expert on hauntings, poltergeists, and psychics.

INDEX

INDEX